THE WOOKEY HOLE AFFAIR

Printed and bound by
Mackays of Chatham plc
Chatham, Kent
Badger Road
Lordswood Ind Est
Lordswood
Chatham
Kent ME5 8TD
Typset in Times New Roman

FIRST EDITION

ISBN (hardback) 978-0-9556027-0-2

THE WOOKEY HOLE AFFAIR

MARTIN MILLER

Heavily Edited By
Kate Courtenay
Illustrations By
Emma Townsend

MILLER'S ACADEMY
PUBLISHING
28a Hereford Road
London W2 5AJ
+44 (0)207 229 5103
www.millersacademy.co.uk

TO -
My wife Ioana who
bears no relation to Gayle
- thank God.

CHAPTER ONE

Glencot House, Somerset

When Tarmin Rimell first saw Glencot House, everything seemed wrong - for many reasons. Maybe the hammering rain didn't help, perhaps the fallen gate, the crumbling pillars and the sodden stone walls, grey and inexpressive. But beneath this unappealing misty veil, it emerged that the house had a controlling lover - a mistress and a guardian. It was overpowered by love, smothered by attention and, like a cosseted child, craved to be set free. With such a depressing mask, Glencot exuded a sense of foreboding mystery. This was a love that would have to be coaxed into a smile, but the rewards would be great, as far as Tarmin could see. As his eyes drifted to the large estate agent's board at the end of the driveway, he inwardly sensed that Glencot would be his.

The mansion itself was elevated upon rocky ground, with a neatly mown lawn sweeping down to the riverside. In the distance, a gushing waterfall ran into the weed-ridden millpond. A lone heron stood still on a rock, watching and waiting. Around the walled entrance, a few cars of dubious pedigree were randomly parked, cluttering the driveway like a child's forgotten Dinky toy collection. Tarmin retreated to the fallen pillar to study the gloomy facade, collecting his thoughts. Just a stone's throw away, a bored face peered through a patched leaded window, gently scrubbing a cooking pot. A sad face, her hands compliant to the dishes, her mind resigned to her dreams. Everyone here - the heron, the kitchen staff, Glencot's walls - needed an injection of life, a blast of new vigour. The house itself was like a jaded millionaire, weary of the glitzy champagne circuit and all the incumbent social inevitabilities. One thing was certain - this old socialite lusted after new flesh, fresh energy and invigorating light.

Flicking streaming rivulets from his coat sleeves, Tarmin pushed open the studded oak door, as instructed by the rain-soaked notice. The day outside was a perfect reflection of the starkly funereal inner entrance. A disappointment to Tarmin, who'd always held a romantic attachment to the English vestibule, and this one was far from matching his ideals. Inside, the smell of damp, mouldy coats clung to the air like wet lichen, the fusty odour exacerbated by a pot of disintegrating hydrangeas, furring up in old water. A line of mud-caked green and black wellingtons stacked the walls, propping up a scattering of walking sticks and dark umbrellas.

The oak door scraped over the Victorian tiled floor in noisy protest, and Tarmin stood for a moment, digesting the vista. As far as the eye could see, there were potted plants with 'Gods Waiting Room' invisibly threaded through their wilting forms. Then, somewhere from behind spreading palm fronds, he caught sight of a bald head shuffling through the Financial Times. A quick glance around the entrance hall confirmed his earlier fears. The sales brochure had positively gushed: 'Private House Hotel, pristine condition and lovingly furnished throughout with a large collection of attractive antiques'. 'Pristine? My arse', he thought. On the other hand, the bald-headed man with the paper seemed to fit half the bill.

'Good morning, Sir.' The voice belonged to a smart red-haired woman, hurriedly crossing the room and shuffling letters in her hand. 'Have you come to see Mrs Jennings?'

It was as if the unlit chandelier overhead had suddenly been flicked on. Life was at hand.

'I have indeed,' Tarmin replied.

Miss Ginger ushered him into the library, a dreary, heavily-panelled Victorian room sporting a literary collection that would have turned Sir Walter Scott in his grave. Despite her advanced years, Mrs Jennings was obviously no literary heavyweight, coveting the collected works of Barbara Cartland, Mills and Boon, Agatha Christie and Alan Titchmarsh. The ultimate decaying romantic.

The octogenarian herself suddenly appeared in the doorway and, with unsteady hands, placed a coffee cup on the walnut side table. In an instant, she disappeared. And then appeared once more to straighten some tulips in a vase. After briefly introducing herself in a diminutive voice with Germanic traces, she scuttled off like a crab through another doorway. Tarmin began to chuckle inwardly at the thought of Mrs Jennings in quick-change mode, assuming the mantle of every member of staff. First chambermaid, then Miss Ginger, then donning the apron of cook and finally back to little old lady again. Eventually, she padded through the door with her walking stick and sat down.

After twenty minutes, the conversation between house-seller and prospective buyer had not progressed further than mere niceties. And over the next three hours, Tarmin experienced what it was like to be the suffocated child of Glencot. Mrs. Jennings invited him to inspect every nook and cranny and, by five o'clock, he'd absorbed the life history of the 1938 Dennis mowing machine, the name of every tedious fish in the river, plus family histories for each and every supplier on the payroll (including the parentage and physical deformities of their various offspring).

'Mrs Jennings, may I ask why you want to sell?' was the longest sentence Tarmin managed to string together. The tour had rendered him a linguistic simpleton, rotating a vocabulary of 'I see,' 'fascinating,' 'really?' and 'amazing,' with an ordered and meticulous precision.

'My husband, Boris, died a year ago,' she answered, showing her guest a black and white photograph of a man dressed in army uniform.

'Of screaming boredom?' Tarmin wondered.

'My children and grandchildren are in Okalahoma and I'm moving there to play nanny and amateur gardener.'

The monotone sales pitch lasted two more cups of Earl Grey tea, seven Bourbon biscuits and a protracted lecture on the history of pansies.

Eventually, the old lady said something that got Tarmin's attention.

'You know, Mr. Rimell, the other extraordinary thing about this house is supposed to be its secret places.'

Tarmin's eyes lit up and he pulled his chair in a little closer. Partly to hear properly, and partly because he was about to pass out from the boredom.

'What about them?' he asked. 'I like things like that'.

4

Mrs. Jennings nodded and swept away some invisible dust from the walnut side table.

'I've never had the time nor the inclination to explore such theories' she smiled back at him. 'But these old houses do have such secrets, I'm told. Just as many have ghosts stalking their boundaries. Who knows? Glencot may have a fossilized monk trapped behind the panels, and on the other hand, it might not. It all adds to the mystery of the place, eh?'

Tarmin had heard, imbibed and eaten quite enough. Climbing into his MG, head bursting with exasperation, Tarmin's thirst was now focussed on a very large gin and tonic. His teeth tingling after the massive caffeine overdose, he swept out of the courtyard, offering several polite hand waves to the frail old lady standing in the porch. He could just make out the door once again viciously scraping the tiles as she banged it shut. Almost immediately, his mobile phone bleeped into life with several text messages, as the car slowly wound its way up the hill. He pulled off the lane, plucked the cigarette packet from his jacket pocket and lit up. Winding down the window and blowing thick wafts of smoke into the fading light, he made his first call.

'Hi James,' he said, inhaling quickly. 'That was some place......and some owner!'

'So what do you think, Mr. Rimell? It's a sleeping beauty, isn't it?' James hoped against hope that a juicy fat commission was heading his way.

'More like a snoring dinosaur, but there's something of quality there.'

'You're the first client through the door, so think quickly,' James urged, mind flipping to his empty bank account.

James Collins was a twenty-something eager-beaver property agent, well acquainted with Tarmin's eccentric ways. This was the third major property that he'd earmarked for his client in the last two weeks, and he felt the need to crack the whip a little. All work and no pay was an unspeakable evil in James's book.

'By the way, do you know anything about secret places?' Tarmin asked, his imagination drifting to the swinging shadows of a hangman's noose.

James felt the bite and knew it was time to reel him in.

'Glencot is like many of the great houses in Somerset. Of course it has a rich history, with many owners stretching back over the decades.'

'But have you ever heard any mention of hidden places?'

'There's nothing written that I know of. But those rumours are always rather intriguing, aren't they? An added incentive!'

Tarmin looked at the house across the fields and decided to move off.

'I'll think things through and call you in the morning. Bye.'

It was now tipping six o'clock and Tarmin fancied a snoop around Glencot's land, and then a quick pit stop in Wells before heading home to London. He drove aimlessly for a while to get the lay of the land, eventually pulling over to check the hotel view from the opposite hill. Here was what it was all about, the pieces of the jigsaw falling into place. Glencot appeared neatly guarded by a cluster of great oaks, their brown reflection sparkling in the water, warmed by the evening sun. The stone-balled gables rose above the mullion windows, half obscured by rampant ivy and wisteria, and all competing for the gardeners' hacking saw.

He remembered being told that the hotel had been built by a mill owner back in the 1870s. It had endured an eclectic mix of owners, the penultimate incarnation being as a private school run by a rather unsavoury character. Finally, Mr. and Mrs. Jennings had bought and run the hotel for thirty years, but had never effectively dispersed its institutional feel. Jaded interiors aside, the magnificent exterior was undeniably impressive and disdainfully shouted: 'I've made a bob or two!' There was nothing prissy or twee about Glencot; it cut a bold swathe, a house that stories were made for.

Jumping back into the MG, Tarmin took in the distant Tor at Glastonbury, looming behind the house. In the blink of an eye, he'd driven through Wookey Hole, straight on to Cheddar Gorge and then turned back in a loop to the city of Wells. By half past six he was parked at the pub, by seven had downed a couple of gin and tonics, before heading out for a quick snapshot of the Cathedral.

As he approached the entrance, Tarmin faintly recognised the strains of music and stood gazing at the stunted towers of the cathedral. On reaching the massive doors, Carmina Burana slipped gently into his senses, the music formed and intrigued. He'd never been to Wells before and its charm was quietly ensnaring. He loved small things, and this city boasted the title of 'Smallest City in England', rendered particularly fascinating by the dominance of this magnificent building.

Tarmin had left a rain-swept London some twelve hours earlier on 'undoubtedly yet another wild goose chase,' as his wife, Gayle, had murmured when he'd slipped out of bed that morning. She gave some pretence of tolerance for his little jaunts but, like all his ideas, they were (in her opinion), as short lived as a flash storm. Maybe he could prove her wrong this time. For years he'd harboured an exciting vision of an exclusive Arts Retreat in the countryside, ideally set in a slightly sinister house with a wild river running though. This would be the place to vent his literary aspirations, as well as being able to give the occasional lecture on his favourite authors: Martin Amis, Oscar Wilde and even perhaps, Dan Brown! Plus, it could also be the first step towards a much-desired marital separation. Maybe it was just another dream to flirt with, but as of today, it seemed like it could just become reality.

He gently eased open the cathedral door, careful not to invite attention away from the ethereal music. A sharp ticket request stopped him in his tracks.

'Sorry?' he stuttered, moving in closer. 'I need one?'

'Yes it's all sold out. Sorry.' The door wallah at least had the decency to appear half apologetic.

'Can't I just stand at the back? I can see it's nearly at the end.'

Tarmin beamed his failsafe lopsided grin at the large lady, whispering his request. Huffing and puffing like an overheated camel, she rose from her canvas chair, and holding onto a stone saint for extra support, threw a black shawl around her ample shoulders. Beckoning him in with a fat jabbing finger, she pointed to the huge transparent plastic restoration fund box, loaded like a coin collectors dream. Tarmin slipped a £10 note through the slot, making sure the puffing camel got full view of his bounteousness, and edged himself along one of the back pews. After a quick glance at the stained glass windows, his eyes settled on a group of female thirty-somethings. You could always find a good-looking woman in church, he surmised. There'd be someone seeking quiet solace on her kneeler, gazing meaningfully at the ceiling or tweaking the flower arrangements.

At that moment, a stunning brunette stepped into the pulpit, ready to sing her aria. Her simple beauty - curvaceous breasts plumping out a vermilion evening dress, long auburn hair cascading down her back - generated a stream of unchristian thoughts. It was great luck that Gayle had a previous lunch appointment at The Wolseley today and had passed on accompanying him. There was no hiding anything from his wife. This morning she'd been wagging her finger in his face and rattling on about some nonsense.

'Bloody well behave yourself, you sex maniac!' she'd shouted after him.

'I'm going to look at a house, Gayle,' he'd fired back, 'not visiting a brothel, for God's sake.' Tarmin was indeed a very lustful dreamer but, as yet, not an active philanderer. Though of course, as Gayle well knew, idle dreamers could always become as lascivious and predatory as the next man.

After a small pause, the choir gave way to the soprano's presence and sat down. Her voice slid gently over the ancient walls, coating them with a soft and celestial beauty. If all church experiences were delivered with such honeyed reflection, Tarmin reckoned he could take up the cloth tomorrow. First though, he'd got a three-hour drive home to get out of the way, aided by his newly acquired tom-tom navigation computer. All that was needed to top such a pressing feeling of perfection was a glass of beer and a steaming curry. Keeping Tarmin Rimell happy was incredibly simple.

CHAPTER TWO

Six months later, April. Glencot House

The early days as master of Glencot had passed by in a flash, with Tarmin acclimatising to his base in Somerset, whilst Gayle was overseeing their West London hotel, Millers Residence in Notting Hill Gate. He'd forgotten how much was involved in managing a proper hotel. Millers was a piece of piss compared to overseeing the smooth operation of a mini stately home. The excuse for a heating system had seemingly evolved through decades of enthusiastic plumbers. These masters of copper piping all seemed to be frustrated sculptors, hell bent on making high profile instillation art out of their metallic tubular creations.

Fortunately, Tarmin had a mania for candles, considering power points in Glencot were as rare as trees in the Antarctic.

THE WOOKEY HOLE AFFAIR

A posse of Eastern European cowboys had since undertaken various building and decorating tasks on site, as the house (post Mrs. Jennings' sparse and antiquated sense of style), suffered from a severe lack of normal decorative necessities. Tarmin ripped off the dark purple wallpaper coating the passages and stripped acres of chipped paint from all the windowsills. All the vile, burnt orange carpets, heavily stained by cigarette ash and spilled liquids, were pulled up to reveal solid oak floors, whilst outside, lawns were trimmed, flower beds tended to and the driveway re-gravelled. Tarmin's hit list of furniture, paintings, bric-a-brac and books had become an endless financial drain. On top of which, new staff came and went as frequently as the changing tides. Most days it felt like rural rats deserting a sinking ship.

Revelling in the quiet comfort of his car and idly cruising northwards to Bath, Tarmin felt more like an escapee from a concentration camp than a respected hotel owner. Bath's history had always fascinated Tarmin - an interesting fusion of Roman influence, the novels of Jane Austen and the health-giving aspects of the spa water baths, all thrown into the mix. This was a special place; the only place in Britain where hot mineral springs spare their thermal and curative waters for the good of mankind.

Architecturally, he knew that most of the best-known streets and quarters had been created by John Wood, who started building in the early 18th century. His son, John Wood the younger, eventually assumed his father's mantle and went on to build the Assembly Rooms and The Royal Crescent - Tarmin's favourite places. But it was the elder Wood's love of elegant townhouse symmetry that became such a hugely admired staple of architectural style during the Georgian times, and which Tarmin romanticised. Bath was a place that transported him back to other times, perfectly exemplifying the clean lines, muted colours and elegance of

The Georgians. Way before then, there'd been the Romans swanning around the place; later, the bustling city streets and crowded bath houses during the medieval period, and then, the 19th century rickety bath chairs with their large-spoked wheels, bowling along the uneven roads. The city of Bath held a key to Tarmin's imagination, projecting historical relevance on every building and rooftop that popped into view.

But today, Tarmin had other things on his mind; he was on a major shopping mission. There were always things to buy for his spacious acquisition - shelves to fill, plinths to adorn, paintings to hang. His idea of a heavenly splurge was to spend a few hours curled up on a threadbare sofa at the local auction room. He loved auctions and auctioneers loved him, their dream buyer. Tarmin found it pathologically impossible to let any bargain escape. And, of course, his interior decorative taste spoke volumes about his personality. People always passed comment on what a wonderfully eclectic mix of styles, periods and treasures he'd amassed over the years. However, anyone who knew Tarmin Rimell and had sat through an auction with him, understood that he bought purely and utterly for decorative effect. He was, for instance, a past master at displaying 17th century Chinese blue and white vases, perched way out of reach and looking a million dollars. Little did his guests know or even suspect (all monetary offers being rebuffed), that these objects were invariably glued, riveted and quite often backless. As expert as his wife Gayle had become at sifting out Jimmy Choos from every charity shoe mountain, Tarmin possessed eagle eyes when it came to anything antique (or at least pretending to be antique).

Arriving in Bath, Tarmin tested out his newly acquired 'positive thinking' skills to muster up a car parking space, but found himself frustrated at every manoeuvre. This was absolutely the last time that he'd waste money on doing that ridiculous 'self-help' course that Gayle had recently dragged him to in Euston. He'd only done it because their relationship was at an all-time low and she'd nagged him like a stuck record.

Tarmin had met Gayle when he was just turning eighteen. He'd taken a summer job as a Red Coat at Butlin's Holiday camp in Bognor Regis, but due to a complete lack of musical and acting abilities, he'd found himself lumped with the twice daily task of dressing up as a green giant. This talentless role involved little else than a fondness for children and the ability to swim about in the sodden giant's cumbersome outfit.

At 10.30 every morning and at 3.30 every afternoon, the young inmates of the camp would assemble in full hunting order and, at the blast of a whistle, were unleashed to hunt down the not so jolly green giant. Tarmin (in his giant guise), would expose himself to the children, who spotting the grotesque figure, would immediately and with blood curdling screams, drag and hurl him into the swimming pool.

He reflected with some nostalgia, that today's stringent health and safety standards would have put pay to such abandoned fun and wet discomfort. But, it was on one such occassion (just as he was dragging his sodden body out of the pool), that a stunning Red Coat, on her first day of holiday camp hell, lent over to give him an elegant helping hand. He only bothered to find out that her name was Gayle when, some hours later, they swapped intimate information at the back of the laundry store, writhing beneath a mass of soiled dining room linen.

Their tryst lasted all summer long and this was the best and only job that Tarmin had happily endured. Summer moved on and so did Gayle - to a Blue Coat with a smart mini cooper. Such was life.

Their paths eventually crossed again some fifteen years

later, back stage a Queen concert in Hammersmith. Gayle stuck out like a beacon, dressed in a skintight orange and white minidress, with a large zip-ring dangling seductively at the top of her cleavage. Neither of them had instant recollection of their seaside romp and, to this day, he still could barely remember the details of their time together. He'd eventually twigged a couple of dates along the way, whilst she'd been regaling him with stories of her early life. But considering she never mentioned the green giant that she'd seduced, he decided not to let on.

They got married in obscene haste at a Brighton registry office, since he was scratching a meagre crumb as runner for the Brighton antiques trade. That was over fifteen years ago, and her once Rubenseque body had since been honed to an anorexic twig by her combined obsession for yoga and rocket leaves. An obsession that Tarmin had initially found irritating, but now, downright repulsive.

Lighting up yet another Marlborough Light, he wound down his window and pondered where to go. Deciding to play safe for once, he headed for the public car park in Charlotte Street, just off Bath's Queen's Square. It was within spitting distance of Bonhams and at least it meant that he wouldn't be in danger of getting one of those infuriating plastic packages slapped on the windscreen. It was only 10.20am, forty minutes before the first hammer dropped.

Today was a weekly low grade 'County Sale' at a place where he'd be just as comfortable as at Christie's. The main difference being that here, his mad impulses cost him a lot less and he could run rings around the buyers. Inspecting the goods on offer, he saw that some four hundred lots covered everything from a crap MFI table, to over-flowered amateur paintings sent in by Auntie Flora's hard-up nephew.

Tarmin stamped out his cigarette butt on the pavement and caught a quick glimpse in the window. It really was time to get a hair cut, he conceded. He'd been growing his wild hair specifically to annoy Gayle, who was forever on his case nowadays, saying that he resembled an Arab pony or an antiquated Johnny Depp. But with a little give and take, he felt pretty happy with his looks. For a forty-five year old guy he was in good nick - no bulging beer belly, a decent crop of hair and no spooky beard. What else could a woman want? Except of course, if that woman happened to be Gayle.

'Why don't you just go the whole hog and wear Pat Cash earrings? Or plonk a Weetabix on your head, like Elton John?'

Gayle had begun to nag him incessantly, a sure sign that she was as unhappy in the relationship as he was. If his wife had her way, Tarmin would resemble Prince Charles - booted, suited and safely staid.

Today, his hair was going to do the Worzel Gummage thing whatever, so he gave up all pretences of being tidy and entered Bonhams. Wandering up and down the lots, he flipped through the catalogue pages, occasionally scribbling down the odd price. As crap went, this really was five star. Disillusionment descended as fast as a rain cloud, and he'd just made a decision to leave a few bids at the auctioneer's office and check out the antiques market by The Assembly Rooms, when an inconspicuous cardboard box caught his eye. Lot 189, written in felt tip pen across the sides, turned out to be a large collection of prints, engravings and documents. Given a princely estimate of £20-30, this was just the sort of pig-in-a-poke that Tarmin loved. He shuffled through the contents and pulled out one of the framed photos. To his delight, he immediately recognised a stained sepia photograph of Glencot House at the turn of the century, the staff forming a stiff line-up at the front entrance, culminating with the house owners by the front door. Flanking them on either side were two butlers in formal dark penguin tail suits and starched collars, staring straight ahead with haughty pride. The line fanned out with immaculately dressed maids clad in sensible shoes and spotless white aprons, all standing to attention, abreast of gardeners, drivers and footmen, dressed in a variety of long brown coats, overalls and neat caps. Tarmin looked at the black front door framed by its neatly trimmed ivy arch and mourned Glencot's historic demise. At least now he'd be restoring it to some of its former glory.

Delving deeper into the box, Tarmin unearthed further photographs, small prints and old papers - all revealing the history and former inhabitants of his new home. He couldn't believe his luck. But at the top of his list was to find a clue, any clue that might indicate secret places. Back at Glencot, his endless forays around the house had all drawn a blank. He'd shaken the panelling to see if it moved and lifted old carpets to examine floorboards, but there was nothing. It was disappointing as he felt like injecting a little excitement into his turgid life. Maybe there'd be a document here that would shed light?

'I'll nab this little lot' he thought, glancing at his watch. '10.35am now. If they push through 140 or so lots an hour then I can get back for 11.30 and be in time to catch the action.'

On his way out to register, Tarmin had a quick rummage through the silver plate section, noting the silly estimates. The downside of silver in this day and age was the time-consuming cleaning. On top of which, most silver polishes seemed to stink like blocked drains - although this point didn't actually bother him unduly, since his housekeepers were the ones to save his own delicate hands from any rigorous polishing regimes.

'Lot 160-182,' Tarmin pondered, putting his on glasses for a closer look. 'If I get back for 11.15, I'll have a go at those too.'

THE WOOKEY HOLE AFFAIR

He added himself to the three-person line, all waiting to register and collect their bidding numbers. First was a tiny foreign lady with an immaculately coiffed hairstyle, reminiscent of the late Jackie Kennedy. She introduced herself to the Registrar as Amelie Prigent and, excusing her poor English, told the bored-looking man that she loved everything to do with 'silvah' and was 'exseeted' at the prospect of the sale. The Registrar gave a gratuitous nod and passed over her bidding paddle. Next up was a man of similar age to Tarmin, wearing a large black leather jacket and slouchy jeans. The final punter was a thirty-something guy with bags full of art books and trade magazines - obviously a serious contender. Tarmin dished up his passport and driving licence for identification, and was issued with a numerical paddle for the auction.

With the ticket safely tucked into his catalogue, he left the auction room and decided on a quick cappuccino at Waterstone's Costa Coffee, in nearby Milsom Street. He could, of course, find somewhere more relaxing, but the bonus of this joint was the crowds of tasty undergraduates who frequented it during term time. He and Gayle had foregone the delights of parenthood, preferring (at the time) to keep their own, adult company. Just as well really, since he'd now be lusting after girls of a similar age to his own kids.

Settling down with a packet of shortbread and cup of coffee, he caught sight of two leggy students coming through the door. Immediately, one of them clapped her hand over her mouth and groaned.

'Chloe, I've just remembered! Can't stay here - this is a fag free zone.'

The other girl winced, tugged her friend by the arm and pulled her out of the shop.

'That's the last straw' Tarmin thought, gathering his bits together. How could he possibly survive a coffee interlude without either nicotine or decorative wallpaper? Luckily he hadn't lit up and disgraced himself. He could just as well have headed off to the oldest known house in Bath and indulged in an infamous Sally Lunn bun.

Finally, when a large heffalump of a girl with oversized glasses politely asked Tarmin whether she could share his table, banged her tray down and promptly spilled tea all over her kilt, he decided it was high time to give up the ghost and get back to Bonhams.

'Lot number 159,' the auctioneer threw to the room. 'A pair of Staffordshire dogs with just a little damage, a small chip to the left ear. Shall we say £40?'

The lot was knocked down to a very rotund woman, bedecked in chains, baubles and turquoise trinkets. She looked like a cross between a Christmas tree and Mary J. Blige. Tarmin wondered what on earth she'd be doing with a pair of china dogs.

Next, the first silver lot was presented as a plated Victorian candelabra, estimated at between £120 and £160. The bidding stopped at £65 and was immediately knocked down to one of four conspiratorial dealers, bantering together in a huddle.

'What's your buyer number?' The auctioneer called to the purchaser, the obvious big mouth of the group, who dismissively waved his paddle card back. Tarmin recognised him as the leather jacket who'd been queuing infront of him earlier.

'I didn't see that.' The auctioneer coughed and took a sip of water.

The dealer waved it again, muttering: 'Blind as a fucking bat!'

A ripple of laughter erupted from the group. Tarmin sighed at their infantile behaviour and drew a large feathery squiggle with a big nose on his catalogue. Without any great consciousness, he scribbled GAYLE in capitals underneath.

THE WOOKEY HOLE AFFAIR

The next lot came in and was knocked down to the same smart-arse from the huddle, who pipped Jackie Kennedy to the post. Cursing her loss with a string of French insults, she snapped her cream handbag loudly shut and left the room.

Tarmin was getting the bit between his teeth. He'd taken an instant dislike to the loud-mouthed 'Lovejoy' impersonator, who was rocking back and forth on the delicate wooden legs of a rather nice Georgian chair. Tarmin wondered whether his self-help course might now come into effect. Staring hard at the mahogany leg, he willed it to snap in two and disintegrate. The loud mouth instantly rocked forward and sat bolt upright. Positive thinking was definitely a waste of time, Tarmin noted, scribbling BUGGER IT in huge letters across the glossy print of a Chinese bird fan. The hammer thumped down.

'Pair of Art Nouveau candlesticks. Who'll start me at £80?'

When the bidding reached £120 (and still below estimate), Tarmin's hand shot up and snagged them for £190.

'Let battle commence,' he chuckled to himself.

The remaining seventeen lots were all secured by the new owner of Glencot House. The gang of four tut-tutted and swore from their corner. Every week they'd managed to maintain a nice little routine that yielded the goods, and now this nonce in a burgundy jumper and London hair had appeared from nowhere and completely messed up their bids. Tarmin didn't give a toss whether he'd pissed anyone off or not. The £3,400 was wisely spent, as far as he was concerned - both with the bargains he'd purchased and the innate pleasure he gained by spoiling the gang of four's day. In his excitement, he very nearly missed the Glencot photograph lot. It became his, in the end, for a mere £22 Tarmin took his exit past the ill-tempered mutterings of the wide boys, provoking a grubby erect finger from the loud mouth. Nice type of bidder in Bath, he noted.

Still, there was plenty of time left for a celebratory lunch. Since Gayle was holding the fort in London and rarely dragging her suburban arse down to Somerset, he'd rediscovered a whole lease of bachelorhood. He could drink like a fish, eat like a pig and flirt with the writing course students who regularly came to Glencot. Today, he'd go to Pimpernel's restaurant in The Royal Crescent and splash out.

A friendly face ushered him to a window seat, overlooking the beautiful gardens. Soon it would be warm enough to open up and sit on the terrace for al fresco dining, but today, he was more than happy to look across the lawns and gaze at the spring blossom. His waiter returned just a few seconds later to take his order and uncork a bottle of Sancerre Blanc from the Loire Valley. He plumped for Foie Gras, followed by seared organic sea bass, string beans and Potatoes Dauphinoise. One hefty slurp of the crisp, honeyed wine instantly hit the spot. It was on days like this that he thought about his old friend, George Kimininos. George was his main drinking buddy in London and, despite some of his Glencot staff being keen contenders for the rural title, it wasn't the same as having a mate on tap who knew him inside out.

Finishing off his meal with a chocolate mousse that slipped down his throat like silk, he couldn't resist a small glass of port to round things off, hoping to God that the entire Bath police force had been alerted to a terrorist threat somewhere or he'd be jailbait at even the sighting of a breathalyser.

Strolling up the hill to The Circle, Tarmin crossed over to the Royal Crescent. With the low afternoon sun streaking across the huge span of beautiful lawns and flower beds, and the impressive curvature of the Crescent sweeping in a line behind him, a thought crossed his mind: 'Maybe a little pad here would be fun?'

Tarmin was a gipsy who never settled. However, his plans

for a swift bit of estate agent window-shopping were quickly shelved when he remembered that he needed to get back to the auction house to pick up his purchases. Plus, he'd be soon be sucked in to rush hour traffic. He checked his phone and there were no messages. It was nearly five now, and he needed to be back within the hour since he had nine new takers on the 'Journalism for Beginners' workshop, due to check in. A somewhat notorious ex-editor from a national celebrity magazine was hosting one of the days, whilst he was personally going to undertake teaching 'art and antiques reportage'. Mary Goodly Smith, his other guest lecturer, was in her sixties now and retired, someone who more than knew her stuff. On top of which, she was a well-seasoned imbiber, which always pleased Tarmin.

Glencot's 'Minima' (as Tarmin like to call it), was one of the hotel's better innovations. The room had been previously used for table tennis, and was an airless space in the basement with some architectural merit, including a fine oak study door with a stone-carved gargoyle topping the embellished arch. It had been a wasted space, dimly illuminated by a naked light bulb, where nobody bothered to venture - the surrounding walls littered with cheap glassless prints of alpine scenes. The fine flagstone floor was covered by a multi-coloured 'Pollockesque' carpet, old enough to show the indentation of each flagstone and sporting a myriad of unattractive drink stains.

Tarmin had contemplated the room on many occasions. It was still a good space, a waste of good space and something needed to be done. Eventually, like all things, it was a simple solution. A proper entertainments room would be built. Soon after, the surrounding whitewashed walls and ceilings were transformed with black paint, the cold flagstone floor scattered with huge, comfy cushions and a state-of-the-art projection system fitted with a large screen to cover the end wall. Ensuring that it earned its keep, he'd charge (as with the sauna), £25 per session for private use. He'd created the perfect after-dinner curl-up room with a range of films showing from 'Roman Holiday', to 'Carry On Up The Kyber'. On top of which, he'd also discovered something pretty incredible about the room.

Only last month, Tarmin had hired out the Minima to a clutch of local girls on a boozy hen night. Somehow it had skipped Anne's notice on reception that this was a girls-only pre-wedding bash, but perhaps he should have been alerted when they'd booked the Minima to show off their 'holiday' movies. When the actual night had arrived, a group of fifteen garrulous ladies descended on Glencot, all bearing beautifully wrapped gifts, all teetering on high heels and squeezed into too-tight dresses, and then had disappeared head-first into the champagne cocktails. The bride's name was Robyn and there was no doubting that her gaggle were an exceedingly merry bunch of women. From behind the thick oak door of the Minima, high-pitched yelps, raucous giggles and cheering, along with the odd ominous thump or two, had ricocheted down the corridor. Eventually, the door had swung open and the inebriated group emerged into the candlelit hallway and headed off to the bar, clutching champagne glasses and cheerily patting each other on the bottom. The bride-to-be's dress had now slipped right off her shoulder as she'd tripped along the carpet, clutching a spare arm for support. The rest were no better either.

'Come on Robyn, get your arse moving! You're like a frigging snail. I'm going to wee all over the carpet'.

Drunken hens were always such a charming breed, Tarmin had mused. He hadn't envied Edward and Rob who'd happened to be on bar duty.

Eventually, the time had come for a mass departure, and none too soon, after various guests and writer students had complained about the uncouth conversations floating up through the windows. Tarmin had herded the unsteady party towards the front door, propping up Robyn, when she'd sunk her long acrylic nails through his cotton jumper. He'd felt like he'd been crucified.

'Good night ladies' Tarmin had yelled, and as they stumbled through the main hallway, a redheaded girl dropping to her knees and screeching like a banshee.

It had become imperative to get them out and he'd gestured towards the oversized people carrier, manned by an equally oversized driver. A large man had already slid the side door open, his bulky frame partially obliterating 'Sam's Carriage Company - No Trip Too Long'.

'Thanks', had slurred a very slack mouth.

'Night', said another, grabbing Tarmin's sweaty hand. 'You can squeeze in the back with me if you like'.

He'd smiled diplomatically, perversely wishing for once in his life that Gayle had been with him. No woman would dare drape herself anywhere near him whilst his wife was in the vicinity. Gayle might not belong to the acrylic nail brigade, but she had nerves of steel and an iron will.

'I'd love to, really, but I have to lock up', was all he'd been able weakly to muster.

'You can lock me up anytime', came her tipsy response as he'd helped her into the van.

If only she'd looked like Angelina Jolie, rather than a juvenile Bet Lynch, he might just have hunched-up in the boot and gone along for the ride.

The very last girl (who'd been sorting out the bill) had eventually emerged, wrinkling her brow and motioning Tarmin to one side.

'I think I should point out that something appears to have died in the Minima. There's a vile smell in there. Made me feel quite sick'.

With that bombshell, she'd slid out into the damp Somerset night and hopped into the front seat. Sam's people carrier had revved up its engine, spraying gravel against the front door and screeched up the driveway and into oblivion. At long last, a comforting silence had descended on Glencot with the blanket of night.

Tarmin had then shut the door behind him, reflecting that hen nights were to be avoided at all costs and begun his nightly ritual of extinguishing candles, flicking off light switches and bedding down the fire. He was just heading off to the quilted comforts of his large four-poster bed, when he'd remembered that the projector in the cinema room was still on. Disgruntled, he'd headed off to the Minima, grimacing at Rob who was taking crates of empties out the back.

'Fuck this for a life; I must be out of my tree', he'd mumbled, wanting to go to bed.

'Indeed you are' was all his barman could offer, which wasn't of huge comfort.

In the Minima, the gently humming projector was still illuminating the screen with its soft blue light, and he'd remembered the girl's comments about a putrid smell. He'd sniffed around the room like an airport drugs hound, pulling out cushions and expecting at any moment to find something unimaginable stuck to the under side of a beanbag. Suddenly, in the darkness of the room, he'd stubbed his foot on something blunt-edged. Bent down in the hazy gloom of the Moroccan wall lights, Tarmin had then pulled away the covering cushions. One of the lines of the enormous flagstones was proud of the others by about two inches, and as he'd taken a closer look, he'd seen that there was also a very thin leather attachment, constructed as some kind of submerged handle. Immediately he tugged on it, a sharp odour had hit his normally under sensitive buds. It could well have been a rat that had disintegrated under piles of mould but, whatever it was, the pungency was unavoidable and needed unearthing.

Flipping the room lights back on, he'd got to work. The flagstone was one of the larger ones - about two feet by three. He'd knelt down and pulled at the leather corner piece. The whole stone had lifted easily in his hands and crashed down to one side, revealing a large black hole and a dimly lit upper step. Tarmin had never been heralded for his bravery or a Livingstonesque sense of exploration, but he'd surprised himself, gingerly descending the dusty hewn steps. Choked by dust and sweeping aside the dangling cobwebs, it hadn't looked like anyone had headed down this way for quite some time. Had Mrs. Jennings known about this place? She certainly hadn't mentioned it. His brain rapidly computed the odds on what he could find and, that was anything from a crypt full of tarnished gold, to a rat-infested scene out of the 'Lost Ark'. Five steps down, in true Glencot style, his torch had failed. Thank God he was a smoker. His lighter took control, five more steps down, his brain bellowing: 'Far enough for tonight!' For a moment, he'd stood still and listened - there hadn't been a sound. The dull light of the Minima glowed sparingly from above.

'What the fuck do I do, if the stone slams down on top of me?' he remembered, panicking. He'd turned once again to look into the darkness. By his left shoulder he'd found an old porcelain light switch loosely wired into the wall. He'd clicked it up and down twice - nothing. The harsh smell had definitely diminished this far down but, as he turned with his cigarette lighter back to the upper steps, he'd made out a dark shape just a few steps up. Crouching low, he passed the flame as near the bundle as he dared, and been able to confirm his original diagnosis - a very dead, very smelly and very mouldy rat.

'I'll really have to reach the bottom', he'd thought to himself. 'On the other hand, why not just wait until morning?'

'You can't come this far and leave a question mark in the air', had spun right back. It had felt like a drug habit that he couldn't contain. He'd carried on step by slow step, the occasional cobweb tangling his hair but, thankfully, no sign of hairy legs scuttling off, no spooky squeaks or sounds from furry bodies - just resoundingly dark silence.

At the very bottom, the naked flame from his lighter had scorched his thumb, and he'd sworn loudly as his light source fell clattering to the floor. More silence and total darkness, except from a small shaft of glowing light from the opening above him, seeping through in a thin laser line. He'd bent down to search for his lighter. Gone. Then he'd remembered the phone in his pocket, flipped it on and let the glowing screen soothe his nerves. Aided by its weak illumination, he'd edged very slowly forwards along the spooky stone corridor. Thoughts of impaling wall spikes shooting out, and screaming pre-historic birds with vast black wingspans, had flooded his overactive brain. Then suddenly, just ahead of him, a large door had materialised by the tiny glow of the phone light. On closer inspection, it had appeared to be a massive plate steel affair measuring over four feet wide, the steel frame strapped down like an Armada wall chest. Tarmin thought about how he'd never experienced his heart beating so rapidly, and with such an audible boom. In fact, he hadn't felt that excited since he'd got a positive response to his first invitation of sex.

He'd tentatively touched the door, expecting an electric charge to incinerate him to ashes. But the shocks had been dead, non-existent. It was just cold, smooth steel. He'd pushed a little harder and nothing. Not a budge, not a creak, just a fine filter of dirt falling onto his now filthy hair. He'd pushed even harder and it moved a jot. He placed his palms firmly on the cold steel and exerted more pressure; the door eventually gave in just an inch, then another, then another. No scrapes on the floor, no screaming of thirsty hinges, just a smooth, silent progress. Straining to see in the weak light, Tarmin had grabbed a fleeting glimpse of fine parquetry inlaid into the panelled wall. The place was incredible! But at least he'd had the sense to concede that it needed a proper investigation, and despite the adrenalin rush, that would have to be conducted in daylight hours by torchlight.

'Tarmin, where are you?' Rob had suddenly yelled from somewhere up above. One thing had stuck in his mind and certainly wouldn't change - he wasn't going to let a living soul know that he had found the secret room at Glencot.

CHAPTER THREE

Christie's, London.

Nathan Hunt sat discretely at the back of the saleroom. In the seat next to him, a girl wearing long black boots and noisily chewing gum, checked through her text messages and flicked her painted nails. The awaited lot was very shortly about to be offered to the room.

An obsession with Anglo Saxon antiquities ran deep in Hunt's blood, inherited mainly via his Nazi grandfather's family line, a lineage that traditionally coveted treasures of art and bookish pursuits. Hunt's grandfather, Helmut Gebbels, had been notorious from his Nazi party connections during World War II, and along with many other key players, had eventually committed suicide in 1945.

THE WOOKEY HOLE AFFAIR

Gebbels had married Helga and spawned just one son, Harald Gebbels.

After the death of his infamous father, Harald had been whisked off to Austria, and grew up under the care of elderly relatives. A strange, lonesome figure, he'd funnelled his lack of sociability and studious nature into a positive love of collecting art, eventually becoming known as one of the key experts on religious arts and artefacts. In 1955 he came out of hiding to marry his second cousin, Alberta Schwarzkopf, who, two years later (and after a pregnancy that nearly killed her), presented her husband with their only child, Nathan.

Following his college years, when his own star had begun to rise in the world of antiquities, Nathan Hunt had made a conscious assessment about his birth name and its damning Nazi connections. It didn't bode well or look good to have the name of Gebbels above the shop door, despite the fact that both the schloss and his major collection were inherited from his grandfather - an invaluable array of paintings and pieces plundered from across Europe during the Nazi occupation. That, along with the fact that he had been unfortunately christened Adolf Gebbels, had made life doubly intolerable. If he were going to operate across Europe with dignity and ease, then he would have to adapt. Combining a lack of originality with his love of movies, it was when his superhero Ethan Hunt battled his way across the screen in 'Mission Impossible', that he found his answer. The name and image more than did the trick, and a small adaptation from Ethan to Nathan made him seem less affected.

Today was one of Christie's biannual antiques sales and Nathan hoped to secure a third century Celtic gold warrior fibula for his museum in Vienna. A similar one had been snapped up by The British Museum in 2001 for a

29

record breaking £1.1 million and, although today's exhibit was known to be an inferior piece, it was still earmarked for sale at around the two million mark. Next summer he'd decided to put on a groundbreaking exhibition of ancient gold jewellery and badly wanted the fibula to add to his existing priceless pieces. Nathan Hunt's personal collection was a growing masterpiece in itself.

'Lot 132, third century Celtic gold fibula, depicting warrior and hunting dog. This brooch is from the Braganza Dynasty. Will anybody start me at £1 million?'

'Thank you, Jane,' the auctioneer acknowledged the raised hand of an eager, pale-faced young woman, confidently clutching the phone to her ear. '£1.1 million anywhere?'

The room remained startlingly silent seconds before the frenzied phone bids and noise from the floor kicked in. Like greyhounds on the track, they were off, and in no time, the bidding had steadily crept to one and a half million before Nathan made his move.

'£1.75 million is a new bid from the back,' the auctioneer nodded at Nathan.

Nathan was a man used to getting his own way. Everyone in the room knew that bidding against him was near futile, and any bloody-minded 'running up' was pointless.

London had always been good to Nathan. Over the years he'd collected a stable of invaluable contacts neatly interlinking the auction trade and the world's most dedicated collectors, but he'd gathered very few friends along the way. Friends just complicated his life - like women. His love was his uncomplicated stash of art, safely tucked away at an exclusive Austrian schloss outside Innsbruck. Nathan's home truly was his castle. Gossip was rife about the many Nazi treasures horded within his fortress home. He conducted his affairs with complete discretion, paid his taxes with obscene punctuality and donated only to the most prestigious international charities. He was indeed straight out the pages of an Ian Fleming novel, but not yet a villain, just a 21st century missionary. He was also a walking encyclopaedia of pre-Christian and medieval religious art, and it was constantly rumoured that behind those walls lay a collection of academic wealth to rival the treasures of the Papal Collection. As a recluse, he never took holidays, never ate out. In fact, eating out to Nathan meant room service. At forty-seven, his life was a solid pattern of self-indulgent artistic and financial quest - nobody else quite understood its nature, only seeing the overt obsession. But professional relationships were paramount in this business and Nathan was a man you wanted in your armoury.

Another few phone calls came in and the figure rose dramatically to £2 million. Nathan's mental limit was two million but this piece of jewellery was the icing on his cake, the piece that he had to have more than any other. Although, with Nathan, there was always a piece of art that must supersede the next and an acquisition that was an 'essential'. His mind was already vaguely drifting to other coveted pieces from the Braganza Dynasty.

'£2.2 million and, that's your final bid?'

Nathan closed his eyes and nodded.

'Thank you, sir. Number 311.'

The auctioneer slammed down his gavel. Nathan acknowledged the rostrum and rose from his chair. After a few cursory handshakes and polite acknowledgements of congratulation, he headed onto the street and straight into a taxi, clutching a small glossy brochure from The Millers Academy in Westbourne Grove. Normally, a successful transaction of this kind would dictate Cristal champagne, sushi and sex in the Royal Suite at Claridges Hotel. But tonight he was making an exception.

Tonight he would not go straight back to Blacks.

Tonight he would make a detour.

CHAPTER FOUR
Same evening in Westbourne Grove

Nathan Hunt arrived at The Academy with eight minutes to spare. He was about to do something very out of character. It would normally have taken wild horses to drag him to a public lecture, but this was special. The benefits, he hoped, would justify the pain.

His elegant Tyrolean green jacket drew a few admiring glances, as he squeezed into a spare seat near the front. How he hated the front of anything. Nathan was a shadows man. Even at school he would be the last to put up his hand, the person lurking at the back of a crowd. It was however, a somewhat disingenuous gesture on his part, enduring being a smart-arsed swot just for cover. He'd learned well

MARTIN MILLER

that you could always get away with more in the dark.

Fortunately, the professor was already in the room and about to be introduced to his audience, although it was actually the Q&A afterwards that Nathan was waiting for. Tarmin Rimell, owner of The Academy, stepped forward and tapped his guest speaker on the shoulder.

'Ladies and Gentlemen. Welcome to the Academy for this evening's lecture, hosted by Professor Richard Bundy, foremost expert in antiquities at Christies. The professor is going to be talking us through a selection of religious paintings and artefacts from the fabled Arthurian period. This has particular resonance for my wife and I, having recently purchased Glencot House in Somerset, nestling in Arthur's very own neck of the woods! Who knows, we might indeed be sitting on our own little treasure! Thank you, Professor, and please, everyone - enjoy!'

The Academy - Tarmin's West London urban outlet for his more social and intellectual interests - had a reputation for producing a varied mix of lectures throughout the year. Only the week before, Professor John Gun had the visiting members nailed to their seats as he described in vivid and gory detail how, 'for the sake of art,' he'd had himself crucified and still lived to tell the tale. Tonight's lecturer (an excellent fallback for whenever someone dropped out), was Tarmin's old friend and mentor, and a seasoned speaker. Professor Bundy was pushing fifty-five, but the combination of a solid physique, brilliant mind, and captivating conversation delivered in a deep, gravely voice, always guaranteed an eager audience of well-heeled women. Predictably, tonight's group happened to be predominantly females, with a smattering of male add-ons. For the next forty minutes, the tall, white haired professor expertly held the assembled members in riveted silence, until eventually turning back to the screen and switching off the monitor.

THE WOOKEY HOLE AFFAIR

'And I think that really does conclude my point about those Celtic warriors. Are there any further questions from the floor, or shall we adjourn upstairs for some wine and dinner?'

Gayle Rimell, joint founder of The Academy with her husband, rose from the front row clapping loudly. She was wearing a too-tight yellow satin blouse, erroneously open at the middle and revealing an unattractive peek of greying bra. Tarmin raised his eyes to the heavens. Gayle however, didn't give a toss. She was a woman who was very comfortable in her own skin - even if the skin in question was rather indecorously on show. She'd embraced The New Age with the enthusiasm of a newly freed slave and was a walking advert for positive thinking. This had also led her to yoga mats and staunch vegetarianism, appalling her husband far more than her recent 'Women's Only Retreat' on Dartmoor.

Despite the health kick, she'd mysteriously lost on a good two stone in weight, which had turned Tarmin to his gin. He married a curvaceous, fun-loving meat-eater, not this whippet-thin Linda McCartney wannabe. Their differences had become so pronounced of late, that the split of Tarmin being in Glencot and Gayle in London had been a blessing. Except for one thing. Tarmin hadn't accounted for the fact that his wife could be unfaithful to him and whatever he thought of her, the idea of being cuckolded wasn't an easy one to swallow. Particularly when the lover in question was reputed to be Teodor Popescu, Gayle's Transylvanian yoga teacher from the Porchester Centre.

He'd caught sight of them sharing a pot of dandelion coffee and couldn't believe his eyes. Teodor was a shade over five foot five, had a long black ponytail, and was dressed in a skin-tight teeshirt and bright orange Hari Krishna pants. He knew that a confrontation was brewing, but right now, he didn't have the stomach for it. She could enjoy the clandestine Down Dog sessions with her lover until he, Tarmin, was good and ready.

Gayle wrenched her bra straps and grinned at Bundy.

'On behalf of The Academy and all the guests here tonight, may I thank Professor Bundy for a very fascinating and well-rounded lecture. I'm sure that there'll be many more questions to ask him, but let's all head upstairs and crack open that wine!'

Applause rippled around the room just as a dark-haired man leaned forward and coughed loudly.

'Could I just ask the Professor a quick question?' Nathan Hunt said, betraying his slight Austrian accent. 'Are you actually able to identify any of these large West Country houses where some of these Arthurian artefacts are supposedly buried or stored? I'd be very interested to check them out.'

Sensing that the answer was not going to be short (nothing was ever brief in Professor Bundy's world), Gayle interrupted again and suggested that they all move upstairs to the buffet, and that the professor could answer the dark haired man's question over chilli con carne.

'I'm sure that everyone has had enough mind fodder for one night and are needing to satisfy their bodily needs. No offence to you,' she smiled, 'but my husband, for one, will be itching to get his cigarettes out! Plus, if he doesn't hit the gin bottle soon, World War Three will erupt.'

Tarmin winced and shot Bundy a glowering look. His irritating spouse was treading on extremely thin ice.

As everyone shuffled along the chair lines towards the stairs, two blonde-haired women at the back of the lecture hall sat tight.

'Wow!' one exclaimed. 'What was that guy rabbiting on about?'

'Who gives a shit' the petit blonde responded. 'I was only paying attention to his eyes, not his mouth. Let's get upstairs before he gets snagged. Susannah Denton told me on very good authority that he's a horny bastard. And I've always fancied having a go at an older man.'

Gathering up his coat, Nathan squinted at the two of them through narrowed and disdainful eyes. He could see that getting his much-needed answer from the professor was going to be a lot more challenging than he'd hoped.

The upstairs salon of The Academy was a recreation of a small Victorian academy of art and science. The sort of place that the blonde duo dreamed about being taken to by such a man as Professor Bundy, and being laid behind the teetering stone busts. From their vantage point by the door, they spotted Professor Bundy greedily piling his plate from the baroque-style banquet buffet. The candlelit room flickered in sensual anticipation, as smartly dressed women buzzed around him, like moths to a flame.

'Shit,' the petite blonde scanned the gathering with shrewd eyes. 'Way too much competition.'

Contemplating her plan of attack, she inadvertently stepped backwards into a plateful of dressed salad being carried by an elegant elderly lady. Instantly, the woman was adorned by strands of greenery dripping down her silk blouse - a piece of curly lettuce protruding from her Victorian brooch.

'Oh no! How awful!' the tall blonde stammered.

At the same moment a voice from behind interrupted: 'Mother! Are you ok?'

'Obviously not, dear' came her crusty retort. 'Look at me. I resemble a damp spaniel!'

The sodden rocket leaves and slivers of red pepper had also decided to jump ship all over the Persian carpet.

'I'll have to leave,' she spat.

'I really am sorry,' bleated the smaller woman, who'd caused the accident. 'Look I'm staying at Millers Residence across the road. Please come over and change. I know I have something to suit.'

Professor Bundy's mother looked her up and down and snorted like a truffle-hunting pig.

'Richard,' she snapped. 'Get me a car will you? I'm beginning to smell like a jar of pickled onions.'

The professor hurried after his whingeing, ancient mother like a calf following the herd, and losing every ounce of macho ruggedness in her wake. The two blondes sank into the nearest couch and curled up in mortification.

'Bang goes my hope of bedding the older man,' the petite one muttered.

'What?' her companion looked perplexed. 'You can't seriously still fancy him now that you've met the dragon mother?'

But it would take a lot more than a soggy salad incident with his relative, to put such a committed hunter off her prey. This was Bethany and, when Bethany fixed her sights, it was as securely as a sealed bid.

Just then, a four-eyed heavyweight with a penchant for crushing sofas to death, slumped down beside the distraught pair. With his weight instantly displacing the balance, he reached for the nearest velvet-tasselled cushion in a vain attempt to cover up his Henry VIII mound. As the sofa springs scraped against the floor, a plate of quiche triangles bounced in the air, the deafening clatter drawing all eyes over to the girls once again. The taller blonde stood up and plucked away a parsley stalk shining with vinaigrette, nestling unattractively in her tights.

'This is fucking ridiculous, Bethany' she snapped. 'I feel like I'm in some kind of freak show. I'm going to get a bloody drink.'

'Look he's back!' Bethany was desperately trying to calm her friend.

'I don't give a toss. You can apologise to your OAP if you like, but I'm out of here!'

The professor was already at Bethany's side and bent down to greet her with a smile.

'I'm so sorry. My mother can be a little acidic and accidents never were her strong point. But she's fine now, winging her way back to Hampstead in a taxi. Did you enjoy the lecture?'

Just then, the tall blonde returned, carrying two full glasses of red wine. 'Sorry, I don't even know your names,' he continued.

'I'm Bethany.'

'And I'm Rebecca,' said the tall blonde, spitting it out like a bitter olive stone.

'Here's to salad days then!' He said, holding his glass up for the customary tink.

The room was thinning now as they settled down on one of the hugely overstuffed sofas located beneath a four-foot high plaster bust of Michelangelo's David. Bethany and Bundy immediately found common ground (of sorts) with a mutual love of porcelain china.

'I know it sounds silly, but I've got a growing collection of china thimbles, which some people say could be very valuable in years to come,' Bethany told him.

'Not silly at all' Bundy answered, wishing they could move onto something altogether more salacious and, just stopping himself from saying out loud: 'Each man to his own, and all that.'

'Actually, I really must be moving on.'

Rebecca couldn't comprehend her friend's passion for this intellectual fossil. 'Fancy a shoenami in the morning?'

'Definitely, I'll come with.' Bethany caught the professor's blue-grey eyes. 'We're holed up in Millers for the night. A hop, skip and a jump away and bingo! Beddy-byes! Fancy a little nightcap?'

'What a fortuitous thing', Professor Bundy thought to himself. He just happened to have been given The Wordsworth room, in payment for the lecture, which just happened to be bang next door to Miss Bethany in The Coleridge.

As they rose from the sofa, Nathan Hunt, who'd been lurking nearby, took his cue and stepped forward.

'Professor Bundy, a quick word, if I may? My name is Nathan Hunt and I'm an antiquities collector from Austria. But I often stay in London and frequent the European auctions. Your lecture was of great interest to me. I appreciate that you're somewhat tied-up right now, but could you just quickly point me in the right direction of those Celtic burial sites in the West Country? Whereabouts are they located? I noted that Mr. Rimell also mentioned that his Somerset abode might house such things. Is this a known fact? I cannot see him now to ask him.'

Professor Bundy was torn. He loved talking about his work more than anything in the world, and of course - although he didn't let on - he knew exactly who Nathan Hunt was. Everyone knew everyone in his industry, and Hunt was becoming pretty legendary. But right now, something else entirely more pressing was stirring from within. Looking across to the door, he could see Bethany smoothing back her blonde hair and applying a slick of wet lipgloss across her pouting mouth. He had to get rid of this tedious Austrian distraction. However, this man seemed ultra eager to get the information. After all, he'd hung on all through the dinner, lurking in the shadows to try and snatch some time with him.

'Mr. Hunt, I really recommend that you meet with a very

good friend of mine, George Komininos. His shop is close to here, just off Portobello Road. George knows more about this subject than absolutely anyone else. I have his card here - check him out. You can always get me at Christies and we can have a chat. It's just that right now, I am a little......tied-up, as you say.'

With that, the professor handed over the business card, shook a few hands on the way out and swiftly followed the curvaceous bottom, swathed in tight black satin, over the road and through Millers red door.

Tarmin had just returned from the loo and overheard their conversation. Nursing his glass of Chilean Merlot, he looked closely at Nathan Hunt. Who was this mysterious dark-haired man who had suddenly taken up membership at The Academy overnight, and was now cornering his friend? Whatever, he certainly wasn't in the mood to be cornered by anyone, and decided to slip out without saying any extended goodbyes. Tapping a short message on his phone, he sent a swift text to Bundy.

'Bloody Mary's at The Electric. Tomorrow at 11.30. Good night and Good luck'.

Outside, on Hereford Road, Nathan's taxi was waiting.

'Blacks Hotel,' he instructed through the front window.

Nathan had a thing for London Cabs. He usually had a driver on call but somehow he still loved the anonymity of a cabby, even though they always talked too much for his liking.

A short while later, as he stepped from the taxi into Roland Gardens, another one pulled up and deposited a school of Japanese wealth depleters. Skipping over a puddle, he checked for messages at reception and took the stairs.

An hour later there was gentle knocking on his door.

'Room service!'

'Over there,' he pointed to a tall chest of drawers.

'Here? Oh my god! These are gorgeous!'

'How are you?' Nathan leaked a half smile, as the woman picked up the black lace lingerie set and sifted the soft silk stockings through her manicured hands.

Amanda was always the highlight of his visits to London. When he was sixteen, Nathan's German-born father had taken him to a small flat in the back streets of West Berlin, whilst the family were visiting his mother's relatives. Nathan's mother, Alberta, was a sweet but ineffectual woman, who had spent her dark beauty on her bullying and control freak husband. It was no surprise that her son would turn out to have the same sexual predilections. Nathan had therefore been introduced to sex in a most Victorian way - with a decent looking hooker in a small hotel. His father, brought up by elderly relatives, had the first same deal with sex, but for him, it was a less salubrious weather-boarded gaming joint in Klangenfurt.

Nathan loved that first German brothel, loved the whole experience of women for money, lapping up the impersonal aspect of no commitment. Sex to him developed into an 'on-demand service', in the same way that he could freely order a plate of Veiner Schnitzel or savour the finest brandy. Old habits did indeed die very slowly.

Amanda, who was in her mid-thirties now, was five foot nine inches tall and had a figure to die for, with surgically constructed breasts and softly rounded hipbones; Nathan's favourite place to lie and kiss her stomach. With her large blue eyes and golden curls, she looked as if butter wouldn't melt in her mouth. How misleading. She actually looked forward to Nathan's short trips to London, ever since the first time he'd shown that he had the balls for her. Hunt was a silent and controlling client, ordering her to dress and undress and to move in a certain way. She'd often harboured the fantasy that he was a contract killer holed up in a garret lair, and that after they'd finished their sex, he might take a gun, move to the bathroom window and assassinate a dark figure lurking on the streets below. He looked like he might handle a gun rather well. One day soon, she might just introduce a dressage whip into their sessions.

But it was frustrating that no such fantasies came true. Afterwards with Nathan, it was a case of pick up the cash and go - normally, a little unsteadily on her high-heeled feet, after all the champagne and frenetic energy. Her visits never lasted more than an hour and a half, but she always got to keep the stunning underwear he bought her and, on a very few occasions, there had been jewels. Nathan got his money's worth and Amanda's body paid the price.

But tonight was different.

Tonight, Nathan was wired and aggressive.

CHAPTER FIVE
Electric Bar and Grill, Notting Hill Gate

Nursing a woozy head, Tarmin Rimell dumped his Marlborough Lights and lighter on the freshly scrubbed bar of the Electric Brasserie on Portobello Road, arranging himself over two stools. He was a troubled man. On the one hand, he had done something that he'd always dreamed of - buying a dilapidated stately home, doing it up and making a great hotel and Writer's Retreat. And it was fun. At least, on some days. But then there was the magnetic tug of city life. He loved his life in London, lording over his other ventures, Millers Residence and The Academy. For one thing, his London friends were always more compliant drinking companions. Did he really want to do the countryside thing as well?

Then on the other hand, Glencot had seeped into his veins, its beauty and constant potential pervading his every thought. When he was there, footling around in Bath, walking in the lush gardens or propping up the bar of local pubs - well, it all seemed so congenial, so stress-free, so…..right. Plus, it gave him a breather from his nagging doubts about his marriage. What he really needed one of those trendy Life Coaches to come and sort him out. Narrow down his options, make him pinpoint his values. On the other hand….Life Coaches cost a lot, didn't they? And he'd always rather spend what loot he had on ebay, buying up bits and bobs for his already over-crammed shelves. Christ! What to do? It always boiled down to one thing and that was, light a fag, have a drink and forget about it. For now.

It was late morning, and he was traversing the delicate lines between cappuccino hour and pre-lunch cocktails, with The Electric still heaving with a residue of yummy mummies and a selection of not-so-yummy trainee rug rats. There was a time when children were never even seen in a bar. The few children that decorated the tables were actually not the problem - more their mothers, constantly commentating on the state of their progenies' appearance and eating habits, much to Tarmin's discomfort. Not to mention the black looks fired his way as clouds of his cigarette smoke drifted over their sweet little curly heads. Stubbing out his last and looking at his watch, he hoped to God that Bundy would get his arse over here, sharpish.

'A large Bloody Mary, please. And throw in a good splosh of Lee and Perrins.'

His head wasn't quite as crystal clear as it should have been. The pretence of trying to get on with his appalling wife was quite literally killing him. The way out was divorce, and divorce meant handing over his money. He'd worked long and hard to make a pile for himself and the thought of some

Transylvanian trainer getting his hands on the fruits of his endeavours, was almost too much to bear. But the obvious conclusion, bearing down on him every minute of the day, was to sell Glencot, pass over the cash and get the hell out.

Ever since overhearing the Austrian art dealer's inquisition of Professor Bundy (between the advances and retreats of that devilish little blonde), Tarmin had become intrigued by the whole concept of buried ancient artefacts. He wasn't quite sure why, except that it fed his love of all things devious. But most pressing, was this pending decision over Glencot, and Bundy was always his sounding board, someone who's opinion he could trust. If he did sell, he wanted to make a killing on it. There had to be some extra impetus and, of course, there was always loads of potential PR to be had from the area's connection with Glastonbury, King Arthur and all that Holy Grail historical stuff.

Just at that moment, a small boy unleashed his Dinky toy car right under Tarmin's stool, and scrambling on all fours to retrieve it, he knocked hard into the steel frame. It took every ounce of Tarmin's mental strength to refrain from taking a swipe, whilst his Bloody Mary slip-slapped over the bar counter.

Bundy had texted back that he'd make it by eleven thirty, but seeing it was now approaching midday, Tarmin was more than a little worried that he might have another form of elevenses on his mind. When they'd sloped off last night, Bundy and Bethany were last seen interlinking arms and skipping across Westbourne Grove, Bundy unnecessarily steering her bottom through the sparse traffic.

Topping and tipping an unlit cigarette on the bar top, Tarmin looked up and saw them crossing the room, hands interlocked.

'Oh shit, he thought. 'Woman in tow.'

Bethany was obviously a well-trained drinker, appearing as

sprightly now as she did at the lecture last night. Unlike Bundy, who looked as though he'd been crushed by a huge juggernaut.

'Thank you, thank you,' she enthused, taking a huge sip out of Tarmin's Bloody Mary, something that was guaranteed to wind him up. 'Sorry, had to do that. Needed a little pick-me-up, you know?'

'Definitely one of my better Academy bookings,' Bundy grinned at Tarmin. 'What a great night!'

'And morning by the looks of it,' snorted Tarmin, noting the professor's piercing pink eyes. He looked a bit like the Don who'd just been caught out by the University Dean sneaking a student down the fire escape. How did these old geezers do it?

'Let's start again, shall we? Good morning Tarmin!'

Bundy certainly sounded a lot perkier than he looked.

'Actually, I just popped in to say hi, thanks and bye,' Bethany planted a kiss either side of Tarmin's cheek. Turning to the professor, she kissed him hard on the lips, whispered 'speak later' and breezed off in a strong cloud of Chanel.

Bundy sat on the stool that Tarmin had been guarding for the last forty-five minutes, and ordered a beer.

'Er, no you don't! I'm the one who gives the lectures.' Bundy anticipated a grilling.

'And very good at it I see.'

'I feel rather out of practice, actually. Is Miss Bethany a regular at the hotel?'

Bundy wiped his beery mouth with the back of his hand and gently belched. Intellectual he might be, a purveyor of good etiquette he was not.

'Never seen her before,' replied Tarmin. 'Although her friend Rebecca is a member and came to the lecture on 'Pornography On The Internet' last week. She knows Gayle too. They're doing a nude life-drawing course together. Get the picture?'

A few nonsensical sentiments were further exchanged, before Tarmin jumped in with his problems. He explained about the need to part with Gayle, her possible affair with the Porchester Centre Yoga Teacher and how he needed to get a ton of money to pay her off.

'This guy she's hooked up with has provided the perfect excuse for me to ditch her, Bundy. He's potentially my saving grace. I've got to use it.'

'Why not just hire a private dick and be done with it? Far easier.'

Bundy's mind was pretty reluctant to focus on the downsides of love at this particular junction. After all, he'd just got laid.

Tarmin stirred his drink with a tall stick of celery and sighed.

'That's not the solution. I don't want the hassle of divorce courts, dramas of detectives tripping her up and so forth. No, it's not my style. I just want to make a ton of money and pay the cow off. Christ, Bundy, it's like living with the worst case of psoriasis you can imagine. I can barely eat my toast in the morning. She sits there, slurping her porridge and embarrassing me in front of the guests, with her incessant diatribes on healthy living. Need I go on?'

Bundy took the toothpick from his mouth and smiled.

'Of course not. I know that Gayle is a thorn in your side and I think you deserve to move on. Find someone else. So, where does your best asset lie, would you say? What can we plunder?'

'It's got to be Glencot. I can't think of anything else, and I am not going to leave the London stuff to her. No way.'

Tarmin and Bundy discussed the pros and cons of filching a bunch of money from elsewhere, but it all came back to Glencot. The jewel in his purse. He loved the place with all his heart - although he did admit to Bundy that running the country operation was a far greater challenge and headache than he'd ever anticipated. Bundy was a scoundrel at heart, Tarmin knew that. If ever he needed to fabricate a fib of some sort or find a way of slipping the net, Bundy was the man. They needed to manufacture a scam; something that would yield the extra cash to release this hefty burden from his clutches. And once you appealed to the mind of a semi-criminal, it never took long for the penny to drop. Bundy, never the greatest Gayle fan, leapt at the chance.

Tarmin had told him in strict confidence about the hidden cellar, during an earlier conversation, and Bundy had asked to come and inspect it when he was next at Glencot. He loved things like that - secret panelling, dingy dungeons. He sincerely hoped that in his next life he'd come back as a twisted spy or a corrupt police inspector. On reflection, maybe it'd be more fun to be a drug-addled pimp? Whatever, it was always a simple, straightforward plot that would do the trick and he laid it out for Tarmin.

Glencot was built in a place that reeked of ancient history; all those tales of Glastonbury, King Arthur and the Holy Grail. Tarmin had to somehow acquire a bunch of ancient religious artefacts - stone carvings, gold symbols, whatever. He would then make it known, via articles on a carefully chosen Internet blog, that an un-named stately home in Somerset was sitting on an incredible untapped fortune of historical worth. But most of all, they would target a buyer; someone with bags of money and someone who was passionate about this period of history and art. That was the simple part, as far as Bundy was concerned. That bloke last night, the Austrian artefacts dealer, Nathan Hunt. This man, he told Tarmin, was worth a complete fortune. He was a multi-millionaire, an incorrigible buyer and his Viennese museum was notorious. Bundy had often thought about visiting it, but had not yet torn himself away to do so. And, as far as he knew from people in the trade, Hunt had a bit of a screw loose. He sounded like he'd be the kind of nutty punter who'd buy up a house, just to get at the treasure hidden within.

'But you have to be clever about this, Tarmin' he added. 'We will indicate that the owner of the house - yourself - has absolutely no idea about what you're sitting on. You're an innocent duck of the first order. A man who is a bit of a bumbler; one sandwich short of a picnic, sort of thing. Shouldn't be hard for you to act out. That way, Hunt will really go for the kill. He'll do anything to get Glencot. Of course, it won't be the house that he's after, it'll be what he believes lies beneath it. You play the besotted owner of a place, pretending that you wouldn't give it up for love or money, and he'll bid through the roof to get it. Eventually, you'll give in. Bingo, you'll make a bloody fortune.'

Tarmin knocked back the last few drops of his drink and wiped his mouth.

'Knew I could rely on you. Where do we start?'

'Go to George's shop and get him to sort out a job lot price on some of his millions of artefacts from there. You only need a couple of the real McCoy to leave around Glencot for Hunt to check out, in the first place. Those can be on loan. The stuff that we'll be hiding in that hidden cellar of yours, the actual buried treasure, will be crap. You won't have to shell out much. Off you go.'

Bundy stood up, attempting to smooth out the multitude of creases in his black jacket, and patted his friend's arm.

'Oh, and by the way. I'm in at fifteen per cent.'

'Bloody hell, Bundy. I'm getting divorced, I'll need every penny!'

'OK, ten percent then, you mean bastard.'

Tarmin saw Bundy off at the tube and headed out to see George over at 'Komininos & Sons'. Suddenly, life seemed rosy and he was stunned to find himself whistling a cheery section from Die Fledermaus. Where on earth had that come from? Oh God, it was from Gayle, of course. She'd been banging on about that sodding opera all last night; the very latest piece of pretentious culture that she'd indulged in. Come to think of it, who had she gone to the opera with? Maybe he should call Sadler's Wells and find out the name on the tickets? Bundy's idea of a private dick suddenly garnered some appeal.

Weaving his way through the swirling hordes, all hunting down Saturday morning antiques and crap junk, Tarmin arrived at George's small shop, which sported a great little flat at the top. He'd called on his mobile beforehand, and was trying to digest the thought that he'd have to stomach yet more food. But it was a done deal that always came with George's unavoidable Greek hospitality. However, Feta cheese and vine leaves were a somewhat tricky concept to swallow so soon after blueberry muffins and scrambled eggs.

George's shop was decoratively manned by a well-educated Polish art student. After a few minutes of congenial conversation, Tarmin could see that the student hadn't been employed for her extensive knowledge of pre-Christian antiquities, or even for her very impressive English speaking skills.

'The punters love Kasia,' George muttered as they climbed the narrow book-lined stairs. 'You'd be surprised at how many come through the door just to get a close-up!'

This was probably a rather necessary addition to his business, since George (an aging Greek with stumpy legs and wiry salt'n'pepper beard, hairs sprouting out of his ears and eyebrows at alarming angles), was decidedly less alluring than even the stone gargoyle adorning his display window. He'd lost count of how many times he'd been asked whether he'd auditioned for the role of Bilbo Baggins, or whether his flat was furnished with antique toadstools.

George had lived above the shop for over thirty years, and it was obvious that collecting, or as some might say hoarding, was in his blood. Downstairs, on the shop floor, it was all about antiquities, but those in the know would ask to go upstairs and talk to him about anything and everything to do with artefacts from the Roman to Arthurian periods, spanning from 55BC to the end of the 6th Century. On occasion, he lectured, like Bundy, at art colleges or private functions but, being a shy man, preferred to entertain his visitors with retsina and strong black coffee in the clutter box that he called home.

The upstairs living room was enormous, leading on to a terrace littered with remnants from the Roman Empire, together with the traces of Boudica's final submission. The occasional tinkle of the shop door kept Tarmin wondering who was coming in and out. Sitting under a shady canopy, the roasting sun filled the sky and their first bottle of sweet red Mavrodaphne slipped down rather too easily. Tarmin secretly wondered if he was becoming an alcoholic. His intake of wine matched most people's daily cups of tea, and Gayle forever nagged that broken red veins were popping out all over his nose. He sincerely hoped not. George made a couple of forays downstairs, returning with a smile and a wad of notes.

'At least this crazy market is only one day a week.'

Tarmin started poking around in a cardboard box sitting on the coffee table, whilst George unscrewed a second bottle.

'What's this lot in the box?' he asked.

'Don't really know yet,' George replied. 'Marian brought it back last week, using her initiative and my money. Fifty quid for the lot, she said.'

Tarmin loved a good rummage - therapeutic release from stress. This one looked as if it had been emptied straight from his grandfather's toolbox with all the rubbish; screws, iron bars, padlocks and so forth, filtered down to the bottom.

'I love all this crap,' he said digging deeper.

Tarmin had been 'in the trade' for years before he jumped ship and went into the hotel business. He decided that he didn't have the dealer mentality, and the ceaseless humping of furniture was no picnic. He'd always had a fascination for antiquity, and frequent trips to George's, eased his cravings. His first real find had been in a box bought at a house sale in Sussex. The sale was held in the home of a well-travelled gentleman botanist who'd lived for over a century, before ascending to the great arboretum in the sky. His house had remained in a complete time warp and the box that Tarmin picked out, seemingly, contained a load of trinkets of little value. It wasn't until he got home and closely inspected the mayhem that Tarmin identified a first period Worcester creamer. The jug had subsequently been sold at Christie's for a handsome £24,000, nearly 30 years ago.

Meandering through past reveries, Tarmin jolted when the shop bell jangled again. Looking at his watch and seeing that George was busying himself with the restoration of a painting at the back of the room, he remembered the real reason for his visit and detailed his dilemma.

'I just want a couple of really good pieces on loan. Maybe something bronze. Then I'll buy some of the smaller stone stuff, you know? Things that look as if they might have come from an entombment, like religious artefacts. I want it to seem as if I'm sitting on some kind of extraordinary burial ground.'

George agreed to sort out the deal and he'd get it ready for later. He wanted to enjoy his retsina and never trusted himself to touch any pieces when he was half cut. He'd once learned the hard way by snapping a Roman iron sword in half and ruining an incredible sale with the Vatican's Main Hall. Calling downstairs to Kasia, he briefed her on which pieces needed to be collected, and a number of religious artefacts that could be found in the basement store. He instructed her to put them all in a box and take them round to Millers after work. Done and dusted.

Tarmin popped his glasses back on and brushed himself down. George's place was so overstuffed, it was like opening an Egyptian tomb.

'Actually, can you hold on a minute?' George waved a large brush, dribbling dollops of watery black paint. 'Since we're on the subject of favours and family woes, I wanted to ask you a small favour as well.'

Tarmin immediately re-seated himself and lit a cigarette. He couldn't remember the last time that George had ever asked anything of him. George strolled over to the fireplace and stood to one side, his hand running up and down the gilded frame of his prize painting. It was a dour portrait of a 16th man, dressed head to toe in black and dated around 1500. George had stumbled across the piece during a trip to Italy in the late 60s and had no notion of what a treasure he'd bought. It wasn't until a visitor from Rome's Galleria Borghese made a ludicrous offer, that he knew he'd hit the jackpot.

'You really love that piece, don't you?'
Tarmin sensed George's melancholy. 'Not just for its monetary value, but you seem to relish every second of just having it.'

'That's exactly the point, Tarmin. This painting is not only my pension, but it's the thing that I cherish beyond all others. And I have a problem. As you know, my fuckwit of a son is forever hassling me to sell up and give the family some money. Melvin is poisonous, Tarmin - poisonous. Nothing on this earth will ever persuade me to give this to him, so I have come up with a plan.'

George walked across the room and pushed aside stacks of books. Reaching behind, he pulled out a large canvas from behind the leather-bound tomes. Tarmin gasped. It was an exact copy of the Dark Man above the fireplace.

'You got it copied?' He was incredulous. 'Let me look at it. It's quite unbelievable, amazing. You're going to have to be very careful keeping your eye on the original - there's no way you can tell that it's a fake.'

'Well, not to the very untrained eye, certainly. I'm very pleased with this. I used a Spanish guy I know, Domingo Dacosta, and he's marvellous. But I need to get rid of the original. I never, ever want that bastard to have the real thing. You can take it, Tarmin - it's a present to my oldest friend and I've changed my will accordingly.'

Tarmin was stunned. 'Are you really sure about this, George? It's not just the drink talking and you'll regret it later?'

George was not to be budged. 'I have enough pension income from other treasures here. Melvin will never learn of this until my death. I will glean just as much pleasure from Dacosta's version. And be sure to store it well. Is there anywhere at Millers?'

Tarmin mulled it over. Millers was certainly not the place to keep this treasure. He was sure there were still rats in the attic and it would be just his luck if Gayle had one of her clumsy fits and put her foot through it. No, this would go to Glencot with him, and he would hang it with pride in his bedroom and enjoy it the way George did.

It was the perfect solution for the troubled George and Melvin would never in a million years think that anything was up. George had begun to distrust Melvin recently. He was sure his son was on drugs and becoming more and more unreliable and aggressive. Melvin had been a shit for most of his adult life, but nowadays he was almost unbearable. George had come to dread his visits and was certain that he had begun stealing from him. His place was such a tip, it always took him an age to find anything, and his son knew that. But George wasn't a fool. He'd noticed that various small paintings, a couple of china bowls and even a mounted tapestry had somehow gone walkabout. He was not going to risk his beloved Dark Man, at any cost.

Tarmin picked up the fake and together they hung it on the wall. George helped him take the real one down onto the street and hailed a cab. Pulling down the window as it drove off, he yelled out: 'See you at the V&A bash tonight!'

George dismissed the comment with an insouciant wave of the hand. He was not someone who lusted after black tie events. At least some of his friends, Bundy and Tarmin included, would be at his table tonight. As Tarmin looked back, he saw Kasia standing in the doorway of Komininos & Sons, one arm propped high on the door, her magnificent breasts standing proud. The breeze lifted one side of her long, wispy blue skirt revealing a beautifully shaped bronzed leg. How very disappointing it must be for George, he thought. To have to work with that creature every day and know that you would never in a million years get further than a polite hello and goodbye. If he were her boss, well, he'd have her over the piano, under the bookshelves and in the middle of everything else. All of a sudden, a bleeping text message pulled him back to reality.

'Where the bloody hell are you?'

'Shit" Tarmin thought. 'I'd better sober up. Gayle's at home.' Straight opposite George's shop, Nathan Hunt downed the last of his skinny latte in Starbucks, closed the Christie's catalogue and wiped the smeared froth from his mouth. At the moment that Tarmin hopped into the black cab, painting tucked under his arm, Hunt (completely oblivious of Tarmin's presence), paid the bill and headed over to Komininos & Sons. Some of the stalls were already beginning to pack up their wares, vans loading with boxes and clothes rails, and rubbish piling up in the gutters. Nathan entered the shop, carefully closing the jingling door behind him. The beautiful girl smiled.

'Is Mr. Komininos in?' He appraised her good looks but couldn't afford to indulge in time wasting.

By the time Kasia gave him her answer, Nathan was already half way up the stairs and out of sight.

CHAPTER SIX

Miller's Residence, Westbourne Grove

As Tarmin climbed the stairs to the first floor reception back at Millers, he squeezed past a young French girl unceremoniously humping an enormous suitcase down the black-carpeted stairway, expertly missing the statue of Julius Caesar. Like the true gentleman that he was, Tarmin stepped aside to allow passage of the bag and its carrier.

'You're off then?' he commented to the couple, who were trailing behind his French manager. The pair, themselves laden with a collection of designer shopping bags, responded with enthusiastic remarks on the incredible array of antiques that resplendently littered the residence and promised to be back soon and spread the word among the musical fraternity of Lower Toddington.

'Bye, and have a great trip!' Tarmin waved, as Virginia valiantly struggled to squeeze the case into the back of their Mercedes. He didn't feel like helping her.

'Zat car company is ooseless and I will not oose them again' she said in perfect Virgineese.

'Absolutely' Tarmin agreed. 'What's happening in the hotel?'

'Is all a mess, all ze people, zey come down at wonce, and ze coffee masheene, she iz broken.'

'Come on, chop, chop. We need to get upstairs.'

The long-suffering Virginia scrutinized Tarmin with hate-filled eyes. He never helped her with the luggage and sometimes, just sometimes, she felt like she could hit him over the head with one of his collection of Zulu clubs and be done with him.

Millers Residence had opened some ten years before on a whim. Tarmin, single at the time and not versed in the finer arts of domestic science, had hit upon the idea of an 'upmarket' Bed and Breakfast in trendy Notting Hill. The building's previous inhabitants had ranged from rats in the sewer-like basement, to a pigeon-infested top floor that even the resident squatter had deserted in disgust. The hotel was now, as one quality Sunday described it, 'A cross between the old curiosity shop and a set from La Traviata'. Tarmin's ethos was a simple one, to give everything away, except the contents. Free booze on tap, day and night, and everything on a 'help yourself' basis, which the regulars soon got the hang off. The guests came mainly from the music, film, media and fashion worlds, and seemed to take to the accessible home style like ducks to water.

Virginia led the way upstairs and into the main drawing room, which Yvonne, the long suffering cleaning miracle, kept mentioning was 'getting a little full.' Tarmin's idea of antiques collecting certainly made maximalism look like a monk's cell. Feeling a little tetchy after too much booze and sun, he eased himself into the office space, grabbing a boiled sweet from the table, and logged on to the computer.

'Ginny, why is this fucking computer telling me to kill it and start again?'

The doorbell rang. Two heads appeared on the CCTV screen. Virginia pressed the entry button.

'Who's that?' Tarmin asked.

'I don't know.' Virginia couldn't actually care less. 'Ze intercom is broken, but I sink zey are check-ins.'

One phone rang, then a mobile bleeped. The doorbell buzzed in conjunction with a head poking around the office door, asking apologetically if there was any more coffee and maybe a car to the airport? Virginia, true to her cool Brittany roots, somehow coped as if doing a jigsaw from the inside out. The couple on the CCTV arrived upstairs to check in, asking for the Honeymoon Suite. Tarmin quietly wondered where on earth that might be, and after they politely requested non-smoking, he hoped to God that Yvonne had removed all ashtrays and liberally sprayed with polish.

'Just married then?' Tarmin had spotted tiny multi-coloured paper hearts in the bride's hair. 'First time?' and without waiting for the reply, slipped into the drawing room to sober up. He really couldn't entertain the idea of listening to someone's tedious wedding details with his head spinning with all that grape juice. And just when his own marriage was likely heading towards the divorce courts.

Flopping back against a cushion, he bit into a crisp green apple and pondered his newly made decision about selling Glencot. It was going to be a huge wrench, but it had to be worth it. He dialled upstairs to their flat, which was tucked away at the back of the hotel, much to the delight of Gayle who escaped all constant administrative duties whenever she could. Between her yoga sessions, pottery and art classes, incorrigible shoe shopping sprees and busy social diary, Gayle was one busy bunny.

No answer. At that moment, Gayle's stick insect form (unattractively attired in a mustard coloured velour tracksuit and dripping sweat), jogged through the door.

'Nice lunch?'

Gayle slid her perspiring body across the room and gave his neat little bum a nip. Whatever Gayle was, she was unfailingly upbeat, which ground the more pessimistic Tarmin into the dust. He must pretend to be nice right now, as the last thing he wanted was for her to guess that anything was up.

'Am I forgiven then?' he muttered, not really caring for the answer.

'Forgiven for what? For being out all day? What have you been up too? God, it smells like someone's tipped half a barrel of Pinot Noir all over you.'

Gayle had clearly forgotten her earlier rage. Thank God he had married someone with short-term memory loss.

'Are we still on for the V&A bash?' Tarmin asked, trying to sound vaguely affectionate.

'Yes and we're expected there at seven-thirty, latest.' Gayle slugged out the room, straightening some lily stalks by the bar and heading for the magic of her makeover room.

Tarmin stretched out his legs and lit a cigarette. It took him all of ten minutes to get ready for a night out and tonight could be interesting. It was the Asian Art annual party for which Bundy had somehow swung a bunch of invitations, supplying good hunting ground for new punters for both the Hotel and Academy. He tipped a good measure of Martin Miller's gin into a bohemian glass tumbler, added Fevertree tonic water over a mountain of ice cubes and threw in a wedge of lime. Time to follow in Gayle's clammy footsteps and put on his best bib and tucker.

Walking past reception, he saw a beautiful young girl walking up the stairs, accompanied by a beefy cab driver. It was Kasia with the boxes of stuff from George. Tarmin took a cursory look at the contents and his heart began to race. His days of bachelorhood might well be approaching faster than he'd thought. He felt like doing a high kick on the staircase. Professor Bundy lived in a top floor flat overlooking the Albert Hall. On the surface, he seemed to be the consummate bachelor with a hectic social life and a lifetime's art collection amassed in one vast studio room. Divorced now for six years, he'd no intention of returning to a life of consideration. Bundy's dictum was that selfish was good; to be happy you had to be selfish. If you were happy, happiness flooded all around. A simple enough philosophy, but it worked for him and that was all that mattered. He was a man who could tie his own bow tie, achieved his own ironing and cooked a mean fish pie.

Giving his jacket one last brush across the shoulders, and smoothing his hair into place, he grabbed his umbrella and headed out of the building.

A short time later, as the metal doors slid open across the lift entrance, he pondered on a couple of misgivings. Bethany had said she was 'maybe' going to this event too. Apparently Rebecca was part of an organised table and someone had dropped out. He was having a mild panic attack. Bundy had enjoyed his impromptu night with the petite blonde, but was he up for seeing her two nights on the trot? On the other hand, should a man of his age and stage in life really be putting women through the one-night-stand syndrome? Once upon a time, he liked having to be accountable for someone by his side. Now, the mere thought of freedom seeping through his fingers was enough to induce heart palpitations.

THE WOOKEY HOLE AFFAIR

The Victoria and Albert museum was already heaving with flame-throwers, stilted white-faced Harlequins doing the meet-and-greet, and the combined drums of the Chinese Army in the background. Over two hundred people were expected at the champagne reception and dinner in the Cast Gallery. Bundy's invitation was plucked from his hand by a mandarin beauty and he was funnelled through to the vast entrance hall. Only hours earlier, the space had been the daily ticket office and now the computer was replaced by a vodka and champagne bar. On high, the Chaconi glass chandelier gleamed above the sparkling jewels of the assembled crowd.

Bundy exchanged cursory nods and hellos with several people before joining a group deep in conversation about Modern Chinese art. Amongst the gathering were the curator of the 'Art In London Foundation', a couple of red faced male sponsors, an expensive looking African woman swathed in ethnic fabrics, plus Tarmin and Gayle. Pleasantries were exchanged just as dinner was announced, and the crocodile started to snake its way in the direction of the dining hall. Presiding over proceedings Michaelangelo's David and a selection of the world's greatest treasures in stone, bronze and marble, were all lit to perfection.

As the diners huddled around the table plan (displayed on one enormous artist's easel), Professor Bundy spotted Rebecca in the far distance, wearing a long silver dress, with her arms draped around a tall man. His eyes scanned the rest of her guests, but no sign of Bethany. Just for a split second, he couldn't make up his mind if he was relieved or disappointed. For some reason, he always seemed to be sat at the table with the highest level of absenteeism. Not tonight. Within minutes it was full of the usual suspects clinking wine glasses and exchanging little pecks on the cheek. Just as the smoked haddock soup arrived, and warm twisted rolls were placed on the china side plates, it became apparent that there was one space empty - the chair just two along from his right. Leaning over, he clocked George Komininos' place card and wondered what was keeping the short man? George was a) never late and b) loved his food with a passion. And Bundy had hoped to see him tonight to ask whether he might repeat the brilliant lecture on Celtic religious symbolism that he'd so successfully given to some of his students last year.

'Where's George?' he asked, leaning towards Tarmin, who was surreptitiously trying to remove a stray pigeon's feather from Gayle's hair. 'I thought you said he was coming?'

Tarmin stopped for a moment and looked at his watch.

'Hum. Unusual for him; we all know how punctual Giorgio is when it comes to champagne and free grub. Maybe he decided to spend the evening with the Polish sex queen instead.'

'Polish sex queen?' Gayle screeched. 'Who the fuck is that? I thought George was more the type to be gagging over Michaelangelo's stone boys?'

'Don't be ridiculous Gayle. He leaves all that sort of stuff to his son. Anyway, I imagine he's nursing a bit of a headache. George is always far too over-liberal with the retsina and for an extremely short man, that can weigh heavy.'

Bundy nodded, recalling some of his own Bacchanalian sessions with Komininos. Raising a glass of wooded Semillon to his lips, his eyes followed Rebecca walking past, her long blonde hair swept high on her head and secured by a beautiful diamante hair clasp. She looked lithe and muscular in her Amanda Wakeley number. Her breasts were small and pert, unlike Bethany's substantial pair, hard nipples showing through the thin silver gauze. At that moment, she glanced back and caught Bundy staring. She smiled for an instant, attempted a gracious little wave and moved off, her shapely bottom swaying like a clock pendulum. Just as she reached the edge of the room, she bent down and said a brief hello to someone. Bundy strained to see. Without his strong glasses, he couldn't actually focus much further than the vase of white roses in front of him, but this person definitely seemed familiar. Where on earth had he seen him before?

On the other side of the room, seated at Table One, Nathan Hunt sat bored out of his mind. This was just one of three such events that he attended annually, together with The Armoury in New York and Art Basel in Switzerland. Even though Asian Art was hardly his field of expertise, he'd inherited many important Chinese paintings from his parents, exhibited in their family's gallery in Vienna. The social events had to have a business purpose, far beyond any possible pleasure. Of course, he was always placed on the 'Top Table', as they liked to call it. Basically, it was reserved for those with the most money and influence. The thing he hated about top tables was that all eyes stared in his direction, and a string of bodies seemed magnetised to pass by, swarming like bees to honey. Just like the thin blonde in the silver dress who was eyeballing him just now. Did he know her? A bunch of worthless introductions flowed straight through him and out the other side without trace. Hunt's mind was far away and his demeanour was particularly nervous. Even the lady to his left impolitely asked whether he unfortunately suffered from shaky hand syndrome. Embarrassed by his lack of social ease, Hunt told her he was coming down with a bug. That it was one of the down sides of travelling so much - he would pick up every ailment on the planet from airplane cabins and hotels. He'd stick it out through the dessert course, make his apologies and leave. After all, he was only in the UK for a short visit and he had a very particular agenda to adhere to. Sourcing certain very important acquisitions.

CHAPTER SEVEN
Springfield Road, NW8

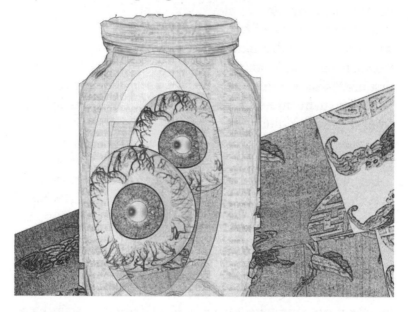

Chief Inspector Jack Donaldson's day had kicked off in a pre-dictably depressing way, his hand stifling the alarm clock just as it was starting to clear its electronic throat. Donaldson's first self-imposed duty of the day was to get up and out without waking his wife, Joan, the amorphous and gently snoring mass in the bed next to him. To add insult to injury, a head full of plastic curlers topped off her bulging shape beneath the duvet. Bloody Hell. Never in his worst dreams (and he was not by nature an optimistic man), had he dreamt that he would finish up sleeping with a woman in curlers.

Sleeping was the operative word, these days. Just over a year ago, Donaldson had found out that she'd been having an affair with one of the kids' art teachers, which didn't, in his opinion, say much for the art department's conception of visual awareness. Ever since the day when it had all blown apart, they'd lived in a state of silent attrition. Then there had been one night a month ago, when she'd been out with her lady friends and came home surprisingly randy and contrite, reeking of gin and orange and wanting to make a fresh start. But that rare mood was rescinded by the following morning.

Donaldson sometimes pondered reincarnation. Was this his first life? In which case, he could look forward to the next few, which had to be infinitely better. Or was this one a punishment for something he'd done in a previous existence? If this were the case, he only hoped he'd bloody well enjoyed whatever gross misdemeanours he'd indulged in.

Donaldson got dressed in the dark, as was his normal practice. He sometimes emerged looking a little strange in the harsh light of day, but did odd socks really account for much when placed against the great backcloth of eternity? He went into the kitchen, boiled the kettle and put a tea bag in a mug. He took a new milk carton out of the fridge, tried to obey the instructions and then lost his temper, spilling milk down his already none-too-clean suit. He wiped away the splashes with a tea towel, realised he'd smeared it into the weave even deeper, gave up and considered the day ahead.

Six years to go to retirement, and his professional life consisted almost exclusively of petty crime and filling in countless bloody forms. Still, he just remembered, there was the sniff of a murder in the air today. Next on the list, was to call his redoubtable side-kick, Detective Sergeant Paul Williams, a man who constantly reminded him that he'd joined the force for higher things than chasing stolen car radios and small-time dope dealers. Williams tended to channel his frustrated ambition into being disapproving of Donaldson's sloppiness. Nothing was said, but the atmosphere was always lingering. Ah well, by the time Williams was fifty and disillusioned, Donaldson had no doubt that he'd have an efficient DS being disapproving of him too. He was just sorry that he wouldn't be there to witness the irritation.

One hour later, Donaldson was at his desk, wondering how best to mop up spilled coffee without prematurely aging all the various paperwork, towards which the brown liquid was seeping at an alarming speed. He put his copy of the Daily Express between the official documents and the rising tide of caffeine, whipped his cigarette packet off the desk (slightly too late), and was hunting for a tissue when there was a peremptory knock at the door and Williams entered, carrying a green folder.

'Ah, good morning, Williams', said the Chief Inspector. 'Just got a call from the lads down on Portobello, and it seems this could be your lucky day'.

'Murder?' Williams asked, hoping against all hope that the answer was yes. It was pretty 'un-pc' for a PC to admit to such a thing, but he found a good old-fashioned murder the best crime of all. At least it taxed the brain, rather than having to deal with all the daily nonsense of busting hookers, prosecuting the same nuisance burglars over and over and overseeing a slew of waste-of-time phone calls from the public who always wanted to report anything that moved.

His best case of all time had been twelve years earlier, when he'd assisted Donaldson on a murder that ended up filling the newspapers for weeks. He'd even been interviewed on Crime Watch, which had thrilled both himself and his wife, Daphne, although on reflection, he wouldn't wear those soft leather grey shoes again, nor his large owl-like glasses. That particular case had started out with a call to Southern Row, after a dismembered hand was spotted sticking through a pile of leaves on the railway. His assigned band of officers stormed a respectable looking house and found the victim's blue eyes pickled in a jar in the fridge, along with her iced tongue in a box, and most distressingly of all, her breasts wrapped in cling film in the deep freeze. On closer inspection, it turned out that the man involved had not only massacred his wife, but also the cat, their ancient bloodhound, and finished up by burning two caged canaries to a cinder. Graham J. Worsted claimed that a personal call from God had told him to do it.

'So what's the case today?' Williams asked.

'PC Atiga will fill you in. She's over there now. Not sure what's happened really. A dead body and a room full of broken glass, that much we do know. I'll be with you in a second. Just have a couple of things to sort out here.'

Williams looked down at Donaldson's desk, saw the spilled coffee everywhere and inwardly sighed. His boss needed a high chair and bib, let alone a right-hand man.

They arrived in a blaze of sirens in Portobello Road, and were briskly waved through to the taped-off crime scene outside 'Komininos & Sons'. Several uniformed officers stood in the road holding back the great British public, eagerly awaiting the appearance of the customary body bag. And judging from the multitude of accents flying around, half the crowd were the ubiquitous tourists, populating every inch of fashionable London.

Chief Inspector Donaldson introduced himself to the nearest uniform. He prided himself on telling the difference between traffic wardens and community liaison officers.

'PC James, sir', the officer answered.

'Who's the senior officer here today?' asked Donaldson briskly.

'Sergeant Pearce, sir. Over there, sir', came the equally snappy response. Sergeant Pearce was already moving towards Donaldson and greeted him.

'Give it to me in a nutshell, sergeant.' Donaldson watched Williams straining to get a look at where the deceased body was.

'This morning, we were called at 9:40am by a Miss Kasia Mindykowski, who, on arriving at the premises, opened up as usual and went directly upstairs for her customary cup of peppermint tea. She found one George Komininos slumped over the kitchen table, his face buried in a bowl of Feta Cheese and salad. Miss Mindykowski initially thought that the poor fellow had fallen asleep after one of his not uncommon retsina binges, but soon realised that it was altogether more sinister. When she tried to wake him, to her horror, the victim's head flopped to one side'. The sergeant paused, 'Not quite sure how he died, sir, although there are definite signs of a struggle. Once we'd pulled him out of the cheese bowl, we could see a huge black eye and various cuts and bruises. He was in a right old state, poor bugger. It seems that Miss Mindykowski ran straight next-door to the Cosy Café screaming blue murder, and that's when they notified the police'.

'Thank you sergeant, and where are we up to now?' Donaldson said looking at his watch. 'It's just on eleven, who's upstairs? Have forensics arrived'

'Where is the girl now, Pearce?' asked Williams, feeling a little sidelined.

'She's still in the Cosy Café with WPC Atiga, who is currently taking her statement. She is naturally in a bit of a state, sir', added the sergeant.

'Williams, why don't you just pop next door and console her a little? You're good at that,' instructed Donaldson, knowing it would piss him off. All Williams would have wanted was to peek at the body. 'I'll join you when I'm finished here. Lead on, Pearce'.

Donaldson and Pearce ducked under the 'Do Not Cross' tape and entered the shop. They were immediately confronted by a white-coated forensic officer, who issued them with sterile suits so that they could proceed to the scene.

'Go carefully on the stairs, gentlemen', the forensic officer instructed the pair. 'This building is like something out of the Ark. And when you get upstairs, you'll find Dr Bill Jacobson who is our duty pathologist today'.

The policemen gingerly climbed the stairs, avoiding the mountains of books pilled high on either side.

At the top, the room was already buzzing with white suits wielding infrared torches, little brushes and evidence bags. The body was still in its slumped position at the table and the photographer was finalising one of the finest photo opportunities of his lifetime. This was like something out of The Godfather - a murdered man with his face tangled in stringy lettuce leaves and smeared with white cheese. Donaldson introduced himself to the doctor, who without any formal pleasantries, launched into his initial thoughts on the cause and time of death.

'It looks like he died at around 9 or 10pm yesterday evening, and from my initial examination, it seems pretty conclusive that no bones were broken. It could actually be a natural death, maybe even a heart attack. Though why he's got all these cuts and bruises is obviously suspicious. I'm just not sure without proper examination.'

Donaldson moved carefully around the room taking in the surroundings. He'd never seen such a junk heap. Books piled high on books, paintings crammed onto every inch of wall space and a multitude of rugs overlapping each other on the wooden floor. Stone busts and columns cramped the outside patio, and from every angle, some bronzed face or marbled creature seemed to be staring back at him. But it was not artfully arranged. No, this was a man who lived alone - someone who left his dirty wine glasses piled high in the sink, and vases of stinking old flowers rotting for weeks.

He lifted up the lid of an ancient chest and half expected a rat to leap out. But something had definitely gone on in here. Shards from a large mirror were lying scattered across the rug, two stone pots had been smashed, books thrown in disarray and flowers from a chipped vase tossed across the floor. It didn't seem likely that his death could have been natural.

'Do there appear to be any signs of forced entry?' he asked Pearce, who was dutifully following Donaldson around like a pet limpet.

'Not as far as we can tell, sir. And nothing seems to be missing, not that you could easily tell in a shithole like this. Sorry, sir - that just slipped out'.

Donaldson was rapidly coming to the conclusion that there was little more to be done at the crime scene and that his time would be best served by checking in with Williams and the young Miss Mindykowski. He went downstairs, slipped off the white suit, dumped it in the bin conveniently provided by the shop door and stepped out from the gloom to meet a barrage of questions from the now-assembled press.

'Inspector Donaldson, can you confirm the identity of the deceased?' a tall man shouted from his right.

'Do you have a suspect?'

'How was he killed?'

'Is Mr. Komininos the victim here, or is it his son?'

The barrage and popping of flashbulbs from every quarter grated on Donaldson's nerves.

'Gentlemen, gentlemen. I can make no comment other than we are investigating a death on the premises, and as soon as we have any more information, which will probably be shared at this evening's press call, then you will all be put in the picture. We respect your patience. Good day'.

With that he was off to join Williams in the Cosy Café, gagging for a steaming mug of tea and a long overdue sausage sandwich.

Williams was in full consolation mode and was obviously not too upset at being delegated the less interesting task of interviewing the discoverer of the crime. Seeing Donaldson walk through the doors and heading towards them, he shot his boss a look to kill. Donaldson could instantly see why. Miss Knockers, or whatever her name was, was one hell of a girl, even in a state of such extreme distress. She had high cheekbones that tapered down to a perfectly sculptured face, jaw line firm and jutting beautifully in defiance. Her snowy skin was soft and clear, not a mark on her young, subtly made-up face. Her body was lithe and shapely, with incredible breasts showing their perfect shape through a tight polo-neck jumper. Large brown eyes framed by jet black lashes slowly blinked soft streaming tears for her possibly murdered friend and, when her delicate hand moved to wipe the wetness from her full, rosy lips, it was almost too much for Donaldson. Imagining her down on her knees, this girl was one hell of a beauty. It almost made him physically sick when he thought of fat Joan back home, rolls of lardy flab filling her green polyamide nightie and filthy curlers topping her blue-grey thinning hair. He would join the gym for this cherubic girl, hike to space and back, just for the chance of a much-needed shag. Come on Donaldson, this is a murder scene, not a lap dancing club. The Detective pulled himself back into police mode by registering the Polish woman's audible distress.

'Good morning, Miss Kno.....Miss Mindykowski', he regained his composure in the nick of time, when Williams shot him a black look. 'This must be a very distressing situation for you and I offer you many condolences for your tragic loss. I'm afraid there are one or two points that I will need to go over with you. I'm sure that Detective Sergeant Williams here will have already asked you the key questions.'

He looked over to Williams and beckoned him to one side.

'What's the story so far, Williams?'

'Well, sir', replied Williams. 'It's just about exactly what Detective Sergeant Pearce said, that the lady seems a bit clueless. As far as she ever knew, Mr Komininos was well liked, having lived in the road for over thirty years, and didn't appear to have an enemy in the world. However, as you came through the door, she was just telling me about a couple of unusual incidents that happened late yesterday afternoon, which may well have bearing on the case. I think I need a bit more time with this lady, sir. Then I can get a proper handle on what's going on.'

'Thank you Williams, I'll take over from here. Why don't you go next door and don one of those pretty white suits? Introduce yourself to the good doctor upstairs.'

'As you wish, sir' replied Williams, torn between his infatuation for the Polish sex queen and the consoling thrill of getting to see the dead body. He could always engineer another interview with Mindykowski later on.

Donaldson returned to the table, and ordered a mug of tea for himself and Miss Knockers, displaying an endearing concern by requesting that hers be 'laced with extra sugar, to help with the shock'. His much awaited sausage sandwich would have to remain in the frying pan for now, with the reckoning that blasting mustardy pork breath near this heavenly creature might be misconstrued as a trifle uncouth. Williams wouldn't do such a thing, he was sure of that.

'My sergeant said that you were about to...Oh, I'm sorry, I haven't properly introduced myself, have I? My name is Chief Inspector Donaldson', he interrupted himself, beaming the sweetest smile he could muster from under his thick grey moustache. 'You were about to tell Sergeant Williams about an incident - or is it two incidents? - from late yesterday afternoon, that you felt might have some bearing on our enquiry.'

Kasia Mindykowski was still blubbing and shaking like a jellyfish, so WPC Atiga moved in a little closer and put a reassuring arm around her bony shoulders. Piss off, thought Donaldson, trying to catch the WPC's eye. He imagined himself in the seat opposite, caressing that fabulous skin, the Polish beauty melting into his once muscular frame, begging, beseeching him to kiss her. 'Don't stop, Inspector' she cried in his imagination. 'Make love to me, take this pain from my body!' God, Donaldson, get a grip, this is hopeless. The Inspector needed to pinch himself to bleeding point, or think of something awful like dying Labrador puppies - anything to keep his mental track on the straight and narrow.

Kasia Mindykowski lifted her tear-stained face and looked up with dreamy brown eyes at the unattractive beer-bellied man opposite her. Taking a deep breath, (which shifted her magnificent breasts a good two inches higher), she told Donaldson about the first visit when a stranger barged his way up the stairs.

'It's probably nothing, but first of all, a man came by that I had never seen before, and walked straight through the shop. I didn't see his face but he was very well dressed, spoke with some kind of Germanic accent and headed upstairs before I could get a good look at him. He must have been with Mr. Komininos for a good twenty minutes or so, and so I popped to the back office to get some stamps and finish the post. When I heard the shop doorbell clang again, I ran back into the shop and saw his driver open the car door for him, and then he was gone. A few minutes later Mr. Komininos came down looking a little agitated and said that if I wanted to leave early tonight, that was fine by him. He wanted to work on his painting restoration and that too much drinking with his friend Mr. Rimell earlier, had made him feel sleepy. I asked him again if he was OK and he said that he was really fine, just too much wine, as usual. Mr. Rimell is very fond of alcohol and he often leads Mr. Komininos into a state like this. I think the English people drink way too much.'

Donaldson nodded in polite agreement and noticed that WPC Atiga was nodding her Muslim head far too vigorously. Bugger off and leave me alone with this angel, he thought.

Kasia Mindykowski sighed, removed a lump of congealed mascara from her waterlogged eyes and resumed her sad tale.

'I asked Mr. Komininos what the man who had walked

upstairs had wanted and he said, nothing much - just had wanted to ask him whether he might be able to sell him his entire store of Roman and Anglo Saxon artefacts. That was his whole life's collection! Mr. Komininos declined and apparently the man was rather pissed off and rude. He was a spoiled brat of a person. That is when he left the shop. I then reminded Mr. Komininos that he had a dinner to attend at the V&A Museum and that I had hung his black tie suit from the dry cleaners in the cloakroom.'

Just at that moment, Williams reappeared and requested a word with the Chief.

'Find out where Komininos' friend, Tarmin Rimell lives,' Donaldson instructed. 'He appears to have been on a bit of a bender with our murdered friend yesterday afternoon. He's not that geezer that owns The Academy, is he? The one that recently reported a fire started by a crazy pissed-up transvestite?'

Williams said that he didn't have a clue, but that Rimell was topping the contact list and that they'd also found out that Komininos was the father of a son who lived in Bognor Regis.

'The son in Komininos & Son, I presume?' Donaldson asked.

'Actually, no. George Komininos was the son, as such. His father, Andreas, was the original owner of the business, having started the family branch in Knossos, Greece and then George moved over here to expand the business to London'.

'So what does the Bognor Regis son do then?'

'He's called Melvin, and he's got a pet grooming outfit on the high street'.

'Pet grooming? Any sign of Komininos's wife?'

'Brenda Komininos died from an angina attack some sixteen years ago. She was from Essex, and they also have a daughter, Melanie, who married one of her Greek cousins and settled in Mykenos. Apparently they only visit with their children every other summer and, this last summer was one of the 'other' ones. Melvin, on the other hand was once upon a time a frequent visitor and often stayed weekends with his father. Not so much any more, it seems.'

'Married, this Melvin?'

'No, gay'.

'Right, said Donaldson. 'Never mind. Bring him up to London, all the same. I must get back to this young lady now - haven't fully finished taking her statement, you know.'

The Polish girl then told Donaldson how not long after Nathan Hunt had left the shop and she was getting ready to leave, that the doorbell had jangled again and Melvin Komininos walked in - that's George's son. This had immediately changed her plans. At this point, Miss Mindykowski banged her beautiful hand on the table and her face flushed with heat.

'His son is a pig, an oaf, _winka! He is a fucking bastard, you understand?'

Donaldson shuffled his feet nervously and gently assured her that he'd got the message. God, this woman really was something - he imagined her storming across the room in a rage, half naked, long hair messed over her face. He would have to forcefully stop her, push her onto the bed and well.......dispense some harsh police discipline. That would do the trick.

'What exactly happened between father and son?' Donaldson asked, grasping at thin air and hoping he'd asked something even vaguely relevant.

'Well I hung around to listen. To make sure that Mr. Komininos was OK. Melvin always wound him up - he was forever asking him to do this, give him that, pay off this that and the other. I hate that man. He always made his father's life a misery. They went upstairs, but left the door open. At first it sounded OK, just a normal conversation. But suddenly Melvin started shouting. He was yelling at his father about the Dark Man portrait that is above the fireplace. It is worth a huge amount of money, apparently. He was always, always telling his father that he had a moral duty to sell it and pass the money on. That the family were all in debt and that it was unfair to sit on such a fortune when they could all have better lives and be rich. Melvin never respected that this painting was everything to Mr. Komininos. It was his greatest achievement in life. I loved Mr. Komininos for the way he loved that painting. It was the sexiest thing about him.'

Donaldson started in his chair. Had he heard correctly? From what he'd seen of the man face down in his dinner, and from various police photos, the antiquities collector had been no oil painting. In fact, he'd not even pass for a substandard water-colour. Perhaps there was a chance for him with this beauty, after all?

Kasia continued. 'The argument got really heated. I think Mr. Komininos was fired up by all that wine with Mr. Rimell, and he really started shouting back. This was unusual for him. But then I heard glass smashing and chairs being hurled around the room. It was frightening, mad! I wondered whether to interfere, but when I heard my boss cry out in pain, I ran up the stairs like I was on fire.'

'What did you see?' asked the police chief, just for a moment concentrating on the story.

'Mr. Komininos was crouching on the floor, his head in his hands. He was shaking and jabbing his fist in the air at his son. Melvin was also hurt; he was rubbing his face and I could see that he'd been hit by a flying object. Probably by the wooden pigeon that was split in half and lying by his feet. I screamed at the son and told him to get out, to get out now! He collected his coat and looked at me as if he would put a dagger through my heart. I didn't care, I would have cut his eyes out, if I'd had a sharp knife. He had hurt Mr. Komininos and I was very angry.'

She finished up the story by telling Donaldson that Melvin had left, and she had helped Mr. Komininos to his feet and sat him down. He told her that he was fine - that they had just had a father and son spat - nothing out of the ordinary - and that he was pissed off with his shitty son, but that the matter had been sorted. The Polish girl had wiped some blood from his cheek but she could see that he was just bruised, nothing too serious. She then left at Mr. Komininos's insistence and went off to meet her boyfriend.

At this point, Donaldson winced. Bugger it, competition was around the corner.

She continued. By the morning time, when Kasia unlocked and came upon the death scene, it looked to her as if much more stuff had been thrown around the room and then of course, she'd found that George Komininos was dead, not asleep. She just screamed and ran. She freaked out and thought he had been murdered.

Donaldson scratched his head. He wasn't so sure either. There had been two men to see the shop owner - both with suspect agendas - but then both had also been seen leaving the premises by Miss Knockers. He would have to ask the pathologist for his verdict. And as soon as possible.

Sergeant Williams agreed that Melvin should be brought to the city immediately for a formal identification of the body and to give an opinion on whether there was anything missing from his father's shop. Upstairs was such a hideous mess, it was nigh on impossible to see how even a cleaner could work her magic there. Williams popped back to the Cosy Cafe to ensure that Miss Knockers was well cared for by WPC Atiga, and to take in the vision of Eastern European beauty once more. Donaldson, slowly nibbling his sliced sausages, had to make do with watching their conversation, heads leaning in closely together, through the windows of his panda car. Sometimes, being the boss sucked.

CHAPTER EIGHT
Next Day, 'Komininos and Sons'

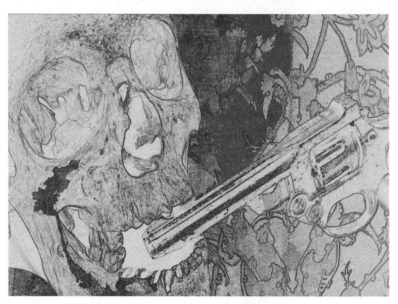

Williams was somewhat surprised to see Melvin Komininos so distraught, although he didn't know that the crocodile tears were more to do with the fact that the son was harbouring a vital truth. Last night, during that huge row with his pathetic shell of a father, George had played his final card to Melvin. He'd told him that his beloved Dark Man painting had been squirreled away by a close friend, for good, and that a worthless fake was hanging above the fireplace for the rest of his life. He'd venomously spat at Melvin that under no circumstances would he leave such a thing of value to his godforsaken son, and that upon his death, his newly changed will had donated the painting to the friend for good.

Melvin had just arrived from identifying his father's body in the morgue, and stared at the table and the large broken bowl - still with remnants of feta and chilli linguine spread over the cloth. How bloody typical that his own father should die in such humiliating and undignified circumstances. And of course, he knew that the dimwit Polish bird downstairs would have grassed up on their row, and that he was going to be a suspect.

Sitting in the large leather chair that overlooked the patio, a million memories flooded back. It had all started out so well in the beginning, with his fun-filled childhood in West London. Then the shit had hit the fan - his mother dying, his sister's big Greek wedding to that arsehole of a cousin, and her desertion to the island of Mykenos. Melanie's marriage had been the only black mark on his family's happiness, as far as he was concerned. He loathed his sister's husband, Barnabas Komininos, a vile bastard of a man, blatantly out to get at his side of the family's money. And to top it all, they'd produced three of the most irksome children imaginable. At least they'd all fucked off back to the homeland. But at that stage of the game, his father had still been his idol, the real meaning of family life for Melvin.

But not long after, the shit had really hit the fan. Melvin remembered the day that he had come out of the closet and told his father that he was gay. Homophobic George had known that his son had many male lovers and silently wished that it was just some kind of unsavoury phase. But the goatee beard, earrings and chains hanging from his jeans were quite a give-away. Maybe his fatherly encouragement for Melvin to go and work with animals (hence the pet grooming) had been unwise and a step too far in assailing his masculinity? Since his beloved Brenda had kicked the bucket and his daughter had left for Greece, Melvin was his only family. But to have a homosexual as a son? That was completely unacceptable - worse than the Holocaust, worse than Hiroshima. When Melvin had introduced him to Sandy, his first boyfriend from the gym (who happened to be Afro-Caribbean, to boot), the tension between the two men had reached breaking point. Maybe he could have built some kind of bridge then, if only Melvin had shown interest in George's artefact collection. There was nothing left to talk about anymore. Melvin, once his sweetest little boy, had zero interest in art. To leave his treasured Dark Man painting to someone who preferred putting silk bows on Persian cats and brushing Shetland ponies, was verging on heresy. George couldn't hide his disgust at Melvin's black nail polish and diamante earrings. It was just too much. And Melvin kicked back. He'd grown to hate his father with the same venom that he hated spiders. There was no forgiving him - particularly after he'd set fire to Sandy's blue Y-Fronts, which had somehow made their way into his laundry basket, and yelled: 'Burn bugger pants! Burn in hell!'

His eyes wandered around the room, taking in the plastic sheets that covered most of the furniture now, as well as various strange bods from the police force who were huddled around the coffee table at the back of the room, discussing his father's possible death. Of course, he knew that it wasn't him that had killed the old bastard. It was his weak heart, that was all. Plus the fact that the pisshead had probably been destroying his liver for the past sixty-nine years. Either that, or a burglar had broken in, had another tussle with the old man and bumped him off. Either way, it didn't help Melvin much. He was number one suspect, he knew. He'd been asked to assess the place, and tell them if there was anything missing, or anything glaringly amiss. Melvin knew the place inside out. After all, he'd spent his childhood playing amongst the Roman pillars, hearing the stories lurking behind every painting and making up his own tales about the various priceless objects that George regularly brought home. Just then, he looked above the fireplace and his heart stopped. There was the fake painting of The Dark Man. If it was the last thing he did, he'd track down the original. And he had a pretty damn good idea as to which 'close friend' had been the recipient.

CHAPTER NINE

Glencot

Tarmin pushed his breakfast around the plate, took a large glug of his coffee and contemplated his day at Glencot. A drizzle was softly falling, the light breeze depositing its sparkle across the grass and packed flowerbeds. A small chaffinch hopped across his view along the lower garden wall and brought his reverie to an end. He just couldn't take on board what had happened to George. It was shocking, numbing. He'd lost one of his oldest, dearest friends and felt consumed with guilt that he'd left him so nonchalantly - sweeping off into the sunset with no thought that he would never see him again. That was the thing about this inconstant life - you never knew when it was time to say goodbye.

THE WOOKEY HOLE AFFAIR

Just then, Anne, his bolshy receptionist, dropped off a bundle of the morning's post. He nodded his thanks, stirred a second spoonful of sugar in his cup and lit up. The letter on top intrigued him. It looked like a very posh invitation - beautiful stiff ivory envelope with a smart crest imprinted on the back. Slicing it open with his Tunisian silver dagger, Tarmin picked out a note.

'Hi Tarmin. Gather you're happily ensconced at Glencot now - Alice and I will definitely be booking in soon! How's Gayle? I gather she's doing the London thing and you're left all on your lonesome. Fancy a night out? Alice is going to St. Lucia for the jazz festival, so you could come to this with me. Good chance to catch up. Priscilla Bedlington is my aunt, and they're great fun! Do come. Tim'.

Tarmin pulled out the invitation and had a look. He considered himself to be a man of the world but he'd never before been invited to a pukka Country House weekend party given by the landed gentry.

It was an invitation completely out of the blue and something that he normally balked at, but right now, with George heavily on his mind, it might be nice to hang out with an old friend for a while. He picked up his mobile and punched in Tim's number.

'Great! I'll let them know you're coming, and we can hook up there. It's a huge old pile in the Cotswolds called Bedlington Hall and…"

Tarmin interrupted him: 'Are you sure your aunt won't mind? It looks and sounds very formal. I'm hardly known for my Oxbridge etiquette'.

Tim laughed. 'Well it's about time we brushed up on those rough edges! Priscilla is a bit nuts and her husband, my uncle John, is the whole tree. It'll be good fodder for that long-awaited novel you keep talking about writing.'

A hard sell wasn't needed. Tarmin was in a foul mood and

needed the change. He'd left London after a humdinger of a row with Gayle, who'd been nagging him about changing the cleaner at The Academy, moaning about the hirsute state of the Miller's hotel guests at breakfast, bitching about their friends and then demanding money to go off and do a fine arts course in Venice.

'And who will run the show in London?' Tarmin had yelled in exasperation.

'Tough titties' she'd shot back. 'I don't give a damn, Tarmin! And what do you care, swanning around the frigging countryside all day and all night? I might as well be married to the Straw Man!'

Tarmin had driven back to Glencot with a thumping headache; grief fogging his mind over George, and a stabbing pain from the persistent nit-picking of his wife. A weekend stint somewhere else with a bunch of new people might just do the trick.

The invitation had arrived on the Tuesday morning and it was now Friday afternoon, the diminishing sun dappling the roads with leaf patterned shadows and streaking through the sheep fields. Tarmin was beginning to get a little anxious and fumbled to find his mobile. It was buried somewhere in the pile of CDs, and he might just need to call Tim again for directions. Bloody Gayle had pinched his Tom-Tom yet again, reason enough to sue her for divorce, if nothing else happened to stick. The best route to Oxford had looked good on the map, but it was now six o'clock and he was due there by seven at the latest. However eccentric this elderly couple were pegged to be, he reckoned they'd still expect punctuality.

As soon as he'd cleared Oxford, the traffic disappeared and he found himself idly contemplating the strange place names as they flashed by. What on earth was a Wold? And who was this Chipping that kept cropping up? He came out of

THE WOOKEY HOLE AFFAIR

Chipping Campden on the B4305 and was just wondering whether to call in at the Fox and Ferret pub for a lightening drink and ask advice for the way to the Bedlington Hall, when he turned a corner and was met by baronial gates topped by a pair of disdainful stone eagles. His destination had been reached.

As the tyres crunched along the immaculately gravelled drive, depositing small stones onto the lawns that swept up to the house, Tarmin pulled over half way up, and drank it all in. The mansion was big and foursquare, with outbuildings spanning as far as the eye could see, neatly tucked away behind high yew hedges. Imposing steps climbed up to the double front door, huge sash windows the size of an average garage door placed at symmetrical intervals across the facade. Tarmin supposed that the house was probably Georgian. Or Queen Anne. Or maybe even Carolean? He was pretty sure that it wasn't Elizabethan, but he didn't know for sure. It definitely wasn't Disney.

Fumbling for the wire that opened the MG, he looked up just as the front door swung open and a gargantuan woman emerged. Dressed in a smart black dress undulating over a Himalayan bosom, she waved at Tarmin and walked over to the car.

'If you would like to park your car over there, sir, I'll take your bag out of the back.'

Female servants - a good sign, he thought. Even if this one looked like the she-devil. Tarmin leant over the back of the passenger seat and grabbed the oversized Gladstone bag, which he fervently hoped contained all the necessary and appropriate things. The housekeeper extended a huge arm and neatly plucked it out of his hand.

'Thank you, sir,' she said blinking through large tortoise-shell glasses. 'I'll wait to show you in.'

Tarmin eased the car into first gear and let out the clutch as slowly as was humanly possible. There was no way he was going to shower any more gravel and disgrace himself. He'd already noticed the giantess picking out some of his earlier mistake from the neat lawn edges. She had got him sussed all right. This one had never visited gentry before, a complete virgin to the upper classes. The instinct of dogs and servants, Tarmin concluded, is infallible and the tall housekeeper seemed to be an interesting amalgam of both species.

He slid the car in next to a gleaming, black Bentley. Finding the door wire, he tugged with such pressure that it chipped straight through all twenty-one coats of paint (or however many they use) on the Bentley's wing.

'Bugger, bugger, bugger!' He desperately hoped the gentry hadn't yet cottoned on to CCTV.

After a quick check to make sure that no one was watching, Tarmin restarted the car and moved it round to the other side of the Bentley, and then nonchalantly strolled over to the lofty harridan who was waiting with his bag. She invited him in, and striding ahead, led the way across the spacious entrance hall, with its polished black and white chequered floor. Right in the centre stood a delightful circular rent table, acting as an oversized flower stand and spewing out lilies, huge furled green and purple leaves, sunflowers and tall-stemmed white roses. Feeling like he was starring in a classic 1920s movie, Tarmin followed his guide up the sort of sweeping staircase that could never have existed outside of a Hollywood imagination. Everywhere he looked, the gilt, crystal and gleaming wood all spelt vast wealth. He could sense it seeping through the panelling and oozing from the oil paintings, an expensive odour that rose from the luxurious flowers.

The silent house appeared to be deserted, but one could secrete a tribe of Hieron Indians here and nobody would know. Tarmin had no idea how many were expected for the weekend party. His hostess, Lady Priscilla Bedlington had extended the invitation via her nephew, Tim, so he could be on his own or part of a whole shooting party, for all he knew. Was this even shooting season? He'd no bloody idea. And what would happen if he was asked to shoot pheasants or rabbits or even a pathetic hedgehog? He had the eyesight of a bat and the cowardice of a lion. He could barely pot shot a scrunched-up envelope into the waste bin, for heaven's sake. At least he hoped that his attire would do. He'd packed white tie, black tie, country suit, blazer and flannels. The complete opposite of his normal over-washed corduroy jeans and Gap sweaters and scarves. He was ready for anything.....he hoped.

The Lofty Lady walked him down a long corridor lined with glass-encased engravings of architectural oddities and occasionally interrupted by mounted blank-eyed marble busts. Tarmin refrained from making comment. One surely didn't. His silent companion eventually turned left at the end of the corridor and stopped at the last door. He was initially surprised that the door wasn't locked, but then remembered that he wasn't in hotel land.

Tarmin gasped at the sheer scale of his accommodation, his heart leaping with joy. This was a place to get settled into, a place that screamed out for misbehaviour! You could plonk his entire residence in London in one corner and still never be found.

Right in the middle of the room stood the most magnificent four-poster bed that Tarmin had ever seen, towering high. How the hell did they ever get it up here? Probably built in-situ, he reckoned. There were enough drapes around it to curtain a row of semis, and a mattress stacked so high that the appealing expression 'bunk up' suddenly took on an altogether more appropriate meaning. Let's hope the shooting brigade yielded some decent girls.

Everywhere he looked, there were masterpieces of furniture design, and immediately catching his eye were a pair of commodes depicting scenes of a great sea battle, as well as a Regency bonheur-du-jour masquerading as a dressing table. Formal portraiture of stiff, grimacing men and unsmiling stern women stared contemptuously down from the walls. There was an enormous marble fireplace, dug into the wall opposite the bed, piled high with logs and topped by silver framed photographs and a small vase of blooming pink peonies. He noticed a jug and ewer. Oh God, no bathroom. If he had to traipse the house looking for somewhere to pee in the night, he might never be found again. That, or be humiliated by pissing into a Ming vase. Lofty Lady swiftly allayed his fears.

'I trust you'll be comfortable, sir. The bathroom is through here'.

Like all good things in life, it was simple really. Pulling on a section of the chair rail that ran around the room, the concealed door swung open. This was Tarmin's sort of room, with no sign of avocado, no gold taps shaped like cherubs, caramel tiling or fake pebbled lino. This needed a degree in engineering to fathom the functioning of the plumbing on the bath alone. The room was only a shade smaller than the bedroom, with the huge white bathtub standing bang in the middle, mounted atop brass lion's feet (if indeed, lions were the size of elephants). At one end of the room, a ballooned canopy shielded a showerhead the size of a nuclear-affected sunflower; a submariner's dream of pipes and knobs. The rest of the fittings were to scale; a pair of enormous marble basins and a thunderbox loo with a vast mahogany seat. And, joy of joys, another well-stocked fireplace which was obviously not just for decoration. As far as Tarmin was concerned, heaven was soaking in a vast foamy tub, glass of whisky in hand and a roaring log fire warming the room and flickering across the mirrors. Add to the mix, a beautiful woman to share it all with and soap up his slippery bits, and everything was picture perfect.

'Mr. Rimell' Lofty Lady's voice jolted Tarmin back to reality. 'If you require anything, just pull the cord next to the bed and someone will be with you.'

Would they bring soap, whisky and a woman? Tarmin wondered.

'And,' she halted for a second by the door, 'dinner will be served at eight o'clock. It's usual for guests to gather for cocktails in the drawing room at seven-thirty'.

After drawing the curtains nearest her, she discreetly made her exit and Tarmin listened to the patter of her sensible heels clip-clopping down the passageway.

Panic. It was twenty past seven already. All his insecurities came back in a rush, jostling to take control. He hadn't tipped Lofty - was that the norm? Where the hell was the drawing room? How formal was it? Should he bring down the gift he'd brought for Lady Priscilla? Why hadn't he asked Tim all this stuff beforehand?

Just then there was a loud knock on his door and Tim walked in.

'Tarmin, get a move on and get changed! We're lining up for some of my aunt's legendary champagne martinis.'

'Christ, Tim. I didn't know you'd arrived. Just in the nick of time! What's the form on the dress front?"

'Whose bloody Bentley did you think it was that you took a chunk out of with that rust bucket?' Tim lowered his spectacles and shot Tarmin a look. 'Anyway, never mind about that now. A suit jacket and a tie will do the trick and we'll go down together.'

'No black tie? No white tie and tails?' asked Tarmin.

'Not on a Friday night. At least, not since the war. Make that The Great War. Come on.'

Tarmin's immediate task was to survive the social obstacle course ahead. With Tim there, he felt a thousand per cent better about the evening ahead. Just stick to general philosophy and don't attempt any bullshit that could be checked out. 'Do as they do'. That would be his mantra, for as long as he remained sober.

Tim ambled down to the drawing room by a route so straightforward, it made Tarmin wonder how Lofty Lady had made it look so complicated and arduous. Perhaps she had wanted a tip? Opening up the panelled doors, the scene within could easily have been filched straight from The Shooting Party or any Oscar Wilde play. About forty people peppered the vast room in small gatherings, sipping from wide champagne glasses, chattering and laughing in deafening unison. Tarmin was beginning to feel quite blase about such vastness and surprised himself by feeling almost (but not quite), at ease.

The two men stood in the doorway for several seconds and then moved towards the nearest group who were involved in a heated political discussion of such intensity, that it wouldn't subside even to acknowledge the newcomers. Rescue swanned over in the shape of their hostess, a statuesque white-haired grand dame, looking effortlessly elegant in a navy cocktail dress and several strings of pearls. She whiffed strongly of floral Granny perfume.

'Timmy! And Tarmin, I presume? How lovely. Oh God, politics.'

She glowered at the group, who took no notice. 'Let me whisk you off somewhere far more interesting. Who on earth wants to talk about Condoleeza Rice or that mad Bush on such a beautiful evening?'

As they followed her across the room (or was this a gallery, or perhaps even the ballroom?), Tarmin studied Lady Priscilla's movements with frank admiration - the way she glided along with the ease and beauty of a professional ice skater. The group that Cilla targeted was (thankfully) all female. Both Tarmin and Tim felt most at home in the company of women. Even unattractive women would be preferable to the Conservative Party hit squad they'd just been saved from, and this lot were certainly not unattractive.

'Let me introduce you all. Ladies, I have some very lovely gentlemen here who are going to entertain you.'

Here we go, thought Tarmin. Let's try and remember two of their names. Tim, on the other hand, was well on the ball. Time spent on the nursery slopes of publishing launch parties had honed his brain to an enviable state of instant recall. Sally, Emily, Alexandra, Camilla, Amanda, Jessica and Bea - the names flowed from Priscilla's posh mouth in an unmemorable blur. Tarmin managed Camilla and Bea and then went blank. What now? His throat dried and he buried his head in the champagne glass. Tim saved the day by introducing Tarmin as the social catch of the season - much to his friend's feigned embarrassment - whilst he surreptitiously twisted the wedding ring off his finger and swapped it to his other hand. Turning to the woman on his left (neatly poured into skin tight black velvet jeans and puckering her brightly rouged mouth), he fired with his opening gambit.

'So, do you live around here, Camilla?'

'It's Jessica, actually, but don't worry. Camilla is the lump in blue who's just ordering her third cocktail. And no, I come from Birmingham, but Bea brought me. She's my cousin.'

Tarmin smiled. 'That's good. I'm in the same boat. I've come as Tim's date.'

'Is Tim your cousin or your boyfriend? No! Don't say anything, no need. I'd already guessed the latter, but didn't want to be rude. There's nothing worse than accusing someone of being gay when they're not. But I noticed your matching wedding rings when you walked over - although you just sneakily took yours off, didn't you? Does Sir John and Lady Priscilla know they've got a couple of steers, bareback riding in Bedlington Hall?'

And before Tarmin could intervene: 'Bea! This is Tim's other half. I think he said his name was Tarmin Rimming. Is that correct?'

Just at that moment, the doors flung open and a small, squat butler with a grey handle bar moustache appeared.

'Dinner is served.'

'It's the chauffeur from Thunderbirds,' Tarmin thought. He even had the trademark droopy black eyes and a protruding lower lip. Tarmin wondered whether he would be expected to give Jessica his arm to lead her into dinner - he was positive that's how they did it in those Merchant Ivory movies. Instead, just as the girls were gathering to walk through, Tim slung his arm over his shoulders and tapped him on the back.

'Great, let's just reassert the gay theory for everyone to see, shall we?' Tarmin thought to himself with some discomfort. 'Why not just ruffle my hair and give me a nice little peck on the cheek as well?'

The grey butler stepped forward and politely ushered Tarmin to the end of the table. Here we go, he thought. Whoever he was foisted on had to be an improvement on mouthy Jessica. She could give Horse of The Year a bloody good run for its money. He dreaded being the last one standing. On the other hand, he didn't want to be the last one sitting down either and made a dive for the bread rolls whilst Latin grace was being uttered. Taking his cue from the other men around the table, he pulled out the chairs for the ladies either side of him, waited until Lady Priscilla was seated and then seated himself.

The table was so vast (with an unbelievable array of hefty silverware, impeccably arranged red roses and thick-set crystal wine glasses), that everyone sitting opposite was effectively out of socialising reach. Tarmin took stock of his immediate companions. To his left, was a lady of very advanced years. The butler had secreted a plump cushion to add padding for her bony bottom, elevating her to dining level. Tarmin noticed that she was dribbling her red wine and had already dropped the fish knife with a huge clatter to the floor. Great - geriatric heaven. She introduced herself as Lady Charlotte Monckton, Cilla's ancient mother.

'Pass us a bun, dear,' she said, holding out a trembling hand and baring a row of uneven yellow teeth. 'And not one of those silly knots with poncey poppy seeds on the top. I'll have a bap, if you'd be so good'.

Tarmin had once read an article detailing the formal ways of addressing a dowager countess, but they didn't seem applicable here. This matriarch had a glint in her eye and a warm manner that was funny and friendly. He felt that if all else failed, at least he wouldn't be short of amusing company.

He turned to the partner on his right and recognised one of the women from his champagne group. She was of medium height, a short blonde bob tucked behind her ears, and dressed top to toe in black chiffon and lace. Grey eyes sparkled underneath dark smoky make-up, her full lips prettied with glistening lip-gloss. As she sat in her chair and crossed her legs, Tarmin caught a tantalising glimpse of sheer black stockings.

'Let me guess', he said, passing her a brown roll. 'You're Emily. Correct or way off?'

'Absolutely wrong', the blonde girl flashed a crooked smile. 'My name is Alexandra - Alex Henshall. But I'll give you half a point for trying. I came with Emily as her guest. We work at Christie's together'.

Tarmin revelled in his good fortune. He fancied the pants off her, and what's more, they had plenty in common. He'd have been well and truly stuffed if he'd been stuck next to Jessica again. She'd turned out to be a National Health chiropodist. He'd mentally prepared to have to resort to his A to Z game with her - a technique that always managed to extricate him from dinner party boredom. It went along the lines of: 'So, do you have any Animals? Have you ever been to Bognor Regis? What do you feel about our Current Chancellor?' And so forth. Unfortunately the technique had its flaws since one letter of the alphabet somehow always managed to throw up a topic of conversation that the bore in question could latch on to.

Alexandra leant over and looked at Tarmin's silver name card.

'That's an interesting name. Emily mentioned that you are Tim's partner. Where do you guys live?'

'You're with my Grandson?' the old Dowager yelled, tuning half an ear into the conversation. 'I always thought Tim had a touch of the fairies about him. How marvellous!'

Tarmin blushed to his roots and felt it was high time to redress the myth.

'No, no! Please let's put all this straight......as it were. Someone at drinks got the wrong end of the stick. I can assure you that I'm as heterosexual as they come, Tim is happily married to Alice and so let's all move on, shall we? Who wants some water?'

Alexandra burst out laughing and put her hand on Tarmin's leg, patting him in a half reassuring, half alluring way.

'That's good news' she said, looking him in the eye. 'I feel like a good old flirt.'

The meal, served by liveried footmen, was simple but dished up in huge portions. A good celeriac and smoked wood-blewit soup, followed by neat squares of salmon in filo pastry and dill hollandaise. Next up, roast pheasant with heaps of vegetables, followed by large bowls of sherry trifle, plates of smelly cheeses and wheaten biscuits - and finally, homemade chocolates. Tarmin felt totally nauseous and was conscious of his leather belt straining to keep his bulging tummy in check, preventing the likelihood of an embarrassing eruption of wind. Cilla's antique mother had no such reservations and let rip with gay abandon.

'Don't mind me, dear', she stage-whispered to Tarmin. 'I fart for Britain when I eat fezzie'

Tarmin had responded to Alexandra's flirtatious knee stroking enthusiastically. He really had the hots for this girl, all thoughts of Gayle being relegated to the Black Hole of Calcutta. They'd laughed about the Dowager's wind problem, discussed their mutual love of antiquities and somehow, at some point, Tarmin had invited her to Glencot for a weekend. She was particularly excited at the prospect of the hidden cellar and demanded a guided candlelit tour. When Sir John Bedlington got up and announced that the ladies would be retiring with Cilla to the small drawing room, she turned to Tarmin and whispered in his ear.

'I can't stand this tedium. Peel away when you can and let's have a game of pool together. Alternatively, I'm holed-up in the fifth room on the left tonight - that's when you're walking down the corridor with the bust of Queen Victoria on your left'.

'I'll never remember that', Tarmin said, his brain already woolly from too much red wine. 'Can't you leave a sign outside? Park your heels by the door and then I'll know'.

With that, Alexandra took the Dowager's arm and helped her through the door, the latter leaving Tarmin to suffocate in a cloud of her undigested blue-veined cheese fug. He grabbed the nearest napkin and gagged.

In spite of flatulence problems, Tarmin decided that he liked the aristocracy. They drank too much, told coarse stories in mixed company and ate white bread with real butter. As the glasses of port were being drained, his steely Republican ideals slowly seeped through the floorboards. Although, he had been pretty pissed off by the mogadon nerd on the other side of Alexandra, who had tried to monopolise her with astonishingly trite conversation. Granted, he was a former political journalist of some standing, but who the fuck wanted to discuss the nuclear threat of Korea or the surge of Chinese capitalism all night? He'd slobbered and leered, drank and dribbled, pawed and spat during a non-stop performance that made Tarmin want to throttle him with his old Harrovian tie. Alexandra, on the other hand, treated him as if he were the most charming individual she'd ever met. The only half decent bit (in Tarmin's now very hazy memory), had been about The Great War, when Tarmin gathered so many tit-bits, he felt he could have fought it himself. Far less tortuous, were his sneering tales of how the young wives of the Guards subalterns had disported themselves during their husband's absence. Tarmin was concerned at one point that Alexandra had fallen for the mind-numbing drivel, until she hissed in his ear: 'If this bastard touches my leg once more, he gets a pitchfork in his hairy balls.'

The port drinking at Bedlington Hall transpired to be of epic proportions. A heavy crystal decanter always seemed to be passed around and his glass always miraculously seemed to be empty. He listened to funny stories that would have embarrassed him in his teens and watched the stupid political journalist do his party act as the one-armed flautist, somehow giving him some insincere but generous applause. Then he tried every way he could to escape back to Alexandra. He slipped off to the loo, got hopelessly lost, and bumped into Lofty Lady who inconveniently steered him back whence he'd started.

'You nearly walked in on the ladies, Mr. Rimell', she smiled. 'They're playing gin rummy'.

THE WOOKEY HOLE AFFAIR

He tried faking that he'd forgotten to raise the roof of his car, but in the blink of an eye, the Thunderbirds butler stepped forward and announced that he'd already seen to it. Third and final plan. He must just phone Glencot to check up on his staff. And he'd only stored the number on his mobile, which just happened to be in his bedroom. What a nightmare it was not having a good head for numbers!

And then bloody Tim stood up and intervened, telling him to use the phone in the study. He knew the Glencot number by heart, no problem.

Sensing inevitable defeat, Tarmin gave in to the sea of port, which Sir John Bedlington (old soldier, legendary philanderer and chronic raconteur), seemed to quaff in infinite measure before evaporation. Sir John lured Tarmin into chatter about a certain Mrs. Annabel Fitzgerald, on whose anatomy he seemed to be an unblushing expert and during which, he somehow managed to wheedle himself an invitation to Millers for a weekend of 'hanky panky' with the curvaceous Bella.

'Good for the old bones, you know, Tarmin. Cilla's rather gone to the dogs, bless her'.

By the time Tarmin and Tim supported each other out of the dining room, the rest of the house had long retired. Belching, slurring his words, sweat matting his hair and with breath that could stop a clock at forty paces, Tarmin felt wretched. He totally forgot to look out for Alex's shoes on the way, and a fat lot of good it would have done him, even if he'd remembered. He could barely raise his little finger, let alone anything else. Tim steered him towards his room and somehow tucked his virtually unconscious body into the massive four-poster.

CHAPTER TEN

Bedlington Hall, next morning

Where am I?' was a feeling that Tarmin had become well acquainted with in his frustrated artist-hits-the-bottle days in Hastings. 'What am I?' was a totally new one on him, but then so was the best part of two pints of vintage port. He'd been awakened at ten o'clock by a soft-footed footman gently placing a tray of tea by his bed and informing him, in a sepulchral whisper, that breakfast was still being served, but that it was quite acceptable not to attend. Or maybe he was actually telling him that if he went to the stables at noon, he'd be tied-up and whipped by Lofty Lady in Sir John Bedlington's leather S&M Club? He really wasn't very aware of anything.

THE WOOKEY HOLE AFFAIR

However, Tarmin was certain of one thing in his uncertain world. Even if he managed to eat breakfast, it would definitely not be the last he saw of it. He opted for staying in his room and falling back into the arms of Morpheus. Even his newly awakened ardent lust of last night had burnt to cinders. And how much of what he had thought about during the dinner and beyond, had he actually said? Oh, God. There was only one thing to do - down the cold tea and shut his eyes again.

After managing to sleep clean through lunch, he woke, washed and dressed himself at half past three, ready to face the world. He'd showered under the Daliesque construction in the bathroom, which was surprisingly easy to operate, put on a white shirt, flannels and a striped boating club tie of his uncle's - hoping against hope that no one recognised it and asked him the significance. Next step was to negotiate the staircase without a shaming mishap.

Seeing there was no one around, he made his way to the flower garden where tea was just being laid out on a large slatted timber table. He was famished by now and even the high class braying from somewhere within (which could undoubtedly be heard all over Gloucestershire), couldn't dampen his ardour for scones and cream. Apparently, Tarmin wasn't the only one who was suffering from a surfeit of port. He was the only man who had made it down at all, apart from Sir John, whose head must have been quite impervious. He was shooting pigeon on a neighbouring estate. Devouring the spread of chocolate biscuits, coffee and walnut cake, shortbreads and brandy snaps, Tarmin felt like a war camp evacuee aching for his first meal. Hangovers were lethal, lethal things. Just as he stuffed a cream-filled scone into his mouth, depositing a vast blob of strawberry jam over the breast pocket of his shirt, he felt a soft tap on his shoulder.

'Mr. Rimming. Good afternoon to you! And where is that lovely friend of yours? He still sleeping too?'

Tarmin had hoped it would be Alex, but sod's law had dished him up Jessica instead. It was like getting a dried-up custard tart after ordering a double chocolate muffin. She giggled at his jam splodge, picked up a napkin, dipped it in a jug of water and promptly made it ten times worse, smearing it deeper into the cotton.

'We only had a tiny bit of a chat last night. And everyone always says that a girl should have one gay guy as a best friend. Where I work in Birmingham, I only get to meet bores with droning northern vowels who do IT jobs, or gardening for old people. What do you do then? Is that a Navy tie you're wearing? Don't tell me you're a sailor?'

Tarmin stared at her in a daze, his half-eaten scone dropping from his hand onto the lawn. Immediately, a King Charles spaniel shot out of nowhere and gobbled it up. How could a hangover get any worse than this? He'd rather appear on Big Brother or be dead in a ditch than talk to this horse-faced bore.

'Come on Rimmy,' she banged on, stuffing a cheese sandwich in her mouth. 'Don't be shy. You're such a man of mystery, everyone's dying to know about you.'

At that moment the devil grabbed his voice box and gave it a hearty old squeeze. OK, she could have her money's worth. Tarmin instantly donned his mystic writer's hat and launched into a monotone monologue, outlining the plot of his latest mythical novel. The masterpiece kicked off with a global forgery scam, money laundering and smuggling, then progressed to incestuous murder, international fraud and the downfall of the Uzbekistan government...and all written in the first person. Jessica's hazel eyes resembled TV satellite dishes by the time his imagination had wrung the final tedious drops from the skeleton plot.

The Wookey Hole Affair

'Did you ever read my first novel - Dogger and the Seaworthy Widgets - by any chance? Oh, what a shame. You'd have got a lot more excited about Dogger In The Manger, if you had. It kind of makes more sense if you're a fan of the series. I'm actually working on Dogger's Backpacking Nightmare, as we speak'.

Jessica had sunk into one of the deck chairs and was neurotically playing with her teacup. Occasionally she had looked up and nodded with acquiescence as his diatribe rambled incessantly on, whilst he gleefully watched her colour slowly draining. Just as she reached for another sandwich and tried to change the subject to sidesaddle riding in the Cotswolds, Tarmin saw a vision in a denim mini approaching.

Alex was looking terrific. The frayed skirt skimmed the top of her tanned bare legs and she wore a plain white T-shirt on top, simple sandals and had pulled her hair into a neat knot at the back, stray strands of blonde blowing about in the gentle breeze. Her smile shone like the afternoon sun, a gorgeous face boasting a smattering of pretty freckles and a blush of pale pink stinging the cheeks. Somehow she looked ten years younger than her vampy self from last night, and was positively angelic next to Jessica, with her bright blue eyeliner and over-plucked eyebrows. Tarmin sucked in hard and felt his heart manically beating, as Alexandra walked straight over to him and, totally ignoring Jessica, kissed him on either cheek.

'A good night had by all?' Alexandra tut-tutted, picking at the now congealed jam on his shirt.

Tarmin felt dumbstruck. 'More tea, vicar?' he nervously quipped, the attempted wit sinking as heavy as lead. 'Fancy a cucumber sarni?'

Why did he say things like that? Surely he could do better? But at least she was still smiling at him. Jessica (who, it transpired, was not totally insensitive), had now picked up her plate of teatime goodies, thrown a custard cream to the spaniel and disappeared off to the tennis courts.

'Why don't we go and sit in the sun?' Alex said. 'It's fucking nippy in the shade.'

God, the upper classes were great. The women said 'fuck' and brought out plates of that unhealthy soft white bread at teatime. For a split second, his mind flashed to London and Gayle, but he wasn't in the mood to be sentimental. His wife had been pissing him off for weeks now. What was wrong with her? He just couldn't fathom Gayle and her moods. She was up and down, like a bride's nightie. No, he was bloody well going to enjoy this cucumber-nibbling girl. For once in his life, he seemed to have someone attractive on his case (but why was she? he wondered with some insecurity), and he decided to take a leaf out of Bundy's well-trodden book and just give in.

They talked and laughed all afternoon. Alex, it transpired, was recovering from a broken engagement to the son of one of England's premier Earls.

'In truth, I was always concerned about our future children. With a father whose chin receded so deeply that he needed a neck brace, you can't help but feel concern for the coming generations. He was also crap in bed.'

This last bit worried Tarmin a tad. Could he swing those rusty joints into action in time? He hadn't brushed up his techniques for as long as he could remember and Gayle's last attempt at a drunken blowjob had sent him fast asleep.

Alexandra had worked for Christie's for six years and loved everything to do with antiquities. She'd spent a year's leave split between Turkey and Rome, and longed to open her own gallery of stone artefacts. In her spare time, she painted huge oil canvases of Campbell soup cans and loved playing netball, tennis and beach volleyball. Tarmin started to sweat uncontrollably. He wanted to eat her. The vision of Alex in a small bikini thumping a ball over the net and falling, legs splayed into the golden sand, was almost too much too bear. He crossed his legs in haste and stroked her hand.

'How about a stroll before dinner?'

They walked hand in hand between the formal hedges, around the walled herb garden and over the stone bridge to an island on the lake, where they found a marble Doric summerhouse.

'Any stately home worth its salt would have had a resident hermit in the old days,' Tarmin mused, as they sat down on the long marble seat. 'That would have suited me down to the ground. I could have sat here and written all day long.'

'Written what? Your Dogger novels!' Alexandra smirked, brushing a straw blonde hair from her eye. 'Come on, we'll be missed - apparently we've got to sing for our supper. Lady Cilla says it's party games tonight.'

In one fell swoop, Tarmin lost his pounding erection.

As they approached the house, Tim and three other male guests were dawdling by the open drawing room windows, brandishing tennis racquets and sipping champagne. Tim lent out and yelled at Tarmin.

'How are you? I've been sick as a dog. Somehow managed to thrash the pants off Andrew and David on court, though. God knows how. Bit of throwing-up went on behind the hydrangeas, after my service game. You managed to keep it all down? Ready for an instant replay?'

Tarmin smiled weakly and grabbed Alex's wrist to stop her from heading off upstairs. He didn't want to share her with anyone. She looked down at his hand and then up to his serious face:

'More tea, vicar?' she said quietly.

Tarmin waited until they were out of sight of the other guests and gently pushed her against a wall. He kissed her, smoothing the hair away from her eyes.

'You're just beautiful, Alexandra,' he said as she softly stroked his cheek and kissed him back. The two of them went into their respective rooms and changed for dinner.

Dinner that night was a repeat of the previous night's, but without the formality. Tarmin started off with a small sherry with Lady Charlotte, who was mercilessly teasing Tim about his crooked nose and telling risque jokes about colonial India.

'We're having curry tonight, gentlemen' she announced to one and all. "And it's the real McCoy. No holding back on the chillies or garlic, my dears, so I hope you all have good old sturdy constitutions.'

Tarmin shivered at the thought, recalling how she'd fared the night before with the relatively harmless roast pheasant. Sir John, the satyr of the Dragoons, was in great party mood. Tarmin was placed next to Bea and Cilla tonight, and enjoyed their easy laughter and eccentricities. He caught Alex's eye several times, but she seemed happy too, snapping papadums in half with Tim and getting in a tug-of-war with Sir John over a piece of naan bread. This time the women didn't leave the men after dinner - much to the relief of Tarmin, who was thinking of starting a society for the suppression of port. Instead, at the end of the meal, a purple faced Sir John stood up, wiped his moustache, rubbed large circles around his huge stomach and announced: 'On your pins, one and all! We're retiring to the drawing room for a game of sardines.'

Tarmin spontaneously burst into loud laughter and everyone swivelled round to look at the party spoilsport.

Like ants in a line, everyone filed into the drawing room and Tarmin and Alex flung themselves on a sofa.

'This is the gentry's version of hide and seek, right?' Alex groaned after another day of too much food.

'Right,' said Tarmin. 'Only, one person gets to hide and when found, you have to squeeze in too. And so it goes on, until everyone has found you and the last person to show up, loses. Riveting stuff.'

'Jesus! How fucking tedious is that?' Alex looked forlornly at the other buzzing groups.

Sir John wasn't giving up. 'We'll have two games on the go at once. There'll be a game of Monopoly going on around the fireside for all the boring old farts who haven't digested their vindaloo, and the rest of us will opt for sardines. Who's snaffling the sedentary option?'

It was with some relief that Tarmin saw Lady Charlotte sit down with Jessica and Bea, and claim her silver boot on the Monopoly board. Sir John lurched towards Tarmin and Alex, hassling the troops.

'Miss Alexandra, sitting over there and looking so very alluring against the velvet cushions! What will you be playing?'

Alex leaned forward and uttered 'Monop....' before Tarmin leapt up and unceremoniously pushed her back down on the sofa.

'We're both up for sardines.'

'Are you bloody mad, Tarmin?' she hissed, going bright red. 'I told you, that sounds like hell.'

A smile slowly spread across Tarmin's face. He'd got other ideas.

They somehow managed to get through two rounds of the childish game (firstly tracking Sir John down behind some crowded bamboo in the conservatory, and then finding Tim lurking behind huge red drapes in the Pool Room), accompanied by much ribald commentary about cheating, peeping and who was the most inebriated. Thank God they'd all consumed a fair amount of alcohol, or this puerile game would have signalled a very early night.

'One more round, and then we can play bridge,' shouted a very flushed looking Sir John. 'Who wants to hide?'

This was Tarmin's cue and he stepped forward and volunteered. As the other all turned their backs so that he could leave the room, he shoved a note into Alexandra's hand.

'Find me quick' he whispered and closed the drawing room door.

Three minutes later, the door to the cleaner's cupboard was gingerly opened and a blonde head poked into the pitch black.

'Tarmin? Are you in here? What the fuck are you doing in a broom cupboard?' Alexandra whispered, just as Tarmin reached out of the darkness and wrenched her arm.

'Shut up and come in.'

'It stinks, stinks of frigging polish in here! I think my curry's going to resurface. You're mad!'

Like all the rooms in Bedlington, the humble broom cupboard was the size of a normal person's kitchen - set with a stone cobbled floor, stacks of shelving, a space for boxes and even a chair in one corner.

'I stumbled across here the other night, when I was wandering the passageway,' Tarmin said. 'Lofty Lady was coming out of the door with her dusters, so I went back and took a peek. There's always method to my madness.'

Alexandra moved a box to one side, skidded on a small brush and knocked over a couple of huge crates, which went crashing to the floor.

'Christ, Alex. Do you want the whole party in here before I've had my wicked way? Come here, you noisy klutz.'

Tarmin grabbed her around the waist and pulled her close. He'd lit a small candle on the back shelf, in amongst the piles of dusters and silver polish. With scarce light and sprinkles of dust falling from the chalky ceiling, Alex and Tarmin shed their inhibitions. Tarmin's hands ventured slowly up her smooth thighs, but immediately her hand stopped him.

'Bugger', he thought, not for the first time this weekend. 'I really have lost my touch'.

At which moment, his self-doubt was instantly erased as her hand forcefully picked out the tail of his zip and tugged. Alex sank to her knees, knocking over a bucket and mop with a huge clatter as she went, and buried her head in his trousers. It didn't take long, but to be fair, they hadn't got long. She expertly put him back together with a parting kiss to his diminishing manhood.

'I want to make love to you right now,' he gasped. 'Alexandra, you're the most fucking gorgeous woman. Come here.'

At which very moment, the door was given a huge tug and Sir John stuck his head into the cupboard.

'Found you!' he yelled. 'And everyone else is behind me, so no need to pile in. Anyone else in there with you, young man?'

At which point, the guilty pair brushed themselves down and stepped, blinking into the bright lights.

'Golly, Alexandra, you're all dirty,' someone gasped.

'Isn't she,' Tarmin concurred, straightening his tie.

Alexandra disappeared upstairs to get cleaned up. The evening subsequently lost some of its magic for Tarmin. He joined in a few more games, somewhat perfunctorily. Alex didn't reappear and by midnight, he said his goodnights and scaled the huge staircase. Passing the bust of Queen Victoria, he quietly counted to himself, knowing that if he got the wrong door it could be calamitous. But there were no shoes outside, no sign of anything. This was the fifth door. He knocked and waited. No answer. He hissed her name as close in as he could get. Silence. Feeling a little let down and with unfinished business clouding his every thought, Tarmin gave up and reckoned on doing the gentlemanly thing. Returning to his room, he opened the door and flicked on the light.

'I'd nearly given up.'

Alexandra was tucked under the counterpane, blonde hair spread over his plumped-up pillows. 'Come on, you. You owe me.'

Alexandra was wonderful in every way. She felt just the right temperature and wherever she positioned herself, her body moulded his perfectly. She didn't fidget, she didn't snore. Her body was, quite simply, perfect and her muscle control exactly what he'd hoped for from a fit volleyball player. This could catch on, thought Tarmin, as he slid easily into her for the fourth time. And thank God, she was not a great talker. Tarmin loathed it when Gayle pondered her vegetable 'wish list' for the weekend Tesco run, the second after he'd come. Alexandra, on the other hand, just heaved a little sigh, made the occasional lovely pornographic grunt and licked her soft lips with appetising slurping sounds. She was heavenly. By the time she left to return to her own room at six o'clock (after all, some proprieties must be observed in Bedlington Hall), they'd hardly exchanged twenty words.

When he woke at nine, feeling that the world was a very special place indeed, Tarmin Rimell realised that he was completely and utterly smitten.

For once Tarmin was a proper weekend guest and made it down to Sunday breakfast on time. And this morning, he felt like he'd run, high jumped and pole-vaulted at the Olympics. Bring on the carbs! But by ten o'clock there was still no sign of Alexandra, when everyone else (apart from Tim and Bea), appeared to be in the dining room. Tarmin wasn't worried. After last night's marathon, she probably needed her sleep. He hated to admit it, but he certainly hadn't lost his touch. Far from it. He'd humped, stretched and twisted like a Romanian gymnast till the cows came home. And for those that gave of themselves with such selflessness, there could only be one reward. Devilled kidneys, thickly cut toast and mugs of steaming black coffee!

Breakfast at Bedlington was a magnificent buffet set along a long trestle table, silver salvers brimming with bacon, ham, sausages, the must-have kidneys, kedgeree, kippers and all the ancillaries. Of course, it was ladies first, which, for once, was a living nightmare in Tarmin's famished book. He estimated that it would be at least twenty minutes until he could get his feet in the trough. Where was Alex? Didn't she need sustenance or was she still in the land of nod? Jessica homed in on him again, champing at her snaffle, and this time there was no escape. Christ, he'd been stupid to feed her all that crap about the Dogger novels yesterday. Now she wanted a signed copy of the Seaworthy Widgets book. She'd obviously swallowed it whole, like he was about to do with those crispy Cumberland sausages.

He brushed her off as best he could and got stuck into some excellent fried bread. Just as he was taking his last mouthful, he heard a car engine kick into life and crunch over the gravel outside. Glancing out of the window, Tarmin clocked the red Jaguar XKR turning the bend by the gates and disappearing behind a large horse chestnut tree. But not before he'd noted the instantly recognisable blonde bob at the wheel. Just then, the Thunderbirds butler lent over and discreetly slipped a small note under his side plate.

'More coffee, sir?' Thunderbirds purred in a voice so low and soporific, it could have induced instant sleep.

111

Tarmin reached for his glasses, unfolded the note and drank in Alex's parting words.

'Dearest T. What's the broom cupboard like at Glencot? Make sure it's stocked with Bolli, some sturdy cushions and several boxes of condoms. I'm coming........Friday at 6. Alex xx.'

Tarmin stood up and helped himself to the largest fried egg he could find.

CHAPTER ELEVEN
Glencot Hotel, The following weekend

The Friday afternoon in question had arrived, and Tarmin spent the whole day in nervous anticipation of Alex's arrival. Sammy, one of his hotel helpers, had arranged a bowl of mixed blooms from the garden, the cut stems dispersing a wonderfully fragrant infusion. At pains to keep his assignation secret, he'd made the reservation in the name of 'Alex Harding', supposedly an old family friend from years back. Obviously, most of his Glencot staff knew Gayle and he was treading a delicate line inviting another woman to stay. Alexandra however, seemed to have no worries about his married status and he just hoped this little dalliance wouldn't backfire. He couldn't afford to be flung out on his ear, certainly not before he'd filed for divorce. Normally he was a 'more talk than action' man but this woman was special. Mind you, he could always blame it on his age, if push came to shove. Not that any such wimpish excuse would ultimately stand up in court. People often had sympathy for late mid-life crisis, conceding that a lost soul could be as helpless in his actions as a drug-addled teenager.

Glencot's weekend was shaping up to be a busy one, with a sixtieth birthday party occupying most of the rooms, and the rest being booked by two sets of London couples. He skimmed down the 'Checking In' sheet. No recognisable names.

Just then, the front door opened and Alex walked into the reception. She saw Tarmin behind the desk and grinned.

'Ready to play, mister?' she whispered.

Luckily Tarmin was rather adept at lip reading, as Anne, his menopausal receptionist, returned at that minute, clasping a steaming mug of tea. Time to down play the connection and dull his rising ardour. Grabbing Alex's suitcase, he swiped the room key from Anne and insisted on taking his old friend to her room.

Just as they approached the staircase, Anne shouted across the hall: 'Mr. Rimell, you have a call. It's Melvin Kimininos again. That's twice he's called today, and once yesterday.'

Tarmin swore out loud. He'd have to speak to George's heinous son at some point, he knew that, but he didn't want that snail of a man creeping around Glencot and looking for his father's painting. He would have to get him off the scent.

'Tell him I'm having a steam bath in Bath,' he yelled, disappearing around the corner. Anne sulked and impatiently tapped her biro on the desktop. That stupid boss of hers could be a complete bloody pain the arse.

On the top floor landing, Alex's heart missed a beat when she walked through the door of Room 12. Tarmin's caring touches had paid off. She flung herself onto the bed and pulled him down with her. This was pure heaven, he thought, praying to every and any of the gods that he didn't run out of oxygen or suffer a heart failure. At which point, Alex pulled open the drawer to her right and blindly fumbled around until her hand picked out the habitual hotel copy of the Bible.

'Just promise me that you won't ever consult this' she said, spreading soft kisses over his neck. He felt like he could erupt at any moment.

'I've long buried my rosary' he replied. 'Just look in the drawer on the other side of the bed and you'll work out which camp I belong to.'

Alexandra rolled across his body, stretched out and tugged open the other drawer. Inside she counted out ten boxes of condoms.

Tarmin smiled.

'Well, you demanded that I be properly prepared and so I am'.

That evening, the drawing room area was unusually busy with four generations from the sixtieth birthday party milling about, and various visiting couples vying for available menus. Feeling exceptionally chipper, Tarmin was uncharacteristically sociable with his guests and expertly moved from group to group, dispensing cheerful pleasantries. He'd perfected the art of delivering short conversations on the hoof and avoided entrapment by appearing to be constantly busy.

'Hello Tarmin,' a voice squeaked from behind.

Tarmin spun round in sweet expectation and his jaw hit the ground. Fuck a duck! It was one of Gayle's oldest

MARTIN MILLER

friends, Jane McCann. How the hell had he missed her in
the reservations book? Of course! She must have used her
married name, Jane Inchbald. It was not the most common
of names and when he'd seen it written down, he'd momentarily wondered but not thought any further.

'Jane, how fantastic to see you!' he stuttered, hoping
she wouldn't grasp his panic. 'I didn't know you were with
us tonight. You do know Gayle's in London, don't you?'

'In London? I obviously know your wife better than you
do, Tarmin! She's in Umbria this weekend at that 'Yoga
Italia' thingy. Do you know her nice friend, Teodor? He's
taken a group of devotees out there. I rather expected you
to be Down Dogging it too. No, it's just little old me here
on my lonesome, I'm afraid. Actually, I'm here for my
cousin Barbara's wedding over in Bath, so I'll be out for
most of tomorrow. But no doubt we could snag a nice drink
or two in the evening. What about dinner tonight? Any
plans?'

'Please, no! Fuck, fuck, fuck,' Tarmin's panic stricken
head was being bombarded with evil thoughts. Through the
corner of his eye, he could just make out Alexandra walking through the door and looking out for him. She looked
beautiful, wearing a simple grey tunic dress teamed with
high black boots, her blonde hair swept to one side. He felt
that ache again. She had a simplicity of style that blew his
socks off.

Rob, his barman, appeared at his side.

'Drinks anyone?' he offered.

Jane snorted like a fractious donkey.

'Absabloodyloutely! I'm gagging for something!'

She quickly perused the drinks menu and ordered a
Miller's Kiss special, an enticingly exotic mixture of gin,
pomegranate and cranberry juices, white grape juice and a
squeeze of lime.

116

'Busy tonight?' Jane continued, turning to Tarmin.

'I'd certainly like to be', he thought to himself. How was he going to sort this hideous mess out? Alex was now by his side, having plucked a glass of champagne from the tray by the door. And then suddenly looming directly in front of him, an overly familiar shape was also busily negotiating his portly frame around the Victorian sofas, lit cigarette and a tumbler of whiskey in hand.

'Bundy!' he shouted, all notions a romantic night falling apart before his eyes. 'What the hell are you doing here?'

The Professor flung himself onto the sofa and introduced himself to Jane and Alex.

'I've been giving a lecture in Glastonbury and the company booked me into a little shit-hole of a place, saying that Glencot was chockablock, the cheap skates! Luckily I never take anything on face value. Checked it out for myself and here I am. I thought you might be stretching your ancient limbs with Gayle at that yoga convention in Umbria? What luck that you're not! We can have a game of chess or two later.'

Tarmin could feel the sweat cascading down under his arms and soaking through the thin fabric of his shirt. His flimsy cover was unravelling before his very eyes, and what with Jane's inquisitiveness and her close link to Gayle, he'd have to change his 'family friend' story somewhat. Instead, he spun her a tale about Alex being an old acquaintance from the antiques world. But as soon as Jane heard that Alex worked at Christies, she made the inevitable connection to Bundy.

'Oh, so you and Professor Bundy must be working colleagues? What a small world.' Jane seemed to be looking with some suspicion at Alex's very close proximity to Tarmin, and didn't appear to be biting.

Following a pregnant pause that stopped the clocks,

Tarmin was left feeling like a rabbit blinded by car head-lights. He shot Bundy a withering look, silently imploring 'don't blow it', and hoping to God that his friend would be on the ball. For once, his luck was in.

'I've definitely bumped into you before,' Bundy said to Alex, patting her arm. 'Christie's is such a hubbub though, and I'm sure you wouldn't notice a bumbling old fool like myself around the place. Actually, on reflection, didn't we have drinks with Chris Morrison once? I have vague memories of a jolly gathering at the Brompton Brasserie.'

Alex laughed, relishing anything purportedly devious, and this man Bundy smacked of just the right kind of naughtiness. Alex was a woman who was born to tempt the unconventional, to take risks and stretch the boundaries of life. Her impulse was to roar not simper, and meeting Tarmin had taken her by surprise. After her previous very aristocratic boyfriend (the chinless wonder), she'd felt free to play the field and let loose. At which point this hotel man had stepped up and surprisingly lit a burning fire within. Tarmin was fun, wicked, romantic and.....married. But that was not a problem. She could tell that this man was not into his wife and that the road ahead, although not entirely clear, was certainly opening up. And also much to her surprise, she was keen, very keen.

After cocktails were downed, the group of four headed into the restaurant with Alex lagging behind, so she could walk with Tarmin.

'What's up?' she said, smoothing his creased brow. 'Chef been caught with his hand in the oven?'

'Worse, much worse. Jane is one of Gayle's best friends and is here for some wedding. Plus, my old friend Richard Bundy has bloody well pitched up, out of the blue. A complete fuck up,' he moaned.

Alex checked that the coast was clear, rose on tiptoes and

kissed his cheek.

'Listen, I've always harboured a secret desire to be an actress and here's my chance! And remember, we have the whole night ahead, under that massive counterpane of yours. Fret not. I can assure you that I am totally unflustered.'

Alex was sweet but it didn't help much. Tarmin knew how the wheels of hotel gossip turned in furious motion, and they would only be fuelled by the presence of an attractive female friend. He had to be very careful and that was inhibiting. But dinner turned into a jolly affair and Alex was a star, bullshitting the night away about their fictitious work connections. Bundy had been quietly put in the picture and played along with gusto. Finally, Jane decided that she should retire to bed, keen to be fresh and perky for her wedding party.

Tarmin, Richard and Alex moved to the balcony overlooking the lake and popped open a bottle of champagne. Tarmin looked at the two of them and realised that he had exactly the right partners in crime to hand. He reminded Bundy about the plan hatched at The Electric of putting a bunch of George's hidden artefacts in the cellar, and enticing Nathan Hunt into the picture. It was slightly more awkward since George had died, but as Bundy quickly pointed out, far better that the artefacts serve George's old friend in some useful way, than be left to that scrounger son of his. They just had to find exactly the right spot to place them. First things first, and Tarmin needed to show the pair where the hidden cellar was.

A few minutes later, having located a couple of torches, Tarmin led the way down to the Minima and winched open the massive flagstone to reveal the gaping expanse below. Alex squealed with delight as Tarmin descended a few steps and picked up another large torch placed on the small shelf under the entrance.

'Come on, you two' he shouted up. 'And there's no health insurance included'.

Tarmin hadn't told anyone else about his secret cellar and had already spent a few lone hours sweeping away the cobwebs and hoovering up the mounds of dust. The three of them moved George's boxes down to the cellar, piling them by the steel door where Tarmin had hooked a large padlock onto the bolt.

The door still needed superhuman strength to open up, but with a bit of pushing and shoving, it eventually conceded. By streaming torchlight, Alex and Bundy could now experience the same excitement of Tarmin's unusual secret. The room was about 20ft by 30ft, panelled from top to bottom with beautiful inlaid timber in pristine Victorian condition, and with pairs of brass chains looping along the heavy brass rails lining the top of the walls. Bundy shone his light around and counted twelve heavy chain links hanging where large paintings had apparently once been.

'What the hell is this place?' he asked Tarmin, flashing his torch up and down the walls. 'It looks like some kind of private gallery? And look, it's been wired up for electricity at one time and someone's certainly made an effort with the floor. This had to have some intention behind it.'

Alex examined the panels closely and waxed lyrical on how the colours of the inlays had retained their vibrancy. She gave Tarmin's hand a hearty squeeze.

'God, Tarmin, what a find! This could clean up so brilliantly. What do you reckon it was used for?'

Tarmin thought back to his initial visit to Glencot and his bizarre afternoon tea meeting with the widowed German owner. She'd feigned ignorance of the cellar's existence, but as soon as he'd found the stone opening in the Minima, he knew that she'd been shielding the truth from him.

The Wookey Hole Affair

'I remember when I first came round to look at Glencot and Mrs. Jennings spoke to me about all the paintings that she and her deceased husband had collected since the war. I suspect that some might well have been of the school of Nazi-appropriated Impressionist paintings that constantly fill various newspaper columns. Whatever, it's possible that they could have owned a stash of dodgy works of art from the last war and stored them down here. Why else hide something away? She pretended that she didn't know where the hidden room was, but this place has definitely been renovated within the last thirty years, so of course she knew.'

'Maybe there's a tunnel somewhere and we can burrow through to Wells cathedral?' Bundy joked.

'Take a look at the ceiling here.'

Alex shone Tarmin's torch over the roughly hewn rock above them. 'This was all carved out years back. I think they installed the actual room not too long ago. This is utterly fascinating; beats sex any day.'

She shot him a sly smile and feeling his warm breath on her cheeks, huddled in close, running her hands down his back and under the belt of his jeans. Tarmin felt her breasts moving against his jacket and gave her a quick cuddle in the dark. It was like being sixteen years old again.

'Maybe they blocked up the old tunnel at some point?' Bundy was standing over by the door and running his hand over the panelling. 'Let's start tapping.'

Moving along each panel, they knocked against the wall, each effort met by a solid refrain. At the end of the room, Bundy swept his torch across the floor and froze his beam on the spot.

'Here' he said, crouching down and pointing to the mosaic tiling. 'Look here - you can see a small scuffed mark in an arched shape. Very slight but there could well have been a door here at sometime.'

All eyes were on the centre panel at the end.

'Reminds me of those Famous Five books by Enid Blyton,' Tarmin said. 'All we need now is the dog, Timmy, sniffing out a secret opening.'

'Take a close look at those chains and the brass rods they're all hanging off. What do you see that's odd about this one here?' Alex said, pointing up high.

The two men looked and saw nothing.

'Okay, look at where the other chains are. They're hanging directly from the brackets themselves. Odd, don't you think?'

The panelling was over 10ft tall and the brass hanging racks were well out of reach.

'Tarmin, can you give me a bunk up? I want to have a closer look. I reckon there's something there.'

Tarmin, more than happy to snatch at any excuse for physical contact with Alex, hoisted her up on his shoulders. Grabbing a firm hold, the rail instantly came away in her hands. Tarmin helped her back to her feet, so that she could give the panelling two hefty shoves, which opened up a doorway. Inside the darkened room was similar to the cellar at the bottom of the Minima stairs. A tiny, cold space, hemmed in by harsh stone walls and a small dugout place on the far side. It was a gloomy space, empty and silent.

'This is your spot, Tarmin', Bundy said, shining his torch around the room. 'What better place could you find to deposit George's pieces? This could easily pass as an ancient place of worship or some kind of burial ground. Let's bring the boxes through and arrange the stuff in front of this 'altar' dugout. We'll have to do a little research as to the precise layout from this period, but it'll certainly lure the Nathan Hunts of this world here.'

Tarmin looked at Alex's sweet face half lit in the illumination. She looked angelic and soft, vulnerable even. This was the girl for him. Time to be rid of the portly dragon once and for all.

'Let's do it, Bundy' he said. 'Time to get this plan on the move'. And with that, all three headed back to the cellar steps to pick up George's boxes.

That night in bed, Tarmin got up for his nightly pee and caught sight of his moonlit reflection in the bathroom mirror. Was he too old for Alex? Could he really face the inevitable wrath of Gayle? Suppose he'd misjudged her lust for the Transylvanian Yoga geek? Maybe this Teodor was just a passing phase? Tarmin wasn't a fighter by nature. He hated confrontation, even though he could be a miserable bastard half the time.

Slipping back under the covers, Alexandra automatically moved over, curled up in his arms and continued her deep reverie. Her body felt like heaven next to his skin. He hadn't experienced this kind of intense feeling since Gayle had dragged him to The Hale Clinic for colonic irrigation.

'Alexandra Henshall, I want to marry you,' he whispered, semi-hoping she wouldn't hear.

Alex grunted and moved her face into his armpit.

One sleepy eye half opened as she looked up: 'Honey, move your leg, please. You're squashing the life out of me.'

CHAPTER TWELVE
Glencot, Two weeks later

Alex and Tarmin reckoned they'd hatched a pretty satisfactory plot to cover their tracks, enabling Alex to freely come to Glencot every weekend. However, checking in for her third weekend in a row, sent Anne's suspicions flying.

'Ah, Miss Henshall.....again. How lovely that Wells holds such a draw for you. Very unusual,' she muttered, pretending to shuffle through hotel bills. 'Will it be your customary room, or would you like to experiment with another, perhaps?'

Alex looked at the middle-aged woman's steely grey eyes, misted with mistrust and censorship, and realised that she'd reached her limit of being 'the family friend'.   'What a bitch,' she thought, but realised that to avoid trouble, she'd have to think of a lightening quick excuse. For all she knew, Anne might have a hot line to Gayle.

'Actually, I'm enrolled on a course at Bonhams in Bath. It's a three-month weekend programme, so I'm very pleased to use it as an excuse to explore Somerset at the same time. Gets me out of the London, you know?'

That seemed to shut her up, although Alex was sure that Anne was the type of dratted snoop who'd ring up Bonhams just to check out her mythical enrolment. She'd have to face that one if it happened, but so far, so good. Her weekend visits had been given a free pass.

Meanwhile, Gayle had previously tipped up on an unannounced mid-week visit to Glencot, ostensibly to check up on some velvet curtains that were being made for the conference room. But Tarmin sensed there was something up, finding her unusually quiet and withdrawn. Even one of Rob's lethal champagne cocktails couldn't get her juices flowing.

'What's up with Mrs, Rimell?' he asked, in the middle of checking the stocks of wines and spirits. 'She's normally a roaring tiger of a lady. Today she's a wounded sheepdog.'

Tarmin was worried. The last thing he wanted was for Gayle to want to come back to him and live at Glencot. Perhaps her ardour for the bendy man was diminishing? Looking at her spindly frame, barely filling her size 4 jeans, a baggy jumper dwarfing her taut tummy, he couldn't imagine how she could even touch her toes, let alone achieve yogic contortions. Guilt suffused his mind - after all, such drastic weight loss was a sure sign of great unhappiness, and could be directly attributable to him. She had even refused Rob's cocktail, after all. It was a thought not worth thinking, but he couldn't ignore her reticence forever. Eventually, he plucked up courage to address the problem with his normal degree of tact.

'Gayle, I'm worried about you. You seem tense, under-weight and very irritable. Is it 'The Change' happening?'

Gayle burst into nervous laughter and then a blinding silence descended as she stared disdainfully at her estranged husband. What she saw was a pathetic excuse of a man. That mass of matted grey hair, his perpetual nicotine crutch in hand, his tatty old trousers and appalling snoring. She knew that he'd mentally left her a long time ago and that there almost certainly would be another woman by now. Tarmin was a man who couldn't exist on his own. He didn't even know how to butter his toast, let alone sleep on his own. No, her husband might just have been faithful in their marriage, but only because she was there to fill the space. When the tide had turned, she was banned from the room like a farting dog. However, she was pretty happy with her new life and though Teodor might not be the ulti-mate partner, he was certainly good enough for now. He would happily bridge the gap between her departure from Tarmin and the next phase of her life and once she'd got what she was after, she'd be happy. And what she wanted was half the wealth of that piss poor husband of hers. That way he'd eventually understand what misery she'd had to endure in his tedious, hurtful company. It was the least he could do.

.Meanwhile, back in London and fired up by his weekend in Glencot and the discovery of the inner sanctum, Professor Bundy got to work on his plan for Tarmin. With the help of one of his fledgling art students, he learnt how to set up a personal blog on the Internet and prepared the written bait for Nathan Hunt. His article gave a subtle taster of his upcoming book on the Ark of the Covenant, or so he would have Nathan Hunt believe. In truth, Bundy had as much interest in writing a book about the Ark as he would on cycling holidays in Senegal. Certainly, it held some fascination, but all the complexities about its origins from the book of Exodus, the Temple of Twelve, and the many different claims for burial grounds and so forth - really, Bundy couldn't give a damn. However, he was informed enough to be able to write an article that should reel in the fanatical Hunt, and that was all he cared about. After all, he had an incentive here ......a ten per cent stake in this whole sorry adventure.

By Thursday he'd got his article typed up and gave Tarmin a call.

'Check out the blog, and see what you think' he told him, at the same time flicking through his address book. He'd received two more messages from Bethany whilst he'd been down at Glencot, and felt the urge to see her again. What on earth was her surname though? He'd got to E and still no sign of a Bethany. Maybe that was one small detail that he'd overlooked?

'How will Hunt find the blog, Bundy? He's not to know you have such a thing.'

'Ah, you dare to question whether I have covered my tracks? My clever little student, who set up the blog, has somehow managed to get the link as a premier listing on google search. Try it when we get off the phone. If you type in 'Articles on Pre-Christian Artefacts', then my piece appears very near the top of the page. We'll manage to alert Hunt to it somehow.'

Tarmin finished the call and moved over to the office in Glencot. He could still smell Gayle's lingering perfume (notably, Yves Saint Laurent's 'Poison'), which was unnerving; a constant dig in the ribs that he was being a bastard of the first order. He logged on, tapped the relevant words into Google and bingo! Bundy's blog co-ordinates had come into view. The article was brilliant, long and complex, and looking and sounding as if written by a man who really knew his stuff - an expert in his field. He called Alex on her lunch break at Christie's, and told her how things were progressing.

'Read me a bit, Tarmin,' she mumbled, tucking into a tuna and salad ciabbata. 'Just a taster; the bit that suggests there's something hidden at Glencot.'

'OK. Here goes.......Bundy writes: 'To trace the roots of all the multitude of potential leads to the Ark, is an obviously complex task - particularly considering the early date from which it was first knowingly hidden. This detail is documented by the prophet Jeremiah, who removed the Ark from the Temple of Solomon during Nebuchadnezzar's siege of Jerusalem - in or around 590BC. From whence it then travelled is open to much speculation, although it is known to have first made its way to Jordan and then on to Ethiopia. A considerable weight of belief states that this is where it still remains, although the larger proportion plumps for Europe, which is far more probable for a number of reasons.' Blah, blah, blah. Bundy then goes on to talk about the complexities of the Ark's co-ordinates, which we'll skip over, and then mentions more stuff about his own local research and findings. Here goes: 'Of late, I've based myself in Somerset during the research period for my book on the Ark of the Covenant. Why? Of course this is a county that's traditionally been littered with many known religious antiquities and relics, and in stationing myself near Glastonbury, I've unearthed an extraordinary amount of literature and local documentation on both pre-Christian and Arthurian pieces from the region. Most exciting of all, has been my own discovery of literature detailing an ancient badger skin and a small menorah allegedly stored in a sealed rock chamber in one of the larger houses in the Somerset region of Wells. This may have particular significance to the Ark, linking to its well-documented inclusion of animal skin coverings. The main covering of the tabernacle was known to be of goat's hair and referring back to Exodus once again, its 'container' was definitively spoken about:

'Five of the curtains shall be the sides and six shall be the curtains of the forefront of the tabernacle, and these shall be doubled to make three.

The remnants of the curtains shall be made to cover the backside of the Ark.

The final covering shall be of ram's skin dyed red and the covering above shall be of badger's skin to shade the Ark from the sky.' That in mind, my own explorations have unearthed both remnants of a couple of badger skins and a tarnished gold Menorah of period significance.'

By the time Tarmin had finished reading Bundy's article, Alex had polished off her tuna sandwich and vitamin booster smoothie. The mix of uncomplimentary foodstuffs was weighing heavily in her stomach but she'd managed to absorb the overall gist. The only problem was the menorah, as far as she could see. The candlestick that George Kimininos had originally loaned Tarmin, was made of bronze and had just four branches. Exodus had described the one from the covenant as having seven branches and fashioned in gold.

Tarmin was unfazed as he'd already thought through this potential hitch. He'd located a metal worker in Wells who had agreed to adapt the existing bronze piece and change the metallic appearance. The menorah would be viewed only in a very dark place anyway, so it was not of vital importance. He told Alex that Bundy had already received quite a few pieces of email correspondence from Nathan Hunt over time, and thought it wouldn't be a problematical thing to subtly direct him to the blog.

Blacks Bar in Rolland Gardens, London, had always been one of Bundy's favourite 'first date' watering holes. It was small, intimate and dark. So dark in fact, that you ran the risk of mistakenly sitting on an unsuspecting lap. Bundy's date that evening was certainly not going to end up on his knee, and if he played his cards right, he would not even have to go through the ritualistic bonding dinner. It had just hit six o'clock and the downstairs bar at Blacks was empty, except for a lone figure sitting at the dimly lit end of the bar. A suitably dark-clad barman was obviously enjoying whiling away his shift with an attractive waitress, both of them giggling flirtatiously whilst half-heartedly stacking newly polished wine glasses.

The lone man flipped the cocktail menu over and over, and chewed on a small cocktail stick. He was elegantly wrapped in a full-length charcoal cashmere overcoat, with a maroon silk scarf loosely tied around the neck. Catching sight of the approaching figure, he nodded in acknowledgment to Bundy who pulled up a stool beside him.

'Nice to see you again, Mr. Hunt', Bundy said, grasping Nathan's outstretched kid-leather gloved hand with some distaste. Being a stickler for etiquette, did this Austrian heathen really not know that it was unbelievably rude to keep one's gloves on for a handshake? On the other hand, perhaps he was worried about leaving fingerprints? It wouldn't surprise him.

'And you too, Professor Bundy', Hunt replied, without a glimmer of warmth showing in his lined, bronzed face.

'Bottle of beer, please.'

Bundy put in his order with the distracted barman and pulled over a plate of assorted nuts.

'Good flight?' Bundy felt that at least a morsel of small talk was required to cut the ice. Perhaps this wasn't too far from a normal date, after all? Hunt sipped his mineral water and dismissed Bundy's attempts at irrelevant conversation, getting straight to the point.

'So, tell me about your recent research, Professor. It sounds most intriguing. You mentioned unearthing a source of artefacts at a particular house in Somerset.'

Bundy further explained in some detail the basis of his assumptions, that three houses in the vicinity of Wells Cathedral were likely candidates as the possible last resting place for the Ark of the Covenant. They were Glastonbury Manor, Wookey Grange and Glencot House.

'And is there any real documented evidence for this theory? Presumably there are a lot of assumptions, as well as falsehoods flying around?'

Hunt felt that Bundy was being evasive. After all, he'd written with some certainty in his blog that he'd actually located a document about the badger skin and a menorah. Now he was just talking in vagaries. Surely he couldn't imagine that Hunt had flown all the way from Austria for a lark? He was beginning to feel irritated.

'Well, yes, there is substance to the documentation I've found,' replied the Professor. 'This is very real. But as you will appreciate, this research has to remain wholly confidential before publication, not least of all because it's taken me many years to accumulate. You'll just have to take my word on this, Mr. Hunt. I agreed to meet you, simply because you contacted me after my blog and expressed an interest to find out more. I have told you all that I can, believe me.'

Believing Bundy was actually the last thing on Hunt's mind.

'You know Tarmin Rimell well, don't you?' Hunt changed the subject. 'And you've obviously told him of your theories and I'm sure he must have had a good look around Glencot to locate any hidden chambers there?'

'Yes, he has. But he maintains there is nothing, or rather, he can't be bothered to look too closely. Tarmin Rimell doesn't care about historical stuff like this. He adores so-called antiques for decorative purposes only and that's as far as it goes. Between you and me, what Tarmin is finding useful about my research is purely a tool with which to hype his hotel business and get the place filled to the gunnels by the world's Ark hunters. And if ever he sells the house, he'll probably get a large 'hope factor' increase in value. You know the score..... 'Impressive country estate with secret cellars, possibly linked to Glastonbury's Arthurian legends, the Ark of the Covenant and so forth'. You can visualise the print.'

'These two other houses? Has anyone properly explored the possibilities there?' Hunt changed track again.

'Yes, both have been properly surveyed and nothing has yet come to the surface. But that was some years ago and like with Glencot, absolutely the only way to find these sealed rock chambers is using modern, seismic technology. That way, you can survey to a greater depth and accuracy. As far as I know, this has not been done.'

'Has Rimell done this with Glencot?' asked Hunt. 'Or could he at least be persuaded?'

'No, he's too damn mean and doesn't care enough, as I told you. For him, it's such a slim chance, that he would rather keep the legend alive and milk the most of the story.'

'Can I be frank with you, Professor?'

'Indeed' replied Bundy, wondering what was coming next. He likened this man's frankness to a wild tarantula on the verge of plunging its teeth into his fleshy parts.

'I would be willing to pay you a retainer if you will furnish me with your latest written research, plus updates as to your progress. I feel that we have mutual interests. If we were to find anything of significance, not only will you share in the glory but you'll also receive a substantial sum which I'm sure would give you a little pension fund.'

Ignoring the veiled insult, Bundy felt a tug on the line. He realised that Hunt reckoned on Glencot being the only location for Bundy's so-called discovery.

'That's an interesting offer', Bundy replied, 'but I feel I must decline. As I'm sure you'll appreciate, I can't be compromised when it comes to my friendship with Tarmin Rimell. That's too much of a line to cross. It's frustrating for me that in this case, the friend in question is particularly resistant to exploring a subject that is so close to my heart, but that's life - sometimes it sucks. And may I also add that you are not the first to have shown such interest.'

Hunt found Bundy a ridiculous bore. He was obviously after something, and he - Hunt - hadn't flown all this way to be palmed off. He wanted him to just get to the point and spare him this fooling around.

'Is your reticence to share information really to do with your friendship with Mr. Rimell, or purely on ethical grounds, as a leading academic?'

'Obviously, Tarmin is a good friend and if I did discover something that would be beneficial to him, then I'd feel morally obliged to pass on the information. As yet, it's still all speculation, and I have much further research to follow up. He simply won't allow a seismic check and that's that. I have to accept it.'

'Are you saying then that friendship is thicker than money? And if that is the case, I'm sure that I would be able to indulge your moral stance.'

Bundy drained his beer and motioned to the sexier half of the bar duo to replenish his glass with a half pint. This playing hard to get was not too difficult a task for Bundy, and he reckoned that a few seconds of silent deliberation indicated careful consideration. He picked at a few nuts in the dish, smoothed back his hair and smiled at Hunt.

'Give me your number please, Mr. Hunt. Your private number.'

Hunt took his wallet from his coat pocket and selected an embossed black card from the pile.

'Thank you, Professor. And if you would like an indication of my seriousness, just text me over your bank details.'

With that, Hunt slipped off his stool, drained his water glass and discreetly clicked his heels before leaving. Bundy watched him go and stared into his beer. That had gone really well, he thought. The hook was well and truly embedded.

Nathan Hunt was no fool. He felt that he'd effectively pierced Bundy's thin armour and despite the Professor's weak attempt at concealment, it was almost certain in Hunt's mind that the reference he'd made to a sealed rock chamber, was indeed at Glencot. In his opinion, the other two houses were simply a decoy to slow up any investigation that Hunt might make. Why involve Hunt? Because Bundy was a greedy bastard and would no doubt be after his cash. Most people were. He knew that it would only be a short matter of time before he got a call passing on his bank details.

Blacks Hotel was Nathan Hunt's favoured place of rest and as he'd only flown into town for one night and this was the suggested rendezvous with Bundy, it made sense to stay put. He'd taken room 007 (their best suite), where he felt at home and at ease. With its huge windows and hand painted white floor, clean beige walls and massive canopy bed, the room was light, bright and lovely. They'd even adapted the original French windows into the entrance. Nathan flung himself in the middle of the massive canopy bed and removed an exquisitely bound parchment book from his crocodile travelling case. Fifty minutes later, he was woken by a call from the reception, informing him that he had a guest in reception.

'Please direct her to my suite' he told the caller, 'and send up a very chilled bottle of Cristal. Thankyou'.

Hunt slipped off the bed and walked to the bathroom to splosh some water over his face. A few minutes later there was a light knock on the door and an elegant woman dressed in a white woollen coat, entered.

'Ah. Good to see you. I've a little job for you, my dear' he smiled.

'You know I only like the big ones,' she replied with a grin.

'I do, my angel. But this one pays a lot better and will put a healthy flush on those pasty cheeks of yours with some wonderfully fresh country air. But first things first, eh?'

Amanda took the champagne glass from his outstretched hand and scrutinised her client's face. She was used to him being mysterious but this behaviour was totally unexpected. But then again, some things don't change that quickly. Leaning over and unbuttoning her coat, Nathan flashed a wad of money and pointed her in the direction of the bathroom.

CHAPTER THIRTEEN

Glencot and Glastonbury

Anne Titchmarsh, Glencot's explosive receptionist, had handed in her notice. There were two things that were bugging her. Firstly, she thought Tarmin was a complete twat, and secondly, his very obvious affair with that smarmy Miss Henshall from London, was hugely offensive to her very devout Catholicism. What kind of an idiot did they take her for, pretending that silly tart was doing some high-falutin' course at Bonhams, for God's sake? She'd seen straight through their pathetic cover from the first weekend that Alex had arrived. And then, whilst delivering a fax to Room Seven, right by Tarmin's quarters, she'd heard an unbelievable noise, like an animal in chronic pain. What should she do do? The high-pitched squealing became so intense that Anne couldn't bear it any longer and banged on the door. Just at the moment, she heard Tarmin answer in a breathless, alien voice, and the penny finally dropped. It was an orgasm! That's what it was, and she mentally congratulated herself that she'd never allowed her husband, Roger, to give her one of those things. After all, it sounded like someone was being spit-roasted on the barbeque.

That lunchtime, Tarmin and Miss Henshall had appeared together in the dining room, the latter confirming Anne's suspicions. Flushed cheeks, hair dishevelled, standing a little too close to Tarmin. A family friend, my arse! Her priest had only just been preaching about the heinous sin of adultery this last Sunday, and here it was in the flesh, brazenly displayed in front of her.

When Miss Henshall arrived for the two following weekends, it was clear as a bell that sin was in the air, and this was not an innocent study of Anglo Saxon antiquities. Little did those nauseous lovebird nerds know, that she had indeed rung Bonhams and found out that the nearest thing to a course they had was a one-off 'Tutored Whisky Tasting' - and that was at Bonhams in London, for goodness sake.

She'd typed up her resignation and marched into Tarmin's office, catching him bidding for a giant porcelain owl on ebay. He'd expressed surprise at her departure, but much to her chagrin, did nothing to dissuade her. Tarmin of course, was secretly delighted. He loathed the harridan from Shepton Mallet and wished she'd just fuck off quickly to her new post at the veterinary clinic. Although, it had left him with a headache to fill the post in a rush (Anne had given no notice). But, at the end of the day, Tarmin had always loathed a snoop. By the close of the afternoon, he'd placed his new ad in the Wells Journal.

Setting off down the winding country lanes from Glencot,

Tarmin stopped off in Wookey Hole to pick up a few stamps. It took him some time to notice, but five minutes or so later, he clocked a dark green car, which appeared (or was he being fanciful?) to be following him all the way to Glastonbury. As he pulled into the car park, the driver, head covered by a floppy hat and wearing dark wraparound shades, strained to see where he was heading.

Suitably distracted, he had a close shave attempting to squeeze his car between a floral painted van sporting matted fluffy bumpers, and an aged landrover. Time to rein it in and get his mind back on the job. It had taken him only ten minutes to drive from Wells and another ten minutes to navigate Glastonbury's ring road. Parking in a metered bay, his two pounds purchased him an hour. In London, he would still be feeding the meter as the first pound was running out.

It was a perfect summer morning, with a soft breeze ruffling through his hair. He spotted the sign for the town centre and soon found himself in the High Street, amongst the many mystical shops and crystal arcades devoted to man's search for inner enlightenment. Warlock cloaks, mystical dragons, and life-sized witches populated the grubby shop fronts, whilst most of the incense-saturated shops sported notice boards offering all manner of courses, workshops and events, and enticing passers-by into their covenesque interiors.

By-passing the meat-free cafes and bars sporting off-putting mystical names, Tarmin eventually came across a discreet alleyway with a faded sign advertising: 'Holy Cod And Cheeses'. At least this place smacked of humour. With the detached superior air of a seasoned meat-eater, he approached the display counter and instantly recoiled at the intense mouldy and fishy smells. After much hoo-ing and ha-ing over the strange menu, he settled on a baked potato with a brown cheese mix, covered with oily peppers and organic baked beans, and served with a glass of homespun green liquid.

Out at the back, he found a terraced area and headed for the only available table nestling under a trellised roof overgrown with vines. Next to him, an elderly hippy sat picking the remnants of a blackened corn on the cob from his teeth and feeding the findings to his equally elderly hound. The terrace was packed by a selection of specimens of dubious sex and nationality, engaging in alienating table manners. Tarmin was in no hurry; he enjoyed people watching and as he absentmindedly stubbed out his cigarette in the baked potato dish, a long shadow fell across his table.

'Mind if I join you?'

Squinting into the blinding sunlight, his eyes half-viewed a tall female wearing an impossibly tight faded t-shirt, advertising a holiday resort on Bondi Beach.

'Please do,' he answered, discreetly placing a paper napkin over the potato and ash mess.

The woman sat down diagonally opposite him and delved into a small leather black backpack, pulling out a copy of the Wells Journal. He didn't flatter himself that she'd selected his particular table, as there was literally nowhere else. The waiter appeared at her side, pen poised, and whilst she deliberated over a brie tartlet with salad, he snatched some sneaky looks at her. The woman was in her early thirties, had large hazel eyes and shoulder length golden hair, shot through with bleached streaks. Her breasts were definitely silicone, Tarmin noticed; either that or she'd been ordering her bras from a porn catalogue. He'd clocked her long legs and knockout figure when she'd sat down, and although not a conventional beauty, she was unusually striking and sensual. The woman spread out her newspaper with immaculately manicured fingernails, and flipped straight through to the classified section. As she circled a particular advertisement, she looked up and caught Tarmin's eye.

'Could you spare one of your cigarettes? They always take an age to bring the food here.'

'Sure.' Tarmin peeled away the cellophane from a new pack and flicked the lighter.

'I always seem to be on the verge of giving up,' she said, flashing a very sexy grin.

Pushing over the ashtray, Tarmin smiled back in complicity. 'Personally, I believe that the attempting of something tends to be the best part.'

He had no idea what he meant, but hopefully she might assume something philosophical.

The woman carried on silently scanning the newspaper, her biro hovering above various entries on the classified ads page.

'What are you looking for?' Tarmin asked, thankful for a sort of valid reason to re-open the dialogue.

'Just a spot of job hunting.'

'What sort of job?'

'One that puts a roof over my head, if I can swing it. I've just left a nanny job in London, which got a bit messy. The daddy reckoned he was part of the bedtime story.'

Tarmin couldn't exactly visualise Pamela Anderson fitting the Mary Poppins mold - more likely gyrating around a pole.

'What takes your fancy then?' he asked, pointing at the newspaper.

'God, there's so little here, it's depressing. Just a couple of waitress numbers, receptionist at a solicitors, fruit pickers and baby sitters.'

'Well, your ship could just have sailed in.'

The words had slipped from Tarmin's mouth before his brain followed.

THE WOOKEY HOLE AFFAIR

'What do you mean?'

'I'm looking for a hotel receptionist at my place in Wookey Hole. You haven't spotted it yet? It's a large ad on the opposite page. Not the most mind blowing of jobs, but it's a great place to work and we can help out with some accommodation, if you want.'

The woman's face lit up and, after a short description from Tarmin about the place and the job, she agreed to come and meet Rob for an interview. Tarmin waited for her to demolish her cheese tart, so that she could follow him back in her car.

'Oh and by the way, my name is Georgia Coleman' she said, climbing into the front seat of her dark green Honda. Just for a second, Tarmin experienced a memory jolt. Wasn't that the same car that had followed him all the way from Glencot earlier? Surely not. All further deliberations were violently swept aside as a huge bus zoomed past, booping its horn with irritation and causing him to swerve onto the pavement.

CHAPTER FOURTEEN

Glencot Hotel

Tarmin's restoration of Glencot was nearing completion. He'd always been a man in a hurry, but now at least, the end was in sight.

Every week, a truck load of art and antiques arrived from London and he felt as happy as a pig in shit, digging into his bag of six inch nails, ranting at the builders, hanging paintings, and filling the glass cabinets with numerous acquistions of 19th century porcelain, courtesy of ebay.

One area that he rarely visited was the kitchen. He'd always held in awe any master of the culinary arts who could churn out endless meals on demand, and yet somehow retain a semblence of sanity. Chefs had come and gone in various stages of neurosis and alcholism, until eventually, a calm and talented one-legged Frenchman had miraculously hopped across his threshold. Poking his head around the door, Tarmin exchanged morning pleasantries with Olivier, who was concocting a thyme and chicken jus and straining the liquid through a sieve. With the smell of freshly baked bread flooding his nostrils and huge pans of vegetables bubbling away on the cooker, Tarmin lost restraint and stole a small handmade truffle from a plastic container. Bliss.

This Sunday morning, Glencot Hotel was looking at its best. Henry the Hoover was ending his noisy foray with a final suck around the reception hall, under the quizzical gaze of several balding deerheads with large, faded antlers. Quiet strains of 'Madam Butterfly' wafted around the sunlit reception rooms and for a change, there wasn't a guest in sight. Double bliss.

The Sunday boot fair held at Cheddar, some six miles away, has become one of Tarmin's cherished weekly habits. The fair was very much an early bird's event with the normal collection of dedicated Sunday devotees supplementing their income by selling off kid's toy cupboards, assorted contents of tool sheds and their other halves' video and record collections. Very occasionally, an antique reared its rare head, to be snapped up by the local collectors' mafia. It was a routine that Tarmin enjoyed, meaning that he could indulge his passion for an hour, for less than the price of dinner at The Ivy.

Today happened to have been a good day for books, and he arrived back at Glencot laden with a carload of literature for his newly constructed library shelves. It had certainly been a lucky day for the charity stall, with Tarmin clearing out their stock and coughing up the asking price without much of a quibble.

Georgia was sitting in the front office, cup of tea in hand, and greeted Tarmin in her inimitably flirtatious way. He still found her kind of odd, but somehow she seemed to be settling in nicely, very nicely. Maybe the oddness was that she seemed so very urban, and that there was something ill-fitting about her being parked in the Somerset countryside.

Tarmin had always recruited his staff from the ranks of friends, or as Professor Bundy often commented, from whoever was at last night's party. So it wasn't unheard of to have found his next member of staff munching a cheese tart in Glastonbury. Having said which, that particular word seemed rather too apt. Anyway, one thing was certain - having a complete change from tweedy, menopausal Anne, with her sensible shoes and lack of humour, was nothing short of a positive. And if he wasn't so afraid of Gayle and so fond of Alex, Tarmin reckoned he would most certainly have had a shot at Georgia himself. Surround yourself with beauty in all its forms and the female form always came top, was his reckoning. Mind you, anything porcelain from ebay came a very close second.

This morning, Georgia appeared to be having a cleavage moment; part of her knack for rotating legs, bum and breast on a daily basis. Leaning forward so that Tarmin had a clear view down her unbuttoned white shirt, she slowly stroked a dangling pendant hanging between her visible bra cups.

'You seem in sparkling form today, boss. Ah, and you've done some good shopping too.'

She smiled as Tarmin stopped by the door, laden with a pile of hardbacks. 'Watch your step now, Henry is........'.

Too late. Tarmin stumbled over the hoover, books flying across every square inch of Persian carpet.

'Can I help?' she asked a little too late, picking up a copy Alex Comfort's 'The Joy of Sex' and holding it to the light.

Typical that particular book should land at her feet, Tarmin thought, dusting down his copy of 'Training The Perfect Puppy'. The charity bin housed a wonderfully eclectic bunch of rubbish.

Ten minutes later, when the books had been carefully stacked, he popped open a beer, settled himself in a corner of the drawing room and tucked into one of Olivier's delicious variations of Welsh Rarebit. Opening the balcony door to refresh the overheated room, he could hear the occasional whirring of the office PDQ machine ploughing through receipts, as well as muted telephone chitchat softly puncturing the silence. Grabbing a copy of The Times, he pulled a biro from his jacket pocket and began the crossword. What on earth was a 'West Indian sea mammal, seven letters and ending in e'? The trouble being that it wasn't too easy to concentrate with that loud mobile phone ringing off the hook in the office. Why the hell wasn't someone answering it?

Just as he was about to explode, the phone was picked up and he heard Georgia's muffled voice penetrating the thin wall. Her conversation sounded a bit strained (with a couple of pleasantries and the like), but then with some insistence she said: 'No, nothing. Nothing at all. Trust me on this, it's not the right time. Listen, please, it's really not good to speak now. Much better later. Can't you call me at two? Why not, sweetheart?'

Tarmin interest was aroused. She was definitely speaking to a man and to his surprise, he felt a sudden pang of jealousy. Was this a boyfriend? He hadn't heard her ever mention anyone. Lucky bastard, whoever he was.

Georgia continued pressing her case.

'Look, it's far easier for me to call you. I'll do it later, no problem. Oh, and by the way - it's way past my pay day. I need the money transferred to my account this afternoon. Can you do that?'

Tarmin was curious, more about who would owe her money, than anything else. He realised that he knew very little about Georgia; no knowledge of her family, friends, or even if she'd ever been married. The only thing that she'd ever spoken of was that she'd previously lived in London, worked as a nanny and that the father of the household had behaved inappropriately. This nanny stuff had never really rung true for him. There was no getting away from her air of sophistication, her overall sexual demeanour and her lustful appearance. She reeked of sex, for heaven's sake, and trying to fit her into the Nanny McPhee box was just plain ridiculous.

Gulping down the last bit of his cheese on toast, he folded up The Times and walked around to the office. Georgia was filing her nails and nonchalantly gazing at the bookings folder. She knew how to play men and she was bored out of her skull. Time for a break, and Tarmin always seemed to be the perfect sucker for her requests.

'Do you mind if I go and stretch my legs for a minute?'

'No problem' he replied. 'Been a bit busy this morning? Floods of punters ringing in?'

For a second she paused, nail file in mid air. She looked away and pointed through the window.

'No, it's all pretty quiet on the western front. I just need to stretch these legs of mine. Never been very good at sitting still for a long time. I'm used to a lot more physical exertion, shall we say.'

They both laughed and Tarmin pulled out her chair.

'Go on then. You need the exercise, fatty.'

THE WOOKEY HOLE AFFAIR

After Georgia had shut the front door, he sat by the computer, checked his email and half-heartedly flipped through a few letters in the in-tray. On the top of the pile was Georgia's mobile phone, taunting him like a red rag to a bull. Out of the window, he glimpsed her wandering by the river and puffing on a cigarette. She wasn't going to be leaping back through the door at any minute.

To this day, he never quite knew why he did it. It was out of character and probably pointless. Grabbing her phone, he clicked through the menu and located the call log. What was he hoping to see? A man's name? Big deal. Even if he did, he would still be none the wiser. He thought about it for a split second, and then pressed for the last received call. The screen lit up in purple writing and the name 'Nathan' appeared. He pressed it again. This time a number appeared as an international number. Seeing Georgia stamp out her cigarette butt and start walking towards the door, he hastily scribbled the number down on a post-it sticker, cleared the phone screen and slipped the yellow paper into his top pocket. Just then the hotel phone rang.

'No, I'm sorry, we're full that weekend. Any other dates workable? No problem. Thanks for calling.'

He put down the phone, just as Georgia slung her cardigan over the back of the chair.

'Good walk?'

'Fine thanks. It's beautiful out here. But I have to confess - I do miss London sometimes.'

Tarmin knew what she meant. 'Me too. Can't do one without a blast of the other. Maybe you should get up there again soon? Grab a lift with me, if you like.'

Georgia looked rather forlorn, as if someone had taken the wind out of her sails. Maybe this Nathan boyfriend was actually a dark force in her life? Whatever, she'd seemingly lost some of her bubble and he hadn't seen her like that before. Tarmin's curiosity was up and following her example, he took himself off into the gardens.

Georgia tapped her fingernails on the desk in frustration. Her period always made her feel ratty and low - there was no getting away from it. And this goddam job that Hunt had persuaded her to do was hardly worth the fucking boredom factor. True, he was paying her truckloads of cash to do bugger all; just spy on a bumbling hotel guy and sitting here mindlessly answering phones and sorting out room keys. But God, how she missed dressing up and being in London, and whilst here in Wookey Hole, she was also losing out on her other regular clients. Thankfully she'd only agreed to six weeks away, with just another two and a half weeks to go. Otherwise she really would end up going as mad as a caged eagle.

Tarmin crossed the bridge and walked up to the far field towards the folly. Nathan. Surely it couldn't be Nathan Hunt? That would be too wierd. He pulled the yellow paper from his top pocket, punched in his 'with-old number' facility and entered the number.

Four long rings and then he heard the voice.

'Good afternoon. Nathan Hunt speaking'.

Tarmin instantly killed the call. His heart beating nineteen to the dozen, he straightaway dialled Professor Bundy.

'You're never going to believe this, Bundy! He's bitten; Hunt has fucking bitten!' Tarmin's raised voice sent two grazing sheep scampering across the field.

'Call Alex and let's get on with our superbait now.' Bundy replied, having listened to to the entire story. 'Your genie may just have granted your wish.'

Tarmin sat for a while by the riverbank, staring at Georgia's frame through the office window. Now it all made sense, now he could understand. And this was quite a revealing insight into that Hunt man too. Georgia was a hooker, he was sure of that now. Shame really, he rather liked her, and she was making quite a good receptionist too, one way and another. But of course, she'd be moving on shortly, that was for definite.

Next, he needed to go through a mental checklist of where they should go from here. Nathan was obviously intrigued by Bundy's blog and his subsequent meeting at Blacks, to be serious enough to plant a mole at the hotel. That was something they'd not anticpiated, not in a million years. (Although, as far as moles went, he couldn't think of a finer specimen). But it was actually a double-edged sword, and he had to remind himself that caution was needed and that with one dangerous slip, they could all be up to their necks in shit.

So the next step was to place the faked documents identifying Glencot as the probable location of the rock chamber, right under Georgia's nose. It would have to be secreted in the box of photographs and letters that he'd bought at the Bath auction all those months ago. Almost immediately, another idea popped into his head. Fired up with renewed vigour, Tarmin hurried back to the house.

By mid afternoon, the hotel was bustling with early check-ins accompanied by a bunch of squealing children. Tarmin wasn't in the mood for infants scrambling over his furniture andscreaming at the top of their voices.

'Grotty little bastards', he muttered, watching a small boy heave himself onto the cabinet and pull at the nose of a low-hung elk head. Little did the child realise that he'd picked out Tarmin's ace. Just as he was about to tug the appendage again, Tarmin pressed the remote control, the elk opened up and burst into a hearty rendition of 'Home, Home On The Range'. As the head shook (ears twitching and teeth bared), the screaming boy scrambled backwards and shot off the cabinet into a crumpled heap. Chuckling sadistically, Tarmin left the howling mess for the mole to sort.

He slipped quietly out of the front door and headed in the direction of the Wookey Hole Club near the caves. It was only a ten minute walk away and he needed to make contact with someone. Immediately after this morning's revelation about Georgia, he'd pinpointed his man for the job, a fellow drinker from the village. After downing a stiff whisky and pocketing a pile of ten pound notes, Mr. John Potter gratefully agreed that he would most certainly be on the case.

At five o'clock, Georgia put on her coat and switched shifts with Sammy. Keeping a distance, Tarmin followed her to the kitchen where she picked up a chicken sandwich that Olivier had left out for her.

'Have you ever been to the Wookey Hole caves?' Tarmin asked, poking his head around the door.

Georgia smiled. Here we go - she knew it would only be a matter of time before Tarmin made his move. All the men around her did. But actually, she didn't mind the idea at all. This idea of sex in a cave was pretty novel.

'No, never. Keep meaning to, but I never seem to have the right shoes. I hear it's a bit on the slippery side.'

Not half as slippery as you, Tarmin thought.

'I always think it's a good thing to take my staff there. You should see it first hand, so you can tell all our visiting inmates about it. What about tomorrow? Are you on the early or the late shift?'

'Late.'

'Ok, let's hit the caves in the morning. Say at about eleven, and we can have a snack at the Wookey Inn afterwards and sample something from the competition.'

150

THE WOOKEY HOLE AFFAIR

Georgia sunk her teeth into the sandwich and a line of mayonnaise dribbled down her chin. She nodded silently and gave him the thumbs up.

Great. The plan was moving ahead.

The next morning at five to eleven, Georgia pulled on some borrowed wellington boots and waited for Tarmin in the vestibule. She watched him crossing the parking lot, inhaling deeply. Georgia winced. This guy never stopped smoking, and although not exactly averse to the occasional nicotine stick herself, she didn't much relish the thought of having sex with a man who stank like the bottom of a litter bin. Nathan Hunt smelled only of peppermint mouthwash.

Together they walked to the Wookey Hole caves, purchased tickets and joined the queue at the entrance. After dispensing chirpy greetings to the assembled crowd, their elderly male guide briefed everyone on the experience ahead. For a second, Georgia wondered about her supposed assignation with Tarmin, trying to figure out how the man would manage to seduce her amongst such numbers. But before she could think any further, they dropped down into the caves and she found herself being transported to another world.

The first witches chambers were beautifully lit and carved out by the swirling underground river, settling into pools. Looking around, Georgia certainly didn't envy the many cave explorers who'd flocked there over the years, unearthing far deeper chambers with names like 'The Lake of Gloom' and 'Tight Squeeze'. The legendary witch dweller (whose image they saw depicted in a well-worn stalagmite), had reputedly taken up residence in the caves during the 18th century and, while casseroling a small child, had her wickedness turned into stone by a passing monk. Legendary or not, the fact that human bones and a dagger were unearthed here in 1912 was quite enough evidence that these beautiful reddish-brown caves were once home to centuries of dwellers.

Back outside, they re-grouped and watched the foamy River Axe gushing over sodden rocks and sprouting greenery. So much for a raunchy encounter with Tarmin, Georgia pondered. Maybe she'd underestimated him? Perhaps this man had wanted to get his rocks off in quite a more literal way.

Their chatty guide, hardly pausing for breath, guided his herd through the prehistoric Valley Of The Dinosaurs - life sized, plastic, and great for kids. After which he ushered them up to the old mill buildings for a demonstration of paper making. Doubling up as a master paper maker, the white-haired man selected Georgia as his guinea pig and offered her a chance to try her hand. Taking great pains to wrap the plastic apron carefully around her ample body, he joked with the other punters that it was days like this, that made his job feel more than worthwhile. Tarmin winced. The old geezer had got closer to those great silicone breasts than he had certainly ever managed. Smart move.

Georgia held the paper tray tightly, and dipped her manicured hands into the white sludge. With her tutor's help, she then pulled the flat soggy sheet onto a paper mat and pressed it hard down. Everyone applauded her efforts and it seemed like the tour was now completed. Gradually the other punters drifted off to try their luck at the penny arcade, or amaze themselves in the Magical Mirror Maze. Georgia and Tarmin were left behind with the congenial guide.

'Fascinating,' commented Tarmin. 'It's the first time that I've been back here since we moved down from London.'

'That right, sir? Where you be living now?'

'Glencot House, down the road.'

'I knows it well. Used to be the Mill owner's home. Special place, that. He built it on the old Wookey Castle site back the 1880s. Bet it's brimmin' with ghosts and treasures? You could be sittin' on a fortune there, young man.'

Immediately, Georgia's interest was piqued. Extending her hand, she smiled at the unshaven man.

'I'm sorry, I don't know your name.'

'It's John, miss.'

'Thank you, John' she continued. 'You've made this a very pleasant trip. Thanks for all the information.'

Walking back to the exit, Tarmin looked over his shoulder and caught the old man's smiling eyes.

'Yes, thank you, Mr. Potter. You certainly did a very good job indeed.'

Professor Bundy was getting addicted to his weekends at Glencot and, after an abortive effort to track down Bethany, he'd resigned himself to this particular weekend being all work and no play. After all, Alex was here again and Tarmin was going to be largely otherwise engaged. It seemed like a good time to further their plotting.

Grabbing various bits and bobs from his room, Bundy wandered downstairs and helped himself to a vodka and tonic from the bar. The idea of concentrating for too long without something to wet his whistle was unthinkable. After that, the perfect place to tuck himself away appeared to be the concert room on the lower ground floor, leading directly onto the flagstone terrace and overlooking the croquet lawn and river. The outside elements would dictate as to where he'd put himself, either sitting within the magnificent portrait-lined interior, or weather permitting, on the terrace outside. This morning had so far turned out to be wet and depressing, so the decision was a foregone conclusion.

Bundy lit the fire and settled down at the Georgian desk by the window, plugged in his laptop and pulled out a sheaf of documents from his bag. He had a special task at hand and Miss Georgia was well within his target range.

During the period of supposed 'research' for his mythical book, Bundy had deliberately appeared fussed about not being disturbed, allowing nobody into whichever room he happened to be working in and making a show of meticulously locking up. But today, he would purposefully have a lapse. Delving deep into his bag, he pulled out the auctioned box of prints, pictures and documents that Tarmin had originally purchased, months before, from Bonhams. This morning Tarmin had brought the box downstairs and given it to Bundy, in full view of Georgia.

'Ah, is this the treasure trove you unearthed in Bath?' Bundy had commented, picking out the top photograph and holding it up to the light. 'And you say there's one or two revealing documents amongst all this mess too? I'll take it away and have a good old rummage. Thank you for this'.

Tarmin caught sight of Georgia straining to catch a glimpse of the photograph and threw in another carrot for good measure.

'Probably nothing of great value for your book, Bundy, but I love all this stuff about secret chambers and the like, and there is quite a lot written on the subject in one or two of those documents. Take it away and let me know what your thoughts are. I'm taking Alex into Wells to buy a couple of DVDs. We're planning on holing up for the afternoon, in all this rain.'

In reality, the box contained nothing of specific historical or architectural interest but, using contacts from her days in the manuscripts department of a London auction house, Alex had constructed a faked four-page parchment, which had proven to be expertly forged. The document outlined the bitter conflict and rivalry held between the Abbeys of Glastonbury and Wells, both having laid claim to recognising distinctive leads to the Ark of the Covenant. It also went on to chronicle some kind of an association to the Holy Grail, detailing an alleged custodianship of the religious artefact by the Druids from Wookey Castle. The author concluded that if this was so, then both the Holy Grail and the Ark of the Covenant were most likely located within the same radius. On page three, a hand-sketched map indicated the position of the former Wookey Castle, showing the land and river at the exact location of what was now Glencot House. On the fourth page, a short paragraph alluded to a rock chamber below Wookey Castle, which had apparently spawned underground passages linking the Bishops' Palace in Wells to the chambers of Wookey Hole caves. This was the final inducement that Bundy hoped would convince Nathan Hunt that Glencot was potentially sitting on top of something of huge archaeological significance.

Bundy spread out his papers and checked the finer details. No room for silly errors here. He was also in the habit of disabling the phone when at work, and he had told Georgia that on no account was he to be disturbed. Doing any work was actually the last thing on his mind. Attempting the cryptic crossword, however, most certainly was.

Glencot was pretty quiet that Saturday morning, with all the checkouts gone and no one due until the early afternoon. With the monotonous rain beating against the windowpanes, Georgia seized her moment and decided to take a quick break. Just around the corner from reception was what Tarmin romantically called his 'Romeo Room' - a small jutting balcony that overlooked the river. She sat down and inhaled deeply on her cigarette. Hunt had been right; the air here was exceptionally wonderful, and this whole experience couldn't be further removed from her normal life as a London escort. However, some habits were a little hard to shift, and today, her dress was better suited to the Soho club scene than a country hotel. But she knew that her flirtatious dress sense amused Tarmin, who liked to administer shock treatment to some of his more tedious guests. The shorter her skirts, the more he'd compliment her great legs. She'd been thinking (since the recent cave excursion), that it was actually rather a shame that she was spying on Tarmin. He was a cool guy; someone she wouldn't mind having as a client in London. On second thoughts (and judging from her limited experience), he'd be a lousy tipper.

The rain gradually petered out, replaced momentarily by sun streaming across the stone balcony. Her eyes blinked shut for a second or two, a welcome moment to doze away the tedium of the morning. At least as a hooker she got to have sex, dress up, drink champagne, and check out the great hotels. Maybe she could find a client or two here? That friend of Tarmin's - Professor Bundy. He always looked like he'd clean out his bank account to have a decent shag.

Her reverie didn't last long, with the phone ringing off the hook through the walls. She ran back in and answered the unwelcome interruption.

'Richard Bundy please,' a slightly muffled voice muttered. Georgia had to strain to make out the words. 'It's very urgent'.

'I'm afraid that Professor Bundy has given instructions not to be disturbed. I can take a message or you can ring back after three.' Georgia's mind was still on sex, as she flicked through her personal filofax. There was Jake Richards. He was a great lay - liked her to dress as an alpine maid and whip the living daylights out of him with her straw broom.

'I mentioned before that this is urgent. You must find him now, you understand. Tell him that it's Graham, his neighbour in London. His flat has been burgled overnight and he needs to speak to the police.'

Georgia's sexual reverie shattered in an instant.

'Poor guy. Oh, that's awful. Of course, I'll go and get him. Give me a minute to run down the stairs and I'll bring him to the phone'.

Out of breath, she knocked on the concert room door and yelled through to Bundy.

'Sorry, Professor. I know you said not to disturb you, but your neighbour, Graham, is on the phone. He says it's very urgent.'

Seconds later, Bundy emerged and affectionately squeezed her arm.

'Upstairs in reception. I've transferred it onto the second line.'

'What the fuck does he want?' Bundy moaned, heaving himself up the stairs as quickly as he could.

'I'm very sorry, but it seems you've had a robbery.'

Bundy grabbed the phone and listened intently to the distant voice, nodding and throwing in the odd response. Georgia sat at the desk and waited for him to finish. After the brief conversation with Graham (better known as Tarmin Rimell), he hung up, banged his fist on the desk and went into deliberate agitato.

'Shit! I've got to go back to London, straightaway. The police had to be called last night, as they've smashed down my door and broken a couple of windows. Graham says the place is in a complete mess. My dear, I'm going to have to leave all my papers here for when I come back, so can you please assure me that you will lock up and keep the room uninhabited until I return on Monday morning? No one's likely to want to use it, are they?'

With Georgia's reassurances and tender sympathies ringing in his ears, Bundy returned to his room to start packing.

Georgia couldn't believe her luck. All the Professor's research was left in her pretty little hands. And that box that Bundy and Tarmin were banging on about earlier in the day, was still sitting on the desk when she'd gone to get him. She'd certainly be earning her keep from Hunt tonight, but she had to wait until the right moment. First off, she checked Bundy out of the hotel and stood in the doorway, politely waving, until his Jaguar disappeared from view.

As soon as she returned to her desk, Georgia called the evening receptionist and arranged to swap shifts, so that she could do a double. At five o'clock, Tarmin and Alex set off for Wells Cathedral, telling her that they were going to drop into a concert and then grab an earlyish dinner at The Odd Spot restaurant, a favourite haunt. They drove back to Glencot shortly after eleven, shared a quick nightcap in the drawing room, said a friendly good-night to Georgia and disappeared upstairs. By midnight the whole hotel appeared to be a sleeping baby.

Georgia waited for a quarter of an hour and taking a torch, slipped the key from the duty office key cupboard and went downstairs to the concert room. Pulling the auctioneer's box towards her, she switched on the small side lamp and started sifting through the crammed contents. What were they talking about? All there seemed to be were old sepia print photographs, letters of no particular interest, the odd postcard and even a flyer from a shop in Wells. Then right at the very bottom she found exactly what she was looking for.

After scrutinising the text and looking at the map under a magnifying glass, she returned to her reception desk and placed the parchments under the photocopier glass. It took a few moments to readjust the toning, but within minutes, three sets of faxed copies were landing on Nathan's tray in Austria. Three for luck. This find was definitely worth a bumper cheque from Hunt with three noughts after the comma. Her covering note read: 'Nathan - this should do the trick. They definitely know that Glencot's land is sitting on the money. Do I get to return to London now? Country air and country bump-kins are wearing pretty thin.'

CHAPTER FIFTEEN

Glencot

Mornings at Glencot were always Tarmin's favourite time. He'd been an early riser for as long as he could remember and, by 6 o'clock, whether in London or in the country, he'd always be out on the prowl. His early mornings were his own, a time to plot, muse and ponder. And it made it easier and more enjoyable that his hangover days were now long gone.

Like most people, he'd had to learn the hard way. On the first night of his honeymoon, when he'd left Gayle in the grand salon of Chateaux D'Esclimant (scribbling all those predictably awful wedding postcards), he'd somehow engineered an escape to the bar and struck up conversation with Mort Walco, a seventy-year-old American with persuasive drinking habits. Hours later, and there were vaugue memories of Gayle dragging him screaming from Mort's arms and into their unused wedding bed. The next three days had been living hell. He couldn't remember whether it was Gayle's fury or his ailing constitution that had ranked top of the list, but one thing was for sure, he'd made a colossal mistake on both accounts and needed neither ever again.

That was then. And now, at 5.30am, with the light just beginning to bleed through the night clouds and illuminate the neatly manicured lawns, Tarmin pulled on a light sweatshirt and slid out of Glencot's huge oak door. Although he was not a gardening man and his knowledge of all things green and leafy was scant, he'd always harboured aspirations to be more competent in that department. His current idea of gardening was plucked straight from the school of 'Capability Brown' - huge JCBs digging up the foundations and creating scenic hills and lakes. Why wait for the trees to grow, when you should do as with all young children and buy them at a sensible size?

He was in the process of building a folly in the far woods and a morning inspection of the works always set his day off well. The folly was being built as a ruined tower, tucked away in a small wooded knoll. His two Polish workmen camped out in a caravan, parked just inside the massive brick tunnel built into the hillside. They'd been working for nearly two months on the ruin and were faithfully following Tarmin's design, based on the folly ruin at Bathampton. Tarmin decided he needed a bolt hole away from the hotel and this was going to be his little oasis. When at Glencot, he existed in a small apartment at the top of the hotel, with his most loved treasures from London - including the 'Dark Man' painting from George.

He'd looked long and hard at where to place it in the hotel, but the black background and dark shading dictated a need for extra illumination; it must be hung in an open space. His bedroom became the obvious choice - above the fireplace and facing his four poster bed. That way he had as much pleasure from seeing it every day, as George had done. Needless to say, Gayle had objected at first sight, slating it as a 'depressing, passe creation, better suited to the downstiars lavatory of a looney bin.'

Half an hour later, he ambled back to the hotel, walking past the cricket pavillion and pitch that had somehow claimed the field across the river, facing the main facade of the house. The village cricket club had a grace and favour arrangement with Tarmin, where the families and supporters could soak up the quintissentially English backdrop, enjoying afternoon tea on balmy summer afternoons. Tarmin crossed the bridge with its stone St. Francis, and sat on the terrace until the sun had fully risen, fresh coffee was bubbling away in its glass pot and the daily newspapers had arrived.

At ten o'clock, Tarmin rose from his seat on the Romeo Balcony, empty coffee cup in hand as he heard Georgia call out his name. Entering the dining room, Tarmin saw her showing a couple around. For some reason, they instantly struck him as rather odd, but he couldn't put a finger on it. The taller of the two men looked strangely familiar, but then again, who on earth did Tarmin know who had a pierced nose? The man was touching six feet tall, had black hair spiked into a tintin quiff at the front, and wore a tight black jumper and Rupert the Bear checked trousers. Was he wearing heels underneath all that? As he moved closer, Tarmin could see that it was a stacked shoe. Who was this guy?

He was so preoccupied, that it wasn't until he felt the hearty grip of the other friend's hand, that he actually stopped to look at him. The brown haired shorter man had eye-popping muscles and smooth, tanned skin. Dark brown eyes, rimmed with kohl, twinkled from beneath his floppy fringe, his full lips shined by peachy lipgloss. On his upper half, he was dressed in a lemon coloured singlet barely covering a hairless chest, with an Egyptian relic dangling low on a long silver chain. Below this he wore a three-quarter length skirt and flower print flipflops.

'This is Mr. Rimell' Georgia said, relishing the uncomfortable look on Tarmin's face and giving him a discreet prod of encouragement.

'Tarmin, may I introduce you to Mr. Dick and Mr. Thompson? They're staying with us tonight and are planning on having their wedding here at Glencot.'

The black haired man was the first to extend a bangled hand and grabbed Tarmin in a hearty grip. The second handshake was Liberace style - gooey, clammmy and a touch flamboyant.

'Congratulations! We put on a good wedding here, even if I say so myself. And we take pride in our after-service too.'

Tarmin dribbled on without a clue what he was saying. He was transfixed by the lipgloss and the large pink tongue that kept licking those fleshy lips, shaded by a stubbly six o'clock shadow.

'After service?' the skirted one grinned. 'Now that does sound good! Jason you little minx, you didn't tell me there was any of that in the brochure!'

Tarmin desperately tried to drive his brain into gear.

'Maybe I was rather over-egging the pudding. After service means that the next time around, we give you a 25 per cent reduction if it doesn't work out.'

'Just joking' he added, noticing black haired man's complete humour failure. Georgia cleared her throat and adjusted the flowers on the sideboard.

'Let's go and have a look downstairs,' she said, catching Tarmin's drift. 'There's plenty of space down there to get up to some naughty old wedding mischief!'

After Jason and Andre's tour of the gardens and reception rooms, Georgia showed them a small selection of the fifteen bedrooms until they eventually reached the top floor.

'We'd like to buy an exclusive usage package for the whole weekend, if you do that?' the older man said. 'Can we take over the entire hotel?'

'Of course. Exclusive that is, excepting Mr. Rimell's apartment,' she pointed at a solid oak door that was signed 'Private'.

'It's just that our crowd are a little on the lively side, shall we say, and we wouldn't want to put any noses out of joint. Do Mr. and Mrs. Rimell live here all the time?' asked Andre, who seemed to do most of the talking.

'On and off,' Georgia replied, hedging her bets. 'Mrs. Rimell is away a lot, and prefers to stay in London during the week.'

The two men looked at each other and Jason nudged Andre.

'I'd just kill to have a good old peek at his apartment. Any chance you can inch that door open? I bet its sumptious - we all love Mr. Rimell's crazy style!'

'No chance, gentlemen,' Georgia answered. 'I'd be skinned alive and dished up by Olivier for dinner. Mr. Rimell is a very private person. On the other hand, buy him a drink or two, and who knows.....maybe he'll issue you with a personal invitation!'

Jason smiled. 'I'd forgotten he likes a drink or two' he said.

Georgia looked surprised. 'You kow Mr. Rimell?' she said, catching sight of Andre kicking Jason's shin.

'No, not at all' he said, rather quickly. 'I think I must have heard silly gossip from somewhere or someone. Oh, look at this beautiful Japanese painting! I'm nuts for silk panels with lotus flowers and tiny birds.'

Jason and Andre stayed holed-up in their suite until around eight, when they came down to the drawing room and settled into the comfy couch, with its dramatic views over the river. Rob jotted down their drinks order and pulled out a cocktail shaker and bag of crushed ice.

'What the fuck are they drinking? Penis Coladas?' Tarmin hissed. Rob grinned and planted two umbrellas in the coconut froth.

'Spot on.'

As the huge orange sun set over the mill pond, the engaged pair stood in the bay window, arms linked. Andre had changed into a long embroidered black and gold kaftan, with bronze flipflops and black nailpolish on his feet. Jason was more demure in a grey suit, but for some reason insisted on wearing wrap around sunglasses. Tarmin found him spooky and untrustworthy and he couldn't tell where the man was looking but, every time he looked up, it seemed as if Jason's black gaze was boring into him. The other Glencot guests were all agog at the unscheduled entertainment and an uncomfortable silence descended when the beefy kaftan kissed his partner with a long, lingering, slurping number.

'Quick! Herd the masses into dinner,' Tarmin whispered to Rob. 'We don't want everyone throwing up their 'Miller's Mess In A Hole' puddings.'

165

MARTIN MILLER

After dinner, the couple returned to the drawing room and sat down in the only two available seats in the inglenook, where Tarmin was already entertaining a couple of wives, deserted by their respectives for a game of snooker downstairs. Jason and Andre introduced themselves to the women, much to Tarmin's irritation, and immediately engaged them in conversation about their footwear. At least that spooky Jason had removed his shades, at long last. If a quiz show existed called 'Name That Shoe', the bridegroom and bridegroom would have swept the board. Tarmin attempted to change the subject.

'Perhaps you can get some tips on marriage from Isabel and Kim, here?' he said, knocking back the last few drops of wine. 'Ladies, these two lovely gents have chosen Glencot for their wedding venue. Longevity and fidelity - hardly the springboards of modern life, eh?'

Tarmin was in one of his unattractive alcohol-induced moods.

'Ooh. You great big cynic!' Isabel laughed. 'And I thought there was a Mrs. Rimell in the picture too. Does she know what a Lothario she's hitched to?'

'Yes, where is Mrs. Rimell?' Jason hissed, looking Tarmin firmly in the eye.

There it was again - something so familiar about this perculiar looking man, yet so unidentifiable. But it was fleeting and the wine wasn't helping his concentration much either. Andre rose from his chair and took Tarmin's glass from his hand.

'I insist,' he said, stopping Tarmin in his tracks. 'Let me top you up while you regale us with your views on marital bliss. In fact, I think that the insitution of marriage calls for a new bottle of bubbly, don't you?'

Very shortly, Tarmin began feeling extremely blurry, quite unlike himself. His speech became laboured and

166

slurred, and keeping his eyes open was a gargantuan task. The others, however, kept in full flow, newly joined by Isabel and Kim's snooker men who had reappeared and were enthusiatically tucking into the booze. Feeling that he might blackout at any second, Tarmin excused himself and, holding on to the nearest table, edged his way along the sofas and, hobbled upstairs to his apartment. There wasn't even time to get undressed before he passed out cold, on top of his bedcovers.

The night was bearer of a cacophony of high pitched screams and booming echoes. Tarmin tossed and turned, his mind and body ablaze, sweat oozing from every pore and soaking the sheets. He could see vast, terrifying dragons blowing gusts of fire across the river, and burning down Glencot. They roared and stamped across the cricket pitch, heads held high, long tails thumping the earth with a ferocity that ricocheted through the blazing house. Suddenly there were devils standing in front of him, pitchforks aimed at his throat, his feet, his balls. Teeth bared, they were inching forwards, prodding their way with razor sharp points. He screamed for mercy as jagged metal pierced his flesh, blood trickling down his forehead and into his eyes. But no one heard him, no one came. Where was everyone? Then he spotted Gayle, all alone and kneeling by the door, her back to him. He screamed her name and her head swivelled 360 degrees, leaving her body still facing the wall.

'What are you fussing about, Tarmin?' she said quietly. And it was then that he saw this wasn't the Gayle that he'd married. Her huge outsized tombstone teeth were deep yellow, protruding over the lower lip like Ken Dodd's. Her bald head sported a comical imitation Hitler wig and, all of a sudden, her outstretched hands grew and grew, waving in the air like giant baseball gloves. Tarmin felt

like screaming, but he was pinned to his bed, suffocated
by strips of sheet that seemed to run through his mouth,
and bindings across his chest that squeezed his breathing
into frantic, tiny gasps.

Just then, two tall black figures appeared and slipped
past him. They were right there - at the foot of the four
poster! The shadows walked back and forth, seemingly
watching his every struggle. When he tried to raise himself onto his elbows, an arm shot out and roughly pushed
him back down again. The figures carried a large dark
square between them, and passed by once again. This was
Jesus on his way to the crucifixion! Tarmin must be rev-
erent, he must savour this incredible moment! Reaching
over to one side, Tarmin found the lamp switch and flooding his passage with light, he somehow flung himself
towards the door.

Consciousness returned as he propped himself up and
gazed in uncertainty at his bed. He was drenched with
perspiration and wondered how it was that all of his bed-
clothes were strewn across the floor? It looked like the
aftermath of a teenage binge party. Christ, what a nightmare. Gulping back the water by his bed, Tarmin pulled
the covers up under his chin and fell straight back into a
deep sleep.

The next morning his telephone rang. It was Alex.

'Darling! What's up? Are you ill? It's ten o'clock.'

Tarmin, rubbed his head and squinted at the clock. This
was unbelievable. For the chief cockerel not to rise at
dawn was unheard of. Moving into the bathroom, he
splashed water over his face and made a clumsy attempt
at brushing his teeth. The mirror reflected back a
hunched, grey figure, looking as though he'd been hit by
a juggernaught. What the hell had happened to him last
night? If he hadn't read so many newspapers over the

years, he'd have sworn that he'd been the victim of a spiked drink. And although he didn't have much clarity, remnants of his night from hell and the vivid dreams of Gayle, flooded his now aching mind.

Back in his room, he took another call from reception telling him that the kitchen were winding down the breakfast orders and would he like to sneak in a couple of sasauges before the shutters came down? Tarmin flopped back on the mattress and pulled his socks on. He was puzzled and distressed. He didn't have hangovers, he didn't get ill from drink. But right now he felt like an indian dog lying in the gutters. His eyes stared blankly ahead at the fireplace, and then he noticed it. The space infront of him was a huge, gaping sore. Slowly, very slowly, the images came back. The Jesus figures carrying something past his bed, the click of his door, and yes, the spiked drink. It had happened. The Dark Man was gone!

He immediately ran for the stairs and was met half way by Georgia galloping in the opposite direction.

'Thank God you're up,' she gasped. 'I've just come on my shift and guess what's happened? The lover boys have legged it! They packed their bags, cleaned out Room 10 of all its bits and pieces, and zoomed off. Must have been sometime in the very early hours of this morning.'

Tarmin felt sick. What was going on? Who were those guys, particularly the black haired one, Jason, who had somehow seemed so familiar?

'They've stolen more than just the room contents and an unpaid bill. They've taken an incredibly valuable painting from my room during the night. And don't ask how they got in......'

His raised hand stopped an astonished Georgia, who stared blankly at him.

'I want you to do two things for me. Firstly, call

Inspector Donaldson at Notting Hill Gate police station and tell him that I need to speak with him. And secondly, assuming that all the washing up has been done from last night and there are no glasses left for testing, get me an appointment with my doctor. I want to pee in a bottle.'

CHAPTER SIXTEEN

Miller's Residence

It was around midday and all was quiet on the Westbourne front.

'Ee's an odd one,' Virginie, the French manager, whispered to Yvonne, the housekeeper. 'Zat man oo iz in Room Eight. Ee has this 'normous case, but it weigh nozink. And ee say nozink at all. Ee give me ze creep.'

She was sitting in her favourite place next to 'Whitey', the albino pigeon who'd apparently been perching on the office windowsill since Roman times. The morning air was warm for this time of year and she had the window wide open to feed Whitey and his feathered entourage with the remains of the guests' breakfasts. Whether the birds enjoyed

Babybel cheese and chocolate croissants was neither here nor there. Tarmin consistently blamed the 'fucking pigeons' for all the computer problems they were having. 'If that damned bird walks over the keyboard again, I'll spray it orange and have it stuffed,' was his usual threat - guaranteed to upset the firecracker from Brittany.

He had to be careful though. It hadn't escaped his notice that most of the regulars came to Millers, not for its service or facilities, but for the outrageously good looking totty that Tarmin somehow managed to seduce into working for low wages and high stress. Indeed, he often wondered if several of the regulars didn't arrange their travel plans solely around the hotel duty roster. At that very moment, the phone buzzed.

'Room Eight, again,' Virginie moaned to Yvonne, the latter busily repairing a green plaster dog, whose face had been inadvertently kicked-in by a clumsy guest.

'Can I 'elp?' Virginie said down the phone, scraping her hair into a scruffy ponytail with the other hand. 'No problem; zuper' she told the gravely voice from Room Eight. Replacing the handset, she silently counted to ten and screamed into thin air.

'Yvonne! More towels for Room Eight! I zink zat ee's filling 'is case with zem, or 'ave committed mass murder.'

It was not one of Virginie's best days, but at least it had followed a good night, even if it had resulted in seriously dishevelled dress and an evil mood. It was nearly 3pm and Kasia Mindykowski was due to arrive at any moment to take over her shift. There was no love lost between Virginie and George's Polish Goddess. She constantly complained that Kasia's fingers spent more time rummaging through her make-up bag than pumping the computer keys.

Kasia tipped up fashionably late and offering no excuses, and looking as if she had come straight from a major makeover session.

'Hello,' she smiled, oozing killer charm and totally oblivious to her gaff. 'How are you today? Tarmin around?'

'Yes, upstairs. And goodbye' were the extent of Virginie's pleasantries as she bolted for the door, stuffing a toffee in her mouth. 'I miss my bus now. Zank you.'

The phone rang. 'Mr. Rimell, please' the voice said.

'Who's calling?' Kasia asked, feeling like she knew that voice from somewhere.

'Detective Chief Inspector Donaldson'.

Ah hah! The flirty, beer-bellied geezer from the Notting Hill police station. What did he want now? She dialled Tarmin's extension and put the call through.

'He can see us this afternoon at four,' Donaldson informed Williams, who was involved with unplugging his earwax. 'Good. That gives us enough time to get a bite on the way. I'm starving.'

They drove to Notting Hill in an unmarked police car and cruised about until Donaldson eventually shouted: 'Pull up and park somewhere. I feel a late breakfast coming on, right here!'

'Take a good look, Williams,' he said as they entered the café and selected a table. 'Here, we have ghastly formica tables, disgusting plastic tomato squeezers, cheap napkins and bottles with brown sauce caked around the top'. He swiftly broke off as the waitress came up.

'Yeah?' she sighed with total indifference.

'Two full English, please, and a pot of tea.'

Donaldson took absolutely no account of Williams' culinary desires. The gloomy waitress tucked her pencil behind an ear and wiping her greasy hands across her apron, stomped off.

'There goes a woman who makes Mrs. Donaldson look

like Kim Basinger,' he resumed. 'Anyway, take a look at this. Sugar held together by tea, and a floor surface that would force Brussels into naming a law in its honour.'

'So why on earth do we have to suffer it, Gov?' asked a puzzled Williams, who was painfully aware that he also doubled up as one of Donaldson's favourite audiences.

'Because, Williams, sometimes you have to look a little further than the immediate decor. Any cafe that's this close to any of those trendy eateries and works this hard at discouraging custom and yet still stays in business.....'.

He broke off again as the apathetic waitress gracelessly delivered the food. '.....just has to be serving a bloody good breakfast.'

They tucked in. It was unspeakably delicious.

'Just remember that, Williams. It's deductions like this, that'll lead you to rise to the rank of Chief Inspector. Never fails.'

Williams wiped the sausage grease from his mouth in slow motion and stared at his plate. From then on, the two police officers finished the meal in silence. Donaldson paid the bill, collected the receipt and returned to the Sierra. They drew up outside Millers at just after four and were greeted by Tarmin at the top of the stairs. The two policemen were more than a little taken aback by the hotel. Their experience of hotels in the area was in complete contrast what lay before them. Here, there was no smell of overboiled cabbage and no grating foreign voices reverberating around sordid corridors littered with over-full waste bags.

'Littered it might be, but not with rubbish,' Williams said afterwards.

They were taken into the drawing room and sat down by the roaring log fire, crackling away in the baronial fireplace. Donaldson felt sweat bubbles popping up across his forehead and reached into his top pocket for a handker-

174

chief. No luck. 'Bloody Joan', he thought to himself. 'Moans that she spends all day ironing, but can't even remember a tiny hanky.'

Just at that moment and, as if cruising down the catwalk, a vision appeared, slinking slowly towards them. Her clipped eastern European accent was all too familiar to the drooling policemen.

'We meet again! Can I get you gentlemen something?'

Two hearts leapt as one as both officers simultaneously rose to their feet in shocked delight. All of a sudden, their day had transformed itself from burnt ashes into a roaring fire. Miss Knockers was back!

'I see you fell on your feet, Miss Mindykowski,' Donaldson blurted out, astonished that he could remember her complicated name. The force of beauty did such incredible things to a muddled mind. In the space of two seconds, his whole body had reacted like a teenager's. He didn't even get this kind of muscle spasm when he played badminton with his brother.

'Yes, my feet and everything else were saved when Mr. Rimell kindly offered me sanctuary after Mr. Kimininos's death. Nice to see you again, sergeant' she beamed at Williams, extending a manicured paw in his direction. Letting go was a problem for the latter, as was disguising the rising bulge between his legs. There weren't many times that life gave you a second chance, and this time he wasn't going to blow it.

'Let me pick that up for you,' Kasia said, noticing the pile of papers that had slipped off his knees and splayed across the carpet. Leaning over, her breasts somehow brushed against his arm, strands of loose hair flopping in his face. Donaldson flushed with impatience. Why the fuck had he chosen the furthest away seat by the fire? He wanted to touch that flesh, savour her honeyed breath on his face.

Joan had stunk of chicken masala this morning and made him feel sick. Sometimes he felt like he could stab that smug son of a bitch sergeant of his, and be done with him.

Tarmin lit a cigarette and tapped the table impatiently with the packet.

'Well gentlemen, shall we get going?'

Everyone needed a reality check when Kasia was in the room.

'As you know, sir, we're here about the theft of 'The Dark Man' portrait that you reported. The Somerset police have circulated details of the picture and it's been posted on the stolen arts register, but is very unlikely to come on the open market, as it's too well known. What tends to happen in these cases is that, in time, the insurance company is contacted asking for a sum of money to return the picture - normally ten per cent of its value, like a reward. Often they pay out against our advice. But as I understand it, sir, this painting wasn't insured and unless you are in a position to raise a large sum of cash for ransom, then I fear your only hope of recovery lies in our investigation.'

Tarmin looked up and spotted Gayle lurking by the window, her decreasing girth swamped by an unattractive mustard-coloured jumper, thighbones jutting through her thin sweat pants. He wished that it had been her that had been irretrievably stolen. What was she doing here? They'd agreed on a truce of some sorts. When he had to be in London, she would stay out of the way and attend her endless courses, hanging out with that idiot boyfriend.

Donaldson was on a roll.

'So far, our main lead is, of course, the gay couple that stayed with you at Glencot and left before anyone came on morning reception duty. We think we've identified the couple in question, and you might like to take a look at this picture here.'

THE WOOKEY HOLE AFFAIR

The Inspector opened a file and took out a news cutting of a wedding photograph that had appeared in 'Sussex Life'. 'It's a long shot, sir, but do you recognise either of the men in this picture?'

Tarmin took the photograph, picked up a magnifying glass from the coffee table and scrutinised the image. The faded snap was dated June 2002 and showed two men dressed in flamboyant 'morning dress', each cradling a ribboned and powdered dog in their arms. He looked below and read the caption: 'Spike Dick and Melvin Kimininos, owners of 'Pussies Galore' in Bognor Regis.'

Suddenly it all clicked into place, that these two were the lover boys all right. How could he have been such a plonker? He deserved to have the shirt ripped off his back and shoved down his throat. At least Gayle was correct on one point, that he was going senile.

'God almighty, this is Melvin, Inspector. Bloody Melvin Kimininos. I was given just one task to carry out for my old friend, George, and I fucked up. Excuse my French.'

Tarmin handed the paper back to Donaldson, slumped back in the couch and took a long drag on his cigarette.

'I'm the one you should be locking up, Inspector, for complete stupidity. Yes, these two are undoubtedly the men at Glencot. I knew there was something about Melvin - who called himself Jason - that was familiar. But then, I'd never have recognised him. It's been years since I last saw him. Probably as far back as when he was at school. Once he'd fallen out with George, he rarely came to London and certainly not when I was ever at the shop. How did you find them?'

'We haven't, sir' Williams chipped in, aware that he'd contributed nothing to the meeting. 'It was a stroke of luck that we even got this close. With your descriptions, combined with some good footwork by the local force, they did some backtracking and the couple's car was captured on CCTV in Wells. Outside Somerfields, actually, and presumably while on their way to Glencot. From there, we managed to gather various other recordings in the area and their pictures went into our system. Quite by fluke, a WPC from Brighton did the match. I say by fluke, because co-incidentally, she'd met them on the gay pride march one year.'

'Sorry, did I just hear you correctly? Who was that, Williams?' Donaldson interrupted, stunned by his colleague's revelation.

'WPC Isaacs, sir.'

'Isaacs marched for gay pride? Why on earth?'

'Possibly because she's a lesbian, sir.'

'Good God. Never have guessed it.' Donaldson's mind suddenly went into overdrive as he glanced at Miss Knockers' voluptuous silhouette walking down the passageway.

'Have you got the painting back?' Tarmin asked, trying to steer them back to the matter at hand.

'No, 'fraid not, sir. Obviously we knew whereabouts to try and track then down. Then it quickly became apparent that some two months ago, they had closed down the Pet Groomers in Bognor, telling friends that they were off to start a new life powdering poodles in LA.'

'And?' Tarmin lit his fifth cigarette of the afternoon.

'Well, sir. American immigration have no entry records, so they could be anywhere on the planet right now. They closed down all bank accounts, credit cards, cancelled their phones and left without a trace. For the last two months or so, they must have been hanging out somewhere in the UK and once they'd got the painting, fled the country. And we have another problem. We've no proof that they actually stole the painting, so we can't do anything more at the moment, until there's something concrete to go on. Interpol and the usual agencies have been alerted but unfortunately art theft is not a high priority - not with all these sodding terrorists bombing the shit out of us all. It's a real 'noses to the ground' job out there.'

'All good news then....' Tarmin sneered, aiming his usual degree of sarcasm at an unreceptive audience.

'Sorry, sir' said Donaldson, 'but this is how it stands at the moment. But look on the bright side. You could always buy the copy of the painting.'

Williams gave him a supercilious look.

'Excuse me, Mr. Rimell. A poor quip. Just trying to lighten the situation,' he apologised.

'Where's the copy?' asked Tarmin.

'Well actually, that happens to be a bit of a mystery too. After Mr. Kimininos's death and when his estate came out of probate, his daughter and grandchildren were awarded the lion's share, with Melvin being put out to grass. Apparently the son was right pissed off, made a lot of noise and eventually his sister got an order banning him from their dead father's shop. He wanted to clean out some of the more valuable items, it seems. Mr. Kimininos's will specifically asked that the shop and contents would be sold in their entirety and the money divided in accordance to his wishes. No one was allowed even a keepsake from the pile. Very odd.'

The Inspector took a sip of his tea and continued.

'It was just going up for auction when the solicitors received a very good offer through a firm of lawyers in Geneva, acting for a private client. He wanted to buy the shop and contents as a job lot. It was so far above the estimates, that they felt bound to accept.

'And?'

'And shippers came in and cleared the place. Didn't even leave a slip of paper behind. The actual shop itself was later sold to one of those wretched coffee chains. End of story.'

'And you've no idea, who bought it? None at all?' Tarmin asked.

'No, sir, none. And to be honest, it's none of our business. All above board and legal. And with regards to your question about the copy of 'The Dark Man', that too remains a dark mystery, as it was all part of the job lot.'

'Where do we go from here?'

Tarmin furiously sucked on a boiled sweet. Before he had a chance to answer, Kasia interrupted with a phone call request.

'It's urgent, apparently, Mr. Rimell. It's the doctor's surgery in Wells.'

'Back in a moment,' he told the policemen and walked through to the office.

The officers stood up and gathered themselves whilst Kasia cleared away the cups. Even whilst doing such a mundane task, she had a way with her body that both of them found impossible to ignore. Her figure was made to be hugged, and today's choice of tight shirt was doing a fine job. Donaldson's gyroscopic eyes kept returning to her braless breasts. 'God', he thought, 'if only the heating was off'.

Wasting no time, Williams sprung to his feet and offered to help; an offer that was eagerly accepted. Donaldson kicked himself. Why was he such a lazy lump? Because he spent so little time at home trying to avoid Joan, he never even thought about domestic procedures. He watched Williams pile up the empty cups and pad after Kasia, like a sick puppy. Donaldson had always admired Williams' winning ways and slickness with women. He watched in envy as his colleague managed to enter the kitchen door at exactly the same time as the Polish Sex Queen, creating a sandwich that he could only dream of being inside. He had to put a stop to this. Maybe a bit of manly authority would do the trick?

'Williams! Bring the car round, will you? I need to go back to the station, post haste.'

Williams raised his eyes to the heavens and tut-tutted. The time was rapidly approaching when he would have to do something radical to precipitate Donaldson's sudden retirement from the force. (Either that or he might jump the other side of the fence and strangle the turd.)

'I'm sorry, gentlemen' Tarmin said, returning to the drawing room. 'But that was quite interesting news. The results came back from my urine test from the night that the lover boys were with us. And my champagne was definitely spiked. They've found traces of rohypnol. I suppose I should count myself lucky that there was no date rape.'

Kasia had started the early evening ritual of lighting up the candles and stopped dead in her tracks.

'That bastard of a man! I always told Mr. Kimininos that he should have had him strangled at birth. I hated him, hated him! And now he tries to take advantage of my new boss. Arrrrgh!'

The three men looked at her in astonishment and thought she was about to explode. Her face was red, her hair wild and she banged her fist on the table as hard as she could. 'I hope you find that creep, you policemen, and lock him up for life. He is a murderer, a thief, a crook and now - possibly - a date rapist. He must be stopped!'

Inspector Donaldson took his moment and moved towards her.

'Miss Mindykowski. Please don't fret, but let's put all of this in perspective too. George Kimininos was found to have died of a heart attack and brain haemorrhage, nothing to do with his argument with the son. We have no proof as yet that Melvin did take the painting, and he certainly didn't profit from Kimininos's will, I do assure you. Innocent until proven guilty, and all that.'

'Pah!' snorted Kasia, as she swept out of the room.

'Nice one Donaldson', thought Williams, trying to hide his smile.

The phone rang again. In the absence of Kasia, who was having one of her many loo breaks, Tarmin picked up the phone.

'Good afternoon, Millers' he barked.

'Hi, Mr. Rimell, it's Georgia here. Will you be back at Glencot tomorrow?'

'No, why?'

'Because the survey team are coming to the hotel in readiness for the free damp-proofing you agreed to.'

He had totally forgotten. He forgot a lot these days. It had seemed a good idea at the time; free damp proof treatment for the whole hotel in return for helping to advertise their products. It was something that Georgia has pushed him to do, and he'd agreed, just to keep her sweet.

'There'll be just two of them apparently, here for the whole day. They need complete access to everywhere in the hotel, but that's ok, isn't it? I did say I'd try and arrange for them to come on a day when you wouldn't be here, so as not to disturb.'

Tarmin would have agreed to anything at this point. He really couldn't be arsed with any other possible aggravation. He was still livid with himself over recent events and felt like he was losing the plot. How could he not have connected Melvin with the theft? Jason, Melvin, whatever his name was, even looked like George, when he came of think of it.

'Six o'clock, Mr. Rimell,' Kasia whispered as she crept up behind him.

'Six o'clock? What about it?' he said, jumping with surprise.

THE WOOKEY HOLE AFFAIR

'Your meeting.'

'Oh fuck, so it is.' Tarmin had arranged to meet Alex at the The Milestone Hotel for an early evening assignation. This was one of London's little gems. The type of hotel that he always secretly aspired to. Very gentile, stacks of style and offered the best tea in London. At least an evening with Alex would jolt him out of this evil mood.

CHAPTER SEVENTEEN

Glencot Hotel Reception

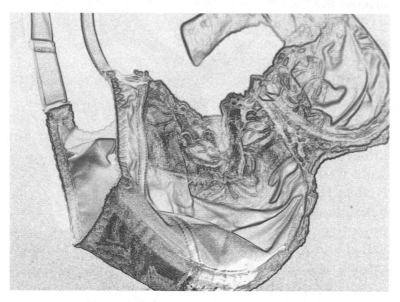

From Georgia's vantage point at Glencot's reception, she could clearly see a bright yellow van displaying the words 'Damp Busters' in bold black letters, driving into the courtyard. The van parked itself awkwardly outside the front door and two men dressed in matching yellow boiler suits got out. Wearing a stunning purple wrap-around dress and high black stilettos, Georgia clicked her way across the entrance and propped herself in the doorway.

'Morning, Miss' said the shorter of the two men, removing his baseball cap to reveal a totally bald head. 'We're the damp busters!' Unashamedly looking her up and down, he tried his best shot at a seductive grin, little realising that he was looking a top London hooker in the eye.

'I can see that,' Georgia snapped back, 'but I'd rather all of our guests didn't. Could you please move your van around the back?'

The second man's jaw was in danger of hitting the ground and to Georgia's disgust, she even detected a line of drool in the corner of his slack mouth.

'Absolutely, Miss. I completely understand. Terry, move the bloody thing, mate.'

Terry and Jim emptied their van, deposited an array of very expensive looking electronic equipment by the kitchen door and then lugged it down to the cellars. The work was underway.

Nathan Hunt had never been a man who liked driving himself anywhere, but on this occasion, he felt he had no option. Discretion was absolutely key. Georgia had called him when Terry and Jim had finished their explorations and after he'd found their report extremely promising; confirmation that his suspicions about Bundy withholding evidence, was undoubtedly correct. Very rarely these days did he get excited about anything, but the slightly fuzzy photograph he'd viewed on his laptop that morning, fulfilled all his expectations. Hunt had to see it for himself and having heard the tip-off from his mole, he also needed to make the most of both Bundy and Rimell being away in London.

His chosen hire car was an average looking blue Megane - hardy enough for those appalling country lanes but not obtrusive in any way. He hated taking time to travel anywhere and rural destinations topped his black list. After driving for four frustrating hours from London (stretching his weak humour to the limit), he eventually drew up at Glencot in the early evening. The car park was full of badly parked pedestrian vehicles, with a large white van in one corner, a swirled Celtic symbol painted down one side.

'So very English' he thought to himself. 'No sense of style or order'.

This was a first visit to Somerset for Hunt. His excursions into the English countryside had been rare and were always exclusively at the invitations of extremely wealthy and sophisticated acquaintances. He parked up and lifted his small leather case from the boot. There wasn't much needed - after all, he intended to stay as short a time as possible. But he'd decided that even though Rimell and Bundy weren't going to be here, he shouldn't take any chances and would assume the guise of a commercial traveller. Feeling distinctly uncomfortable in a cheap dark suit from Marks & Spencer, blue tie and shirt, he consoled himself that anonymity was pretty essential for a good outcome.

Standing by his car for a second, he took in Glencot's exterior. It was unexpectedly beautiful, stately and elegant, and on entering, he was immediately hit by the warm and welcoming candlelit interior and the haunting Gregorian chants piping through the sound system. He looked around for Georgia and smiled to himself when he spotted her behind a desk and on the phone. This was a different woman from the one he'd packed on a train from Paddington all those weeks ago. Georgia was looking relatively demure and strangely innocent. He actually strangely fancied her in 'straight' clothes. The simple checked shirt, green cardigan and loose fitting grey woollen trousers made her look vaguely elegant. It was a revelation.

Georgia caught sight of him and broke into a huge

smile. Thank God he was here now, a slice of sophisticated London life. Then she remembered a slight hitch. What she hadn't dared tell him this morning was that the hotel was nearly fully booked by a strange West Country religious sect. The air all around the entrance stank of sickly incense, and peeking around the drawing room door, Hunt saw the small gathering of cream linen robed figures sipping from silver coated goblets and picking at the occasional wafer from a wooden trencher. He hadn't believed that these people even existed outside of film sets of Middle America.

Georgia left her desk and walked towards him, relieving him of his bag.

'Mr. Hunt, I presume?' she teased.

'How are you? I didn't realise you had a coven meeting here tonight. A small omission from our telephone call this morning? How about some coffee?'

Georgia ushered Hunt into the library so that he could be alone, and disappeared off to the kitchen to sort out a cup and some biscuits. It felt all wrong somehow. Normally, it was him plying her with champagne, paying her for her every move. Now she was expected to be domesticated and play the housewife. It irked, however much she was getting paid.

Hunt wandered around the library room, tweaked the lily blooms on the table and checked out the shelves of books. Standing by the bay window, he watched half a dozen more hooded figures ambling beside the river, their hands clasped firmly together and each one holding some kind of symbolic object that he couldn't make out. He had no idea of their sex, age or even race; they were just anonymous white-robed figures, looking like ghosts. He turned around as Georgia entered the room with his coffee.

MARTIN MILLER

'Who are all those crazy people?' he asked her. 'I'm not expected to break bread with them tonight, am I?

'Don't worry. There are four other regular guests booked in, besides yourself, and you'll be dining in the pink dining room.'

'Thank God for that. They give me the creeps. How long have they been here?'

'They came yesterday morning but I have my suspicions that they're up to something. They're supposedly talking about putting together a film or documentary of some kind, but there is something very strange going on. They've taken the top floor of the hotel and turning down all offers of housekeeping. I bet they're actually making a porno movie. Maybe I should offer my services?'

Ignoring her attempt at levity, Hunt's mind was racing. Perhaps they were after the buried artefacts too? Georgia moved closer and whispered:

'Look, I can't fill you in on everything right now, as I'm still on duty and have a few more hours to go. You relax, have a drink or two and some dinner and chill out. I'll come to your room as soon as that weird lot have gone to bed and then I can show you what you've come to see.'

Hunt was shown to his room by a spotty lad in need of a good dose of steroids, to kick-start a serious growth spurt, his long green apron skimming the floor. Hardly the smooth, slick working force of a Blacks Hotel, he reflected. Tarmin Rimell was a total eccentric, as far as he could ascertain; he had a hooker on reception, a pizza-face lugging the bags and an intellectual nerd as a best friend.

Flinging his coat on the bed, Nathan spent a couple of hours in his room before dinner. He loosened his tie, had a quick shave and glimpsed at Sky Sports. There was no way he was getting involved with a bunch of weird misfits over dinnertime.

At nine-thirty he sat down in the library dining room, just as the other four guests were finishing up, and scanned the menu and wine list. At least this looked more promising. Selecting local gravalax, followed by pork chops in cider and burnt cream, he turned his attention to the carte de vin. The list was surprisingly adequate but still not up to his ridiculously high standards. One of his greatest pleasures was the evening ritual of visiting his vaulted cellar in the Austrian schloss and spending half an hour or so toying with his wines, carefully turning and rearranging the Margaux, Saint-Emillion and Latour-Paulliac.

'Not tonight' he mused. He chose a very acceptable 2002 Sancerre instead.

A small knock on Hunt's door woke him from a dream.

'Come in' he shouted.

The door opened and Georgia stood in the light looking at him. She had changed out of her receptionist's gear and stood before him, tight straight-legged jeans and pert braless breasts beautifully moulded by a remarkably thin black polo neck sweater. Her hair was scraped back into a high ponytail and her curvaceous waist pulled in by a nine-inch silver studded leather belt. Her cheeks seemed appealingly flushed and her eyes on fire. This woman was ready for action.

Nathan was a man who rarely mixed business with pleasure but right now, he was having one of those 'before or after?' moments. It was a no-brainer really and he went for the 'before'. Georgia crossed the room and stood at the foot of his bed, where he was lying propped up on an outsize white cotton pillow. Having got out of his twice-daily shower only ten minutes before she arrived, his hair was still damp and his heavy white robe half spread open, showing that he was stark naked.

'They're all tucked up and silent in the hotel,' she said.

'That's good, Amanda, very good. Best we leave it a while though, just to make sure we don't get interrupted.'

She didn't move. He stared at her breasts gently rising to the rhythm of her heart, whilst she stood silently, looking down at his tanned muscular body, now fully exposed to her view. The single bedside light cast a strange shadow across his manly frame. He was motionless, expressionless. He said nothing, but then he didn't have to with Amanda. The tricks were up to her.

Amanda's breathing became deeper and in the cold room, her erect nipples protruded through the thin black fabric. She slowly lifted her right hand to her hair and slipped off the band allowing her tresses to fall around her shoulders.

'Your call Mr. Hunt' she said, watching his thick penis stiffen.

'Yes, my dear, it is, and don't you ever forget it. You seem to have become rather too comfortable down here. Georgia is totally gone; Amanda will now return.'

His steely eyes lightened a little. She never knew if he even possessed such a thing as a sense of humour and had decided long ago not to attempt to find out. It was always serious business with Hunt. Taking a couple of steps forward, she stopped at the foot of his bed, hands tucked into her belt. Making sure that he was watching her every move, she rolled her sweater over her head and let it fall to the floor. She followed this with a slow unbuckling of her belt and then peeled off the tight jeans and, with her right foot, neatly kicked them to one side. Her striptease left her in a tiny black leather thong and nothing else. Hunt was mesmerised, his erection beginning to throb painfully. What was she going to do with him this time?

The mattress of the four-poster was a good three feet off the ground, and in one cat-like movement, Amanda jumped at his feet. She slipped off the tieback securing the curtains to the great Jacobean post on his left side, and leaning across his body, did the same on his right. Taking both rope bindings in her hands, within a few seconds, she'd secured both of his feet to the end post. Going around to the head of the bed, the process was repeated with the other two tiebacks until he was securely restrained. The final touch was a stocking tied around his mouth. For a man coveting such control, she could never comprehend his love for submissive restraint. Finally, she pulled the drapes fully around the bed, encasing him in her prison. Like a bitch on heat, she grabbed his cock in her mouth and almost instantly withdrew again, repeating the tantalising manoeuvre several more times, occasionally caressing, sometimes violently slapping his thighs and always withdrawing before he caved in.

She killed the bedside light and the room filled with the eerie light of the full moon glowing through the leaded windows. Still the silent man never moved or groaned in his bindings. Amanda peeled away her thong and disappeared behind the drapes for a moment. Drawing back the curtains so that he was in full light, she slid her naked body over his, slowly licking, kissing, scratching and sucking. Still he could do nothing, say nothing. It was time to get a reaction and so she plunged her index finger fast and furiously up his arse.

Hunt couldn't restrain himself and screamed. She left it in there, moving, sometimes gently, sometimes roughly, and, eventually, bringing down her mouth to engulf his neatly circumcised penis. Amanda was a past master at keeping the climax at bay, but as her full lips slid back and forth, Nathan Hunt made sure that he got more than his money's worth.

The cellars at Glencot were pretty extensive and the only area that Tarmin had so far utilised was the large room at one end that he'd turned into his Minima. There was no interconnecting door between the cinema and the rest of the cellars, so Hunt and Amanda had to find access via the main cellars, through the old boiler room. The entrance was tucked away behind the main boiler and revealed a succession of vaulted rooms stuffed with years of discarded rubbish, broken furniture and ripped, decaying mattresses. Amanda led Hunt to the second room - once the proud home of many impressive vintage wines, stacked inside the stone slab bins covering the walls. All that remained were a few empty and broken bottles and wooden cases stencilled with intriguing vintage marks.

Amanda walked to the far corner and lifted up some old sacking. Underneath was a clear patch with a large piece of gaffer tape stuck in a cross shape. Amanda peeled back the tape. Hunt looked over her shoulder and could clearly see a small round hole neatly bored through the stone. From the small holdall that she'd brought with them, Amanda removed a coil of flexible metal tubing, larger than the diameter of a one-penny coin. She attached a small lens to one end and plugged the other part into a small flat screen computer. Nathan Hunt looked on in fascination, impressed at her aptitude. This trip to the country had certainly expanded her horizons. She flicked the hair from her eyes and looked up at him.

'Not quite Tutankhamun, I know, but just you wait.'

'Your guys did a good job this morning. Apparently this hole is some fifteen feet deep and no one at the hotel suspected anything. That was well done.'

'You should have seen them. They looked like they wouldn't know how to change a light bulb between them, but at least they had the right equipment.'

She carefully threaded the tube down the hole until only three or four feet of coil was visible from above ground. She flicked on the computer and the screen came into neon life. A few taps on the mouse pad and then an image of a round, dark circle appeared on her screen. Keeping the screen in her view, Amanda gently pushed the remainder of the tube down, heading towards the rock chamber. Inch by inch it moved deeper down until suddenly, the screen showed some form of life apart from the endless blackness. The images were dim and expressionless due to the limited endoscope lighting, but what they showed was magic to Hunt's eyes. It was difficult to work out the size of the chamber, as all he could see were slabs of hewn natural rock but, directly beneath the hole made by the damp busters drill, he picked out what appeared to be some kind of casket. Next to that was the clear image of a branched menorah and beyond that, smaller stone objects. Hunt slapped his thighs with satisfaction.

An hour later, Hunt and Amanda emerged from the boiler room, brushing away dusty grime and cobwebs. Elated, they quietly made their way across the terrace towards the front of the hotel, and although all the rooms were dark, the full moon illuminated the gardens with crystal clarity. In the far distance, Hunt watched as a deer suddenly jumped by the fence. What had startled it? Then, almost immediately, they spotted the cause. On the far side of the lawn, a naked figure appeared through a pair of columns, half shrouded by the late mists hanging over the weir pool. The two of them stood silently fascinated. Within seconds, the lone figure was joined by another, another and yet another. In all, six naked figures formed a circle and moved around, swaying their hips, hands clasped.

'They must be fucking freezing,' Amanda whispered.

This was more than a little out of Hunt's comfort zone and he couldn't for the life of him imagine anything more absurd than being involved in such a ritual. As they observed the group more carefully, they could see that their bodies had been painted with long, diagonal streaks of colour, and that one of the group was passing around a large cup of some description.

Nathan Hunt had seen enough. Taking Amanda by the arm he encouraged her to turn away and head for the bedroom.

'We've some unfinished business' he said. 'I have some rituals that I'd like to introduce you to.'

CHAPTER EIGHTEEN

Glencot

On their return from London, Tarmin, Bundy and Alex settled themselves on Tarmin's favourite balcony, clutching heavy tumblers of iced Millers Gin and preparing for an amusing few minutes of candlelit bat watching. Glencot housed a colony of long-eared, wide-mouthed bats, happily ensconced for many years in the cellars. As was their wont, they came out to play late in the evenings, re-enacting the Battle of Britain by dive bombing through the front door, navigating around the candles and eventually exiting via the balcony window.

After a while, pretending to be David Attenborough wore a little thin for one and all. Tarmin stood with his back to the river and took a glug of his drink.

'Ok, back to business. How are we going to let Nathan Hunt know that Glencot is available for sale, and more importantly, how are we going to get him to pay a shit load of money, and I mean a shit load, without appearing too suspicious? Let's face it, at our crazy over-inflated asking price, no agent is going to touch it.'

Alex draped herself over the stone balustrading and gazed in the direction of an amorous barn owl, noisily searching for a quick bonk in the branches. Leaning against Tarmin's shoulder, she squeezed his hands and gave him a quick peck on the mouth.

'Bedtime?'

'Not so fast,' Tarmin smiled. 'Is that owl getting you all razzed up? Look, I'm sorry but I just want to get my head around this sale scenario. We're getting tantalisingly close now. I reckon that what we have to do is make Hunt believe that someone else is interested in buying Glencot, and that there's a specific reason to pay way over the odds. This way, we get a bidding war going. So this is my idea, based on the fact that our trump card is Georgia. If we let her discover that we are about to sell the property to someone who both has a specific reason and is obviously very wealthy, then Hunt could offer to buy the property with a valid objective.'

'What sort of specific reason, can you think of?' Bundy asked.

'Well, like there's some amazing planning potential, or something that gives stacks of added value to the property' said Tarmin.

'Or that you've struck oil' Bundy joked.

'Oil in Somerset, that's rich!' Alex placed her glass on the floor and sat down again.

'Not so mad as you might think,' Tarmin continued. 'In

fact, you've hit the nail on the head. Hang on a sec, I've got something to show you.'

He disappeared off to the library and came back a minute later, clutching a copy of the Wells Chronicle.

'Take a look at this' he said passing the dismantled newspaper to Alex and Richard. 'The headline: 'Somerset Locals up in Arms as Oil companies stake a claim.'

'What's it all about then?' asked Alex, unwilling to strain her eyesight in the weak candlelight.

'As you will read' said Tarmin, 'this oil idea might not actually be so far fetched. What this article is saying is that an American multi-national, multi-grabbing outfit called Victory Oil Inc, has been purchasing exploration rights and executing test drillings all over Devon and Somerset. They've been petty clandestine about the whole operation and are apparently approaching the owners of various properties to sign confidentiality agreements. But now the cat seems to be out the bag and this article blows the lid off the company's little game, quoting their head of exploration, Charles Moreland, who seems to be a man of incredibly few words. There's not even a picture of him in the paper.'

'Ah ha. Not so stupid, after oil.'

Bundy reckoned himself to be king of the crass puns.

'But how are we going to get this guy a) to prospect, b) to make sure that there is oil in your hallowed land, and c) give shit loads of dosh to buy Glencot?' Alex asked.

'Actually, I know exactly how we're going to do this' Tarmin said. He poured them all top-up large measures, opened a fresh packet of Marlborough Lights and began to set out his grand scheme.

Georgia (reverting to her work name, of course) was

unwittingly playing a pivotal role in the future of Glencot, being the trump card and lynchpin for their out-right success. The morning post arrived punctually after lunch, and, as she was the duty receptionist that morn-ing, it was up to her to receive the banded batch of let-ters from the postman.

'Nice little bundle, you got there' the postman smirked as he handed it over. He was not the only tradesman who lusted after a job as Georgia's keyboard and had an annoying habit of teasing, offering and withdrawing his little package several times in succession.

'Thank you Pat,' came her terse response as she snatched the letters from his chubby little hands. She really couldn't be arsed to fool around with this unattrac-tive fuckwit.

Georgia sifted through the bundle, putting aside the obvious bills into one file, then those with 'private and confidential' into another, and anything addressed to Mr. Rimell or the hotel, into a third. She half-heartedly made her way through the third pile until one particular head-ing caught her attention. The ivory envelope sported an engraved crest with 'Victory Oil Inc' embossed on the bottom left corner. Extracting the paper, she saw that this was marked 'Strictly Confidential' at the top of the letterhead. Quite clearly, this was one secretary who would soon be looking for further employment. The let-ter read:

'Ref: oil exploration rights.

Dear Mr. Rimell,

Further to our telephone conversation and with regards to Glencot's oil potential, we can confirm that from a geological stand point, certain acreage of your land could well support partial reserves of oil that are of interest to our company. We would therefore like the opportunity to discreetly undertake a more complete geological survey of your land. In the event of success, we would also like to initiate a full mineral analysis within the next seven to ten days. Would this be convenient? Taking into consideration the hotel environs, I can reassure you that the methodology employed is very discreet and unobtrusive. I'd be grateful if you could phone me directly on my private number.

Yours sincerely

Charles Moreland

Georgia swiftly took a photocopy, which she placed in the back of her personal file, then slipped the letter back into the envelope, making sure that Tarmin could see that it had been opened in error. She then carried on with her daily chores until Tarmin appeared in the entrance hall, effusively chatting up an impossibly chic Chinese PR lady with hair half way down her back. After closing her car door, he returned to the office and rifled through the post.

'Anything interesting?' he asked.

Georgia handed him a letter marked 'confidential', as well as the oil company communiqué.

'I opened this one' she said. 'Sorry. It didn't have any private marking on the outside for some silly reason. It's a letter from some oil company saying that they're interested in undertaking oil tests at Glencot. Sounds rather exciting!'

Tarmin scratched his head and watched Rob, laden with an armful of logs, walking past the window. He took the letter from Georgia and scanned the contents.

'No harm,' I suppose, as long as they really don't make a mess of my land and a load of noise that'll disturb the guests. Can you give them a ring for me and sort it out? Try to arrange it for a day when we're not too busy'.

Poking his head around the door a second later, he added:

'And try and do it on your day off. I know what these jumped-up oil men are like and I wouldn't want to lose you to some Stetson-headed fool.'

Georgia made the phone call and sorted out the business. Just three days later, a gleaming silver Range Rover Sport breezed into Glencot's front courtyard, towing a large low covered trailer. Within four hours they were gone again, with neither the guests nor the staff of Glencot being especially aware of the dull drilling sounds buzzing from a distant field. The deed was, to all intents and purposes, done and dusted.

A week later and Postman Pat delivered another letter for Tarmin, this time clearly marked 'Private' on the envelope. Georgia could barely contain her curiosity. She waited to hand it to Tarmin at a time when she might be able to get a peek at the contents, but no such luck. Tarmin seemed particularly cagey and despite a bit of prodding, refused to divulge anything further. Had they found oil or not? Judging from the smug look on his face, Georgia reckoned that the answer was a resounding 'yes'.

Later that evening, the moment presented itself when he popped next door to have his dinner. Extracting the letter from Tarmin's private folder, she had a quick read and ran it through the copier. The evening sun was setting low over Glencot and its secret. And it seemed that tomorrow afternoon, a certain 'Charles Moreland' was expected to make a visit.

In fact, Tarmin had been introduced to an actor called David Mann, an immaculately dressed and coiffured American in his late forties, whose claim to fame had been a tiny speaking part in a grisly 1980s 'B' movie called 'Sunday Spinach Pie'. Mann was an ex-lover of Tarmin's old friend, Carole Ashby, a vivacious ex-Bond girl who had her sexy fingers on most of the thespian pulses in London. Mann had been carefully briefed that for this particular role, he was to pass himself off as the oil exploration chief who would pitch an absurdly high offer to the owner of Glencot, based on its ascertained oil reserves.

Three-thirty the next afternoon and 'Charles Moreland' drew up in his Porsche Boxster, checking in with Georgia. Tarmin instructed her to bring him into the drawing room, playing on the knowledge that the biggest of Georgia's many substantial assets were most definitely her ears.

Moreland settled himself on the sofa opposite Tarmin, in close proximity to the door and from where their conversation would easily drift though the open window. It didn't take long for Georgia to get the full picture; after all, this Texan oil magnate's drawling voice boomed about like a foghorn. In a nutshell, Moreland was offering seven and a half million pounds for Glencot, including its land, but what really surprised her was Tarmin's less than enthusiastic response. Why was he being so strange and refraining from not leaping at the chance? Surely he must see that this was an extraordinary opportunity? Their conversation continued with Tarmin bargaining for a higher sum and playing hard to get, whilst Moreland was pressurising to seal the deal.

'I'd love to say yes, Mr Moreland, but obviously, I need some more time to discuss this matter. This is all happening pretty fast and I'd never even considered selling Glencot until this discovery. I'm sure you can appreciate my position. May I get back in a day or so?'

Moreland sounded pissed off, Georgia thought. He was

coughing with irritation and forcefully blew his nose. Then she heard the sound of a chair being pulled out of the way.

'The sooner the better, Mr Rimell. I'm back in Texas next week to take a board meeting, and would appreciate your decision by then, one way or another.'

They exchanged goodbyes and Georgia watched the taillights of the Porsche disappear around the corner and out of sight.

Tarmin sat back, drained his lukewarm coffee cup and waited for Georgia to enter the room. She leaned against the doorway and gave him a coy smile.

'Do you mind if I just stretch my legs for a minute or two?' she asked.

'Stretch away' Tarmin replied, watching her walk off, mobile phone in hand. He knew only too well that it would buzz into action within a couple of seconds. Good.

It didn't take long for the inevitable to happen; it came with a light knock on the library door.

Georgia came in looking pale and somewhat agitated.

'Tarmin, I'm so sorry. I've just had some terrible news. My sister has had an accident somewhere in the north of Scotland. A stag jumped out and smashed into her car and it's extremely serious. I've got to get up there immediately; there's no one else that she can call on.'

Fake tears welled in her pretty hazel eyes.

'God, she's good,' Tarmin thought. If ever he were to be appointed as head of MI5, Georgia would certainly be top of his wish list. But this is what he'd wanted, and it was time to say goodbye. This wasn't about Georgia any more, it was about Alex's and his future.

'I'm sorry, Georgia. I completely understand, of course. Are you ready to go? Do you feel that you've finished everything that you'd hoped to achieve at Glencot?' He threw down the gauntlet.

For a moment, Georgia looked startled. He'd caught her off guard.

'Er. I think so, yes. Sammy is in at three to take over and said she'd cover my shifts for a few days. Look, you've got my number - maybe I can come back in the future? I really am sorry to let you down.'

'So am I, Georgia, very sorry. You've been a great asset, one way and another.'

Tarmin gave her a hug and squeezed her hand gently.

'It'll all be OK, and don't rush back'.

Georgia had actually turned out to be a great receptionist, despite being the spy who never loved him.

Everything had gone swimmingly well over the last week, and as expected, an anonymous offer arrived courtesy of Credit Suisse, with an unconditional amount of ten million pounds for Glencot. The offer was dependent on immediate exchange and a seven-day completion period for the hotel in its entirety.

'Wow, that man worked fast.'

In his wildest dreams, Tarmin hadn't expected everything to move so quickly and it was all still seemingly legal. Possible little moral issue of fraudulent claims to deal with, but so what? Hunt was a dealer and to win some, lose some was all just a game to him. Plus, he hadn't really done anything wrong. If the shit hit the fan, he could genuinely claim to have been scammed by a false oil report himself. They had nothing on him. The actor was long gone and it would all remain a complete mystery.

Tarmin had responded to the offer immediately and telephoned his solicitor to set the wheels in motion. Before Georgia left, Tarmin had instructed her to make an appointment with his one-man band legal beagle at Frost Holdings, who, she subsequently informed him, was leaving that day for a Himalayan trek. She quickly added that Simon Frost had arranged with her for a locum to cover his two week absence; James McCreedy-Smith from McCreedy & Gareth in Wimpole Street and, that she had made an appointment for Tarmin at 3 o'clock the following Tuesday. The sale was on its way. That was all too easy, Tarmin thought to himself, walking out of the small office at McCreedy & Gareth. He'd barely been in James McCreedy-Smith's office for twenty minutes when he completed all the formalities and was informed that contracts were now formally exchanged with the Zurich solicitors acting for the anonymous buyer. McCreedy-Smith had also informed him that £500,000 had been wired to his client account as an initial 5 per cent deposit for the transaction. Tarmin felt a mixture of relief and chronic apprehension. He'd put to the back of his mind the possible consequences of what he was doing, which seemed to be outweighed by the enormous financial benefits. Now they'd reached the end game. It was critical that Nathan Hunt had no access to Glencot any time prior to completion. Not easy. He had seven days in which to keep him at bay, seven days until completion. During the next week, Tarmin dropped ten pounds in weight and doubled his alcohol consumption.

On day six, his phone rang at 10.30 am.

'Mr. Rimell,' James McCreedy-Smith muttered down the line. He sounded like he was in Outer Mongolia. 'We completed the transaction ten minutes ago.'

'When does the buyer want to take possession?'

'Twelve noon, tomorrow. He's flying in as we speak.'

As it was a lock, stock and barrel sale, all Tarmin had

THE WOOKEY HOLE AFFAIR

to do was pack a couple of suitcases with his personal possessions and he'd be out of Glencot once and for all. However, fear of retribution was still a niggling pinch in his side and, now that the deed was actually done, the fear rapidly re-surfaced. How would Nathan Hunt react when he discovered the chamber of deception? There was no time to dwell on the 'what ifs'.

Tarmin hastily called a staff meeting, including Olivier, who was hopping mad at being dragged away from his latest souffle creation. The place had been bursting with rumour and speculation for some time about this possible sale. Everyone gathered in the library and Tarmin gave his address like a good general dismissing his troops after victory, offering endless booty and furlough in compensation. Unfortunately, his clammy hands and sweating brow were a dead give-away.

'This may come as a shock to some of you but, as of today, I have sold Glencot. The person or persons are unknown to me at this time, but I was offered a substantial sum that made it impossible to refuse. The parties who are purchasing the hotel will not be continuing with its existing operation and on that note, I have good and bad news for you all. The good news is you will no longer have to suffer my interminable drinking, smoking, swearing and abusing of the guests. The bad news is that you will all have to leave the premises today and, I hastily add, clutching fat little farewell cheques in your hands. Thank you all for being with me, and I really am sorry for the rather rude exit.'

The assembled staff were stunned into silence, completely unprepared as to how to react, and launched into a torrent of questions. 'How could the turnaround be so fast?' 'Why hadn't he forewarned them?' 'How the fuck were they meant to find alternative jobs at such ridicu-

205

lously short notice?' Tarmin recoiled from Olivier's spitting venom, expecting a meat cleaver through his skull at any second.

He tried his best to explain that he'd already paid off all their suppliers, had prepared generous redundancy cheques and emailed cancellations for all future bookings. All services and bills would cease in their account names from the end of today. Rob would be left in charge to turn off lights, lock up and leave keys with local solicitors.

Right now he needed to conjure up some of Georgia's handy fake tears and, to his immense surprise, they suddenly appeared. It was enough to satisfy the warring faction. They looked at their boss in astonishment. Perhaps, after all, the loss of his hotel was something that he was finding harder than they'd imagined. In the end, handshakes were exchanged and even Olivier submitted his olive branch in the form of a cup of foaming coffee. The general had effectively won over his militant troops.

Shortly after the meeting, Tarmin went upstairs and carefully packed all his worldy goods into two suitcases, grabbing a handful of brochures as memorabilia. He looked out of the window and watched the heron standing by the river, listening to the gushing waterfall in the distance. Turning back to his bed, the huge space above the fireplace showed where the 'Dark Man' painting had once hung and now stared back at him with empty insolence. Was all of this hassle really worth the divorce from Gayle? It suddenly seemed an extortionate price to pay. He loved Glencot and its land with a passion.

Driving off, he couldn't afford himself even the merest glimpse backwards. Nostalgia was never meant to be part of the deal. This was the end of a chapter and he could only look forwards.

THE WOOKEY HOLE AFFAIR

It was only 6pm but the Blue Bar at the Berkeley Hotel was already bursting at its trendy seams. Alex was pouring Tarmin a glass of Moet as Bundy joined them at their table. As they worked their way through a second bottle, Alex began having a serious attack of champagne-induced paranoia.

'I'm really scared, Tarmin. What would you do in Nathan Hunt's shoes if you'd been conned out of ten million pounds, for God's sake? You'd want blood, wouldn't you?'

'That's always been a risk. That's why I've decided to keep my head below the parapet for a while. Remember, Hunt doesn't have a legal leg to stand on and in the worst case scenario, the only one he's likely to cut up rough with is me.'

'Exactly,' Alex started to rant. 'How do you think that makes me feel? Do you think I want to spend hours picking your skeleton out of a concrete slab at the bottom of Lake Geneva? It's not funny.'

Alex was inconsolable; she'd never been able to hold her booze, Tarmin thought to himself. Unlike Gayle who could match him pint for pint. She snuggled up, gripping him tightly.

'Is it all worth it? You've a great life, friends, enough money to do almost all you've ever wanted and now you'll be looking over your shoulder for the rest of your life, or ours, should I say. Is it really worth all this?'

'With all due respect, sweetheart, it's a bit late in the day to worry about the mafia. Much too late. On the other hand, if you're deadly serious, I could of course ring Hunt and say 'Sorry old man, it's all been a joke. Here's your money back'. How does that sound? I've got his number here somewhere on my phone. But you and Bundy are both OK, remember. You were not even in the

207

frame. It's all on to me at the end of the day. Come on, let's get the fuck out of here and have some fun. It may be my last night on planet earth. And in case it's Bundy's too, he needs to find a very desperate, randy woman.'

Bundy, ever the philosopher drained his glass and stood up.

'I always say one thing. A man without money is like a woman without a vagina.'

CHAPTER NINTEEN

Glencot

It was more like a military operation than a house moving. The convoy of vans snaked their way around the narrow Somerset lanes, taking the ring road around Wells heading for Glencot House. Turning into the Wookey Hole Road, they drove past the secret Ministry of Defence compound, comprising a collection of wire fences, temporary huts and low-level buildings, before turning down the hill and then sharp left into Glencot's drive. The convoy was headed by a large black Mercedes with smoked glass windows, followed by three plain vans, and brought up at the rear by a large Securicor van. As the vehicles parked in the court-yard, Hunt spotted a bedraggled man in a trench coat huddling in the doorway, sheltering from the drizzle. He quickly stubbed out a cigarette as the uniformed driver moved around to the rear door of the Mercedes and opened it for Nathan Hunt. Hunt took a moment to find his footsteps, carefully sizing up the various muddy puddles and protecting his shiny shoes from the thick country mud.

'Mr. Jacobs, I presume?' Hunt said, hyping up his Austrian accent for effect.

'Good morning, sir, and you must be Mr. Hunt?' the man in the porch looked bemused. He'd notched up many a sale under his belt and effected as many handovers as a dog had bones, but never before had he witnessed the Mafia arriving, mob-in-hand, at payback time.

'My client, Mr. Rimell, has left everything intact, as requested, and if you would like me to show you around to agree the inventory, it would be my pleasure' Jacobs added.

'Not necessary, thank you. Just the keys, please'.

'No key needed, Mr. Hunt.' Jacobs indicated a discreet panel, punched in a four-digit code and pushed open the door for Hunt to enter.

Jacobs handed him a business card.

'The code is on here, Mr. Hunt, plus my number, should you have any questions.'

Hunt took the card with a cursory nod to Jacobs and turning back, signalled to his driver. Within seconds, eight men alighted from two of the vans. Hunt issued a barrage of instructions to the assembled group and the men divided into three groups with military precision to set about their pre-ordained tasks. Two men, carrying steel boxes in either hand, walked briskly towards the entrance gate to start their task of installing a temporary infrared security ring with video surveillance around the property. The second group began unloading one of the vans and carried an assortment of drilling, cutting and digging equipment, which they unceremoniously dumped on the fine oak floor of the entrance hall. Another two men stood guard by the vehicle, smoking and idling away the time.

Hunt had no intention of spending any longer than necessary at Glencot. He settled himself down in the drawing room while the bulk of furniture was being cleared, and spread out various files across the great Victorian library table. Deep down he understood that it would likely be several hours before his surveillance team could accurately locate the entrance to the chamber, although he was convinced that there had to be an easy way in there. For instance, there already existed endless authenticated accounts of connecting tunnels between the Abbot's Palace at Wells and the Wookey Caves. Then there were the Holy Grail legends and various sources that put Glencot House as having been built on the ancient site of Wookey Castle, where legend persisted that the druids were custodians of the actual Holy Grail. The chamber must have a proper access and now, with his team in place, and with state of the art sonar survey equipment being set up in the cellars, all would be revealed.

'Mr. Hunt,' a skinny man in his early twenties tapped on the door of the drawing room. 'Just to say, we're setting up our equipment and intend to scan from one end of the cellars through to the cinema room, which we estimate will take between five and six hours.'

Hunt, with little knowledge of the technology, had assumed this process would only take an hour or two. Dusting down his jacket, he wandered around the house, now totally devoid of guests and chilly from lack of heating. The place had a depressing atmosphere that was reminiscent of Jack Torrence's entrance in 'The Shining' and he wondered whether he might encounter a child hurtling towards him at breakneck speed. He couldn't wait to get out of the place. His plan was to strip the chamber of its contents before any semblance of authority got a whiff of what he was up to, and then get out. After all, this deal was never ever going to see the light of day. If the chamber contained what he thought and, if it ever became public knowledge, it would be harder to transport than gold from Fort Knox. Time was not on his side.

Three o'clock chimed from the great grandfather clock, then four and, by six, Hunt was feeling irritable and impatient. Wandering into the library, he saw that his two surveillance men had turned the room into a mini operations centre, with half a dozen screens arranged over a pair of trestle tables. Their cameras covered every approach to Glencot. Hunt sat for a few moments, eyeing up the monitors, where the only recordable life form appeared to be meandering sheep grazing the fields.

'Get me cognac, will you?' he instructed a tall, burly man, who poked his head around the door. The drink arrived and Hunt drained the glass with one swift gulp. He was strangely fixated to the screens, when, all of a sudden something caught his eye.

'What the hell was that?' Nathan yelled, as a head passed directly in front of the camera scanning the rear terrace. 'Who is that man and where's he going?

One of the surveillance men had jumped to his feet at the same time.

'I'll check immediately, sir. I've got no idea how he slipped the net.'

A frenzy of tapping and clicking instantly had all the screens focussing on the rear of the hotel. Hunt could see clearly now that the rain had lifted, and an elderly man was being filmed ambling along the terrace, an overweight black and white collie dog snuffling at his heels. Hunt ran from the library, hopped down the stairs and headed straight for the terrace doors.

'Stay there,' he called back to the men. 'I'll deal with this'.

Approaching the glazed terrace door, he picked out a wrinkled, wizened face pressed against the glass pane, right hand held high to avoid reflection. The old man instantly recoiled when he saw Hunt's silhouette advancing and unbolting the glass doors.

'Can I help you?' Glencot's new owner barked as politely as he could. The absolute last thing he wanted was some bloody snoop buggering up his work. 'The hotel is closed, I'm afraid.'

'Well, maybees you can,' the old man drawled, 'and then maybees you can't. I'm lookin' to say 'ello to the new owner.'

Hunt went back upstairs to the library. It was now seven-thirty and his patience had worn paper-thin. A few minutes later and the door burst open.

'Mr. Hunt,' the man said excitedly. 'I think we've found it'.

Hunt leapt to his feet and straight away followed down to the cellar, where he found two other men sitting on the floor of the Minima, poring over their equipment. One of the seated men handed Hunt a print out, which to his untrained eye, looked more like the workings of his intestines than a rock formation.

'You see here' the man said pointing out a dark grey shadow on the sheet. 'The entrance appears here and travels across the cellars, eventually dipping down to a depth of fifteen feet. We're pretty confident that this is the entrance, actually here in this room. You can also see the undulating shadow at this mark which looks like a staircase.'

'Great work' Nathan said. 'Get Craig down with his men and start digging.'

Within minutes, the boffins were replaced by the brawn, unpacking pneumatic drills, hammers and picks and flexing impressive muscle. Hunt couldn't contain his excitement; he was on the verge of the most thrilling find of a lifetime and wanted to savour every precious moment. He sat in silence as the Minima erupted to the sound of the first drill cracking the flagstone. Almost immediately the man in charge screamed:

'Hold it, hold it!'

The drilling ceased and Craig peered down at the split flagstone. He'd just spotted the leather strapping that worked as a lever for the flagstone entrance. The men all stood back as the stone was lifted, revealing the dark stair-well that Tarmin had stumbled upon all those months earlier. Nathan Hunt stood beside them peering into the void.

'Give me a torch someone, quickly.'

With the powerful beam allowing him to pick out his way down, he retraced Tarmin's steps right through to the marquetry-panelled room where his torch swept across the empty space. The disappointment was overwhelming. This was not what he'd been expecting. He ran back up the corridor stumbling and cursing on the stairs until he emerged back into the Minima.

'Come back down with me' he ordered Craig and another couple of men. 'Bring some tools and the floodlights. And the print out.'

Within minutes, the marquetry-panelled room was completely illuminated and Nathan Hunt was analysing the print out with Craig. The younger man swivelled the paper round 90 degrees and pointed to the wall on their right side.

'It appears that this room is actually larger than the scanners have been able to pick up on and, working on this assumption, I think that we should find what you're looking for beyond that wall.'

'Then get on with it' said Hunt. 'Rip it down. I don't care about sentimentality.'

214

THE WOOKEY HOLE AFFAIR

Hunt stood back as the men proceeded to tear the panelling away and within minutes, the small inner chamber was revealed. As the last of the panelling was taken off the wall, Nathan could clearly make out a short passageway hewn out of the rock, leading to the outline of the chamber and its shadowy contents.

Once inside the small chamber, measuring five by four metres, the powerful lead lights had revealed his worst fears. The shafts of light picked out an imitation set from the London Dungeon, minus the animatronics. He stood in stunned silence, the other men standing close behind him. It only took a cursory glance to realise that the contrived arrangement was constructed of totally worthless artefacts, and when viewed from above, had been arranged entirely to deceive. Of course, it would have been a suspect bet for anyone to bank on the visuals being convincing enough on their own. The camera could never have delivered an authentic enough image. However, it had been the deluge of small talk beforehand that had enticed him into this whole futile journey. Had Tarmin Rimell set the whole thing up or had this particular aspect been the legacy of a previous owner playing some practical joke? And if so, why? After all, Amanda had unearthed all those documents from the photograph box, and those had looked genuine enough. A stream of questions raced through Hunt's head with no answers. It was like Japanese torture. He could, however, see that the chamber had obviously been created to house something of value, once upon a time. The carefully carved altar place in the far wall had certainly been dug to hold something of great significance. Maybe this chamber was a priest hole or even a refuge from Cromwell's Roundhead thugs? Hunt took a deep breath, looked at everything one more time and swiftly left the room, followed by Craig and the men holding the lights.

Dumping his lead lights in a pile at the top of the stairs, he waited until the full group had reassembled.

'Get your gear together and pack the vans. We're out of here. There is no more to be done in this place.'

The men scurried about gathering their equipment, and dismantling leads and cameras. Hunt went upstairs into the drawing room, poured himself a large brandy from the still fully stocked honesty bar, and walked through to the Romeo balcony. He felt emotionally drained and, in his heart, he felt foolish. Of course, deep down he knew that he'd been stalking a dream, but men without dreams were like the sky without sun. Nathan Hunt was no fool - his iron-fisted father had taught him well: 'Plan for the worst, but hope for the best' had been drilled into him from a very early age. It was a lesson that Hunt had executed to perfection but maybe this obsession with acquisitions had blurred the important lines of reality?

Brandy swirling around his glass, there was little left to do now and he turned back inside. While the vans were being re-loaded, he ventured downstairs and out on to the flagstone terrace, strolled across the stone bridge, past the cricket pitch and up the hill. The sheep barely bothered moving from his path as he picked his way through the mangy flock, trying in vain to get phone reception. The Japanese torture painfully continued.

'Call failed', 'Call failed' appeared again and again. He was just approaching the front of Tarmin's half-built folly when finally he got a signal.

'McCreedy & Gareth Solicitors, can I help you?' a chirpy voice perked up at the other end.

'James McCreedy-Smith, please'

'I'm sorry, he's with a client right now', the chirper carried on squeaking.

'Was with a client' Hunt interrupted her curtly. 'Put me

through, it's Nathan Hunt. He will take my call.'

A second later and James McCreedy-Smith was on the line.

'Mr. Hunt' the solicitor sounded somewhat surprised to be hearing from him. 'What news? Everything alright?'

'This is total shit. There's no way I'm going to complete that purchase. Luckily, we will have got away with just the deposit. I will be leaving it at that.'

'I understand,' his solicitor responded quietly. 'The other side have been on the phone all morning demanding the transfer of the full completion funds. I've been stalling them on your instructions. Luckily they didn't get through to the agent, so you were incredibly lucky to have got in there today, without full completion.'

Hunt killed the phone call. He'd already taken a huge hit to his pride today, not something that he was in the habit of doing. He slipped his phone back into his pocket and sat down on the one of the stone slabs in Tarmin's half-built folly. Still clutching the brandy, he downed the remains with one huge gulp and then furiously hurled the glass at the stone lintel in the centre of the folly. The glass shattered into a thousand pieces and, watching the fragments flying at all angles, Hunt suddenly froze. His eyes were fixed on an inscription carved into the stone surrounds. Perhaps there was something here after all? He ran across and studied the carving. It was a bunch of broken up Latin words, a fat lot of use to Hunt. Yet another red herring. He'd barely passed his German language exams at school, for God's sake, and German was his first language.

Tarmin froze on the spot. He grabbed a cigarette and lit up.

'You're telling me that you gave the keys to Glencot without completing the purchase?' he screamed down the phone to his solicitor. 'I don't fucking believe it. I thought you told me that you had completed?'

A string of excuses piped down his mobile.

'You complete wanker' Tarmin exploded. 'I'm sorry, but you're a complete wanker!'

'Please look on the bright side, Mr. Rimell' McCreedy Smith tried to placate him. 'You've half a million in the bank and can always go back to Victory Oil and do a deal with them. We can also put the hotel back on the market if you like, don't forget.'

Here was the sticking point. There was no way that Tarmin could tell this frazzled locum solicitor, who he barely even knew, that the oil company was as much a figment of his imagination as was the chamber of deception. Now it was his turn to go silent.

CHAPTER TWENTY

St. Lucia, Caribbean - One year later

The evening sun had just begun to dip, spreading streams of pink across the still, warm waters. An endless string of bronzed couples, hand-holding and barely clad in colourful lightweight clothing, sauntered across the heated sands, trailing their toes in the Caribbean sea. Half way along the beach, a small band of sweating Rastas made tuneful noise on undulating metal drums, notes drifting out to the linen sails, idly skimming the water's surface in front of the low level hotels and white washed villas.

'Belle Coco Villa' stood right at the end of the line, two huge palm trees marking its territory and overhanging a small wooden veranda, smothered by mixed vermilion and white bougainvillea twisting around the rails. The peachy sunlight coloured the glass windows and tiny singing birds peppered the leafy branches of a smattering of fruit trees, lining the sandy path around to the front.

Melvin Kimininos and Spike Dick lounged at a small marble terrace table, staring in a daze at the various beach lovers and clusters of families. Both men were nut brown and beautifully worked out, defined muscles glistening with suntan oil, wet hair slicked back off their darkened faces. Through the open door behind them, soft strains of reggae filled the air.

'Do you think he thinks about us at all?' Spike said.

He fingered a packet of cigarettes that was propped against a wine glass and then withdrew. It wouldn't be any good smoking after all that expended energy pumping iron and clubbing. There were some incredibly fit guys here in St. Lucia and both he and Melvin still felt like little kids in a sweet shop, even though they'd been living here now for over a year. Melvin had found the house about four years ago, and had the sense to snap up a bargain when he'd seen it. Just as well, taking into consideration what had happened in the ensuing years.

Their particular beach was not one of the most popular on the northern most tip of the island, hence the very reasonable purchase price. However, as a long-term hideout it was tiny and far too small for two strapping men to make as a permanent home. The interior was no better than a basic beach hut - one bedroom, a small shower and toilet, a reasonably sized kitchen that opened up into an eating area, and a neat garden at the front. Melvin had always promised Spike that this would just be their starting point until the money came through, but the reality had become something entirely different. They were men on the run; they'd cleaned out their various bank accounts before leaving, squirreling away a small bunch of money in an offshore account in anticipation of moving on when things died down. Of course, that account was untouchable whilst they were still on the run, but it wasn't this money that would fund their new lives. It would have to be the oil painting - particularly since Melvin had been cut out of his father's will. Privately, Spike had blessed each and every day that he'd remained in St. Lucia undetected. For the first few months, at every minute he'd expected a plain-clothed police guy in dark shades and fluorescent shirt to emerge from the beach and snap a warrant in his face. Somehow, someone always seemed to know where everyone was in the world - no one ever remained undetected.

At least they had some semblance of their pet grooming business here, which was a slight comfort. A mongrel called Snoopy, who had wandered into the kitchen on their second day, swollen pregnant belly and gagging for water, and subsequently given birth to three puppies, one of which they'd also kept. As long as he had animals around him, Spike could just about cope. His boyfriend, on the other hand, seemed to be reaching his limits. Melvin had become increasingly bad tempered and restless. He had been the initiator, hatching this plan, and it was all centred around that fucking drab painting, hanging completely out of place, above the greasy cooker inside.

'Do I think 'who' ever thinks about us?' Melvin eventually answered, tearing his eyes away from a six foot black guy who was adjusting his boxer shorts as he emerged, dripping wet, from the water just a few feet away. 'My father? That old bastard is nothing but bones and dust now, thank God. He didn't deserve to live after cutting me from his will. That fucker didn't leave me a single penny.'

'I meant Tarmin Rimell, Melvin. I wonder whether he has put two and two together?'

'Of course he bloody did, fuckwit. What do you expect? He might be a pisshead but he's no fool.'

'I still don't know why we're here' Spike persisted. 'There is no work for us here and we can hardly sell that godforsaken painting on the island. Everyone's far too poor. What do you plan to do with it?'

Melvin stood up and looked out to sea. The black guy was towelling himself off and rubbing oil into his skin. Christ he wished he could be with someone else right now. Spike was wearing horribly thin these days. Without a business to run and with none of the creature comforts of home, the cracks in any relationship would start to show and, in their case, the boredom was stultifying. The cracks were rumbling like an almighty earthquake.

He walked back to the table and poured two glasses of red wine. Evening shadows danced across the patio, a bird hopped over to his feet and pecked at blown grass seeds, a gentle breeze flipped the deep green leaves of the fruit trees.

'How many times do I have to explain about this painting, Spike? How many goddam times? It's fucking hot property and that means that, until the heat dies down, we can't risk touting it around the dealers and dodgy markets. Before too long it'll be safe to go to the European markets and then we can sell it. I've organised for Lexi Bousquet to ship it out for us, and he'll do it at the drop of a hat. Then on in, we can go anywhere, do anything and live the life of Riley. It's hardly too damn distressing, living as beach bums in the Caribbean, sun burning our backs every day of the week, is it? Or are you counting the one too many wrinkles popping up?'

Spike wished he could take a swipe at the smug son-of-a-bitch and make him bruise and bleed. How dare he treat him like Snoopy? In fact, in that very last moment, he could see exactly where their relationship was headed. He - Spike - was turning into Melvin's father and the abuse that had once been expended to him, was now being vented at Spike. If he wasn't careful, he too would end up in a wooden coffin. He watched his feckless partner staring at the black guy, licking his lower lip and smoothing out his crotch. The guy on the beach was stretching his perfectly flat and tensed torso, as he pulled on a sexy white shirt, completely aware that his every move was being monitored. Just then a bikinied beach babe, long beaded hair flowing half way down her back, jogged by and slapped him on his bottom. Spinning round, he grabbed her by the waist, kissed her hard and the two ran off across the sand. Melvin's peep show was finished.

'I'm sorry Spike, but you're not making this easy. Every fucking day you question me about our situation. We're in deep shit, man, and well you know it. Come inside - I want to show you this painting and show you, once and for all, what all this is about. How our lives will drastically change from selling that badly painted black canvas. You have to trust me and you have to shut the fuck up.'

Spike looked out to sea.

'Come inside. Bring your wine glass and look at our fortune.'

Spike heaved his bulky frame from the chair and barefoot, padded into the house behind Melvin. They stood in the small, wooden panelled room and stared at the painting, lit by the fading sunlight.

'This is a 16th century masterpiece, Spike. As little as I know about art, I remember when Dad got the call from the Galleria Borghese in Rome, and the utter excitement after they'd out-priced what he thought was just a worthless painting. He then always maintained that this would be our family's inheritance, and that's right. I am his eldest child and son, and that bastard cut me out of everything. Everything except this. This is what is going to buy us a fuck-off mansion in Miami, the cars, the lifestyle that you are forever whingeing over. Just accept that it's going to take some time to get this right. I'm not going to blow it now because of someone getting ants in his pants.'

Spike had moved over to the 'Dark Man' painting, and adjusted the frame gently with his huge hands. It always seemed to be hanging slightly askew, which was part of the reason that he'd lost patience with it.

'If you respect this so much, why the hell do you hang it so near this slimy cooker? The smoke and shit is already griming up the frame. It's ridiculous, move it somewhere else.'

Melvin glugged back his wine and looked out across the bay. He wasn't in the mood for an argument, and anyway, Spike was fast becoming history in his eyes. He knew, but hadn't shared the details with his boyfriend, that Lexi Bousquet was gearing up to take the painting to France in just short of a month. He'd sourced some dealers who were arranging a meet and although he, Melvin, wouldn't be able to travel, he had no problem in trusting that Lexi would bring the money back. After all, he was blackmailing the Minister of Health with some incredibly damning drug evidence. If the scandal broke, (and Melvin had the absolute power to effect such a thing), Bousquet would not only face utter disgrace but jail too. In true Melvin style, he had also ensured that the 'happily' married Minister was also filmed shagging him on the conjugal bed. Consequently, he had it all sewn up. As soon as the fortune was delivered to him on Bousquet's return from Paris, he would buy Spike out and leave for America. He wasn't worried about not being able to travel, but didn't want Spike to know that. That was another useful sideline of bribing a government minister;

obtaining a fake passport had been a piece of piss.

Right now though, it was becoming apparent that to avoid any suspicion, he'd have to placate the stupid fucker. He didn't want to piss him off to such an extent that Spike foiled any of his plans. He flopped down on the sofa at the far end of the room, and smiled.

'You're right, of course. Take the painting down, by all means and hang it where you like. I only put it there because, as we both know, there isn't exactly a huge opportunity when it comes to wall space here, and we obviously don't want to hang it in full view of the world. But be my guest, put it somewhere that pleases you.'

Spike lifted the painting down and tut-tutted loudly as he examined the grease stains along the gilded frame. He walked towards Melvin and propped it up on the sofa arm.

'Jesus! There's a bloody great hole right here along the back lining, where the frame has been disintegrating. Are you aware of this?'

Both men looked at the split frame and the canvas showing underneath. Melvin took over and examined it carefully. It was at that moment that he saw what looked like a piece of paper stuck inside. Using a large kitchen knife he very carefully prised the top part of the frame apart and stuck a fork in to keep the gap open. Then with the tip of the knife, he edged the paper upwards until the whole sheet had fully emerged. It was folded in two. He sat down and looked at Spike, his stomach churning with sickening butterflies.

'I have a feeling about this,' was all he could say.

The note read:

Dear George,
It is with great pleasure that I have painted 'The Dark Man'
for you. It has been a difficult quest to ascertain such a

likeness when the quality of this fine painting is dependent on the extraordinary mixing of such delicate dark hues and subtleties. I have never before encountered such a challenge!

I hope that this copy brings you as much happiness as the original and that it remains in your hands until your dying day, as you so wished.
Your very good friend
Domingo Dacosta.'

Melvin leapt to his feet and ran over to the laptop, Spike standing over his shoulder. He tapped Dacosta's name into Google and instantly a string of relevant lines appeared, all bearing his name. The top one looked the most interesting; a small article taken from The Times just five months previously. Melvin read it out loud: *European art dealers and private collectors heaved a sigh of relief today, when one of the primary forgers from a group of painters known as 'Milagro', based in the Spanish city of Barcelona, was jailed for five years. Domingo Dacosta, whose duped clientele have included an art collecting rock megastar, several Hollywood actors and a consortium of London hedge fund managers, was tried at the International Court of Justice in Barcelona. Others from 'Milagro' who were also tried were......* It was not necessary to read any further. Both the game and their futures were well and truly up.

Innsbruck, Austria
One year later

Nathan Hunt loved the summers in Austria, particularly now that he was spending all his time there, shunning the UK. He'd been on a bit of a roller coaster over the past few months, one that had stripped him of his dignity, ripped him

226

off to the tune of half a million pounds and made a grand adversary in the shape of Tarmin Rimell. But he was over all that shit now, although, as he sat down in his 18th century Venetian gilt chair, glass of wine in hand, his mind couldn't help but drift back to just under a year ago and the unpleasantness that had ensued. The awful day at Glencot when his scanning team had discovered the scam in the cellars, had ended with him dismissing his men and summoning Amanda.

'How could this have happened to me?' he'd asked her, and she'd just stared back. For the first time she'd experienced pity for the man who always had seemed so indomitable, in total control. Now she saw the shell of a small boy, a person who had been cowed by humiliation.

'It's not the goddam money. Half a million is nothing to me. It's the fact that he went to such great lengths to do the scam, to create such a ....such a ridiculously contemptuous plan to catch me. Do I really look like such a crass fool?'

Somehow Amanda had seemed turned on by his agitated state, and that had angered him even more. She'd brushed the cellar dust from his hair, squeezed his grime-stained hands and smoothed out a tear that had appeared in his formerly pristine shirt. It was the best she'd ever seen him, she said, her voice annoyingly cooing. In her eyes, he'd become a far sexier and more human version of the velvet-coated, control freak that normally ruled the roost. She would look after him now, take care of him. Did he want to go to bed with her?

How fucking insensitive that bitch had become, he'd thought. He never wanted her to take up that loving tone, to become integrated so deeply in his life. That was another reason to hate Rimell. He'd made this situation so bad that even Amanda had changed beyond his control. Now he'd have to find another woman to be on tap, someone who he'd have to train all over again to deliver to his every whim. He couldn't be arsed.

He'd given Amanda her marching orders, ignoring the piteous tears and pleas for her livelihood. What did he care that she had lost precious clients, being down at Glencot for so long? Serve the bitch right, he'd thought. He wasn't her father, for heaven's sake, barely her keeper. Afterwards, he'd returned to London, sewn up the rest of business with his lawyer, let go of the Glencot purchase and flown straight back to Austria.

But last year was not a total waste of time, when it came to Rimell and his hotel empire. It was indirectly because of him that he'd got to meet George Kimininos, just before his death, and had taken a look at Kimininos's extraordinary artefacts collection. It was easy thereafter to trace the final auction of Kimininos & Sons and put in his bid. Looking around his room now, his eyes ran over various stone pieces and Roman weapons that were artfully displayed. Then he smiled. That was the best bit, the bit that had made it all worthwhile. The masterpiece. Above his fireplace, hung The Dark Man portrait. The auction catalogue had it listed as a copy, but it had taken just one inspection by his elderly mother and she'd ordered him to get it properly checked out.

'Nathan, my son. That painting is as authentic as I am, I'm telling you. The English are so often careless with their things. Take it to Jan Reimann in Basel. He will know and you will find out that you have more money in that one painting than you could ever dream of.'

His mother had been correct in her assumptions and now he owned a treasure that had very spectacular meaning to him. But still it didn't ease the grievance that he felt in his heart. No one took Nathan Hunt for granted. No one had cheated him of his money, or made a fool of him.

He drained the last drop from his wine glass and picked up the phone.

'Ah, Kaufman. Come into the drawing room, will you? And bring a notepad and pencil with you.'

A few minutes later there was a gentle knock on the door, and Hunt's manservant came in. Kaufman was a tall man with distinguished silver hair and a neat beard, closely clipped. He discreetly placed a tumbler of mineral water and a plate of cheese and crackers by Hunt's side, then stood infront of him.

'Tell me what you'd like me to do, sir.'

Hunt picked up a morsel of bleu d'Auvergne cheese and wafted it beneath his nose. It was strong and tasty. A perfect accompaniment to the red wine he'd been drinking. Kauffman always got it right.

'Kaufmann, I want you to call the airline in the morning. I need to book a flight.'

The servant jotted down the relevant numbers and said his goodnight, leaving Hunt alone by candlelight. Hunt smeared some cheese on a pumpkin seed biscuit and chewed slowly. This cheese was damn good, he thought, looking across at the Dark Man. And life will be very damn good again too. He would make sure of that.

CHAPTER TWENTY ONE

Summer at Somerset - One year on

It was more than a sense of déjà vu that Tarmin had felt when he'd returned to Glencot, a mere six months after his disastrous departure. After Hunt had pulled out of the sale and jumped ship, he and Alex had decided to lay low in the South African sun, hopefully well out of Hunt's vindictive radar. Stuck with what to do with an empty hotel and no staff, Tarmin had initially tried to deflect negative attention by putting word out that Glencot had been sold to a developer who was now awaiting planning permission to turn it into a retirement home.

In just six months absence, the interior had been bestowed with an unmistakably Havershamesque atmosphere; local spiders having a field day with their own particular brand of lacy interior design, mice running riot in the lower rooms. There was even a couple of pigeons nesting on the Romeo balcony. Alex and Tarmin had revisited their memories, wandering from room to room and brushing dust from the surfaces, remembering how it had all come to this. But at least they'd returned to Glencot with a concrete plan.

After realising that his original quest for millions to get rid of his heinous wife had spectacularly failed, there was no choice but for Tarmin to change tack. With a heavy heart, he'd swiftly handed over both Millers and The Academy to Gayle as part of their divorce settlement. Gayle, a highly sensitive soul, and feeling jubilant in victory, had instantly sold the lot and buggered off with Theodore to Los Angeles. Since then, Bundy had reported back that after serious plastic surgery, she'd become belle of the LA fitness circuit and was making shit loads of money teaching Pilates to the crazy body beauti-fuls. Tarmin didn't care about Gayle's new life but it did irk that Millers had since morphed into a BT outlet while the Academy had become Westbourne Grove's very own branch of Dorothy Perkins.

Six months of Alex in South Africa had eventually healed his past anxieties, such as they were, and he was now ready for his next venture. Luckily he'd not heard a squeak from Hunt and decided that, with the coast apparently clear, Glencot returned to him, a few hundred thousand in the bank from his divorce and half a million courtesy of Hunt's misfortune, it was safe to come back and resume Somerset life.

Over the next few months, he and Alexandra had worked twenty-four-seven on the new project and this one just had to be a sure-fire winner. Over time, they'd transformed Glencot, spending most of Tarmin's available cash and totally depleting his creative and inspirational bank balance. All leading up to today, the very grand opening.

The cream of Europe's most motley press had been invited

along, and by the look of the assembling crowd, Tarmin could see that the response had hit a universal chord. Word had somehow leaked even further afield, he realised, when introductions were made to Nelson Patterson junior, from the El Paso Times. Alex pulled back from their bedroom window and nudged her lover in the ribs.

'Can you please help me with these godforsaken buttons? And by the way, this is the first and last time, I am ever going to wear this.'

'God, it's so sexy,' Tarmin drooled, slipping his hand inside her open top.

'Don't press those buttons, just do me up. Look outside; we've got to go tinkling with the press.'

Luckily, the June day hadn't disappointed and the broad red ribbon, barring the front entrance to Glencot, fluttered in the soft breeze. Gathered behind it and sipping from small golden goblets of champagne, several dozen of the world's press, chatted amongst themselves and studied the press releases being handed around by Tarmin's staff, all suitably attired.

Tarmin, followed at a distance by Alex, joined the now huge throng, picked up a microphone, clicked it into action and gingerly mounted a giant spotted toadstool. After loudly clearing his throat, he began to address the crowd.

'Ladies and gentlemen' he announced. 'Thank you all for coming along today, and a very warm welcome to ....Gnomeland!'

At which point he invited the Mayor of Wells, Mr. Harold Halpern, to step forward and do the honours. Picking up an over-sized pair of red and yellow scissors, Halpern nodded to his wife to pull his barrage of chains out of the way, and leaning over, made great show of snipping the tape. A ripple of applause, several hoots and a few appreciative whistles accompanied the ceremony, and then in they poured.

Alex looked resplendent in her lime green and orange gnome

outfit, the long cap tinkling a silver bell at the tip. Hell, who cared what people thought? She couldn't look more of an arse than her lover, she thought, watching Tarmin posing for photographers in his large multicoloured felt suit and tin watering can. Glencot of old was no longer. Glencot had been reborn, dressed in Disneyesque garb and could now officially be called Gnomeland. As the press streamed up the wooded drive, gnomic creatures appeared from all directions, displaying their prowess by swinging upside down, star-jumping off rocks and somersaulting through the sea of legs. This was something more akin to an Apache ambush than a welcome party. Living gnomes were everywhere, every size and every colour.

'Could that be Danny De Vito over there?' a tall lady asked her colleague from the Daily Express. 'How odd if it is. He's handing out mushroom vol-au-vents from a large leaf.'

Glencot's Jacobean facade had been expertly cheapened by festoons of gnome themed balloons and, at the point of entry, all guests had to pass under the legs of a twenty-foot high super dwarf. Within, the whole of Glencot (apart from its fine panelling) had been painted in the most vibrant colours that Tarmin could source. Tables, chairs and even chandeliers were all constructed as gnomes, mushrooms or woodland flowers. He'd designed toadstool carpets to cover every inch of flooring, and adorned the wall space with oil portraits of generations of gnome lineage, all presented in traditional gilded frames. Guests were invited sit upon wooden gnomes, eat off gnome china and even sleep with inflatable gnomes, if they so wished. Upstairs, the bedrooms were furnished with magnificent poster beds, their drapes embroidered with white bearded folk throughout the centuries. Tarmin's attention to detail was precise and inspired. Scattered around the place were reproduction gnomes with 19th century patterning; every room had thin smoking pipes in the ashtrays, and pairs of soft fleecy slippers were parked in the bathrooms. Glencot's Gnomeland was designed as a place that would satisfy every possible desire for the gnome maniac. For evening entertainment, Tarmin and Alex had managed to locate an elderly retired actor living in Wookey Hole, to sit in the drawing room and read aloud some traditionally melancholic tales from Northern Europe. Cherubic gnome choirs wafted soprano ditties from watering can speakers that hung in clusters throughout the building. And last but by no means least, the dining room tables were permanently laden with good old gnome cooking. What more could anyone want?

Though of course, this wholly commercial venture grated heavily against Tarmin's love of finery. The riot of colour throughout the house was completely tasteless and designed to disturb even the most visually inarticulate eye. Out of desperation, Tarmin had carefully conceived a style that he was sure would generate the worst possible press, but at least the world would know about it and come to gawp. It was the way these things worked.

When Tarmin had first explained the idea to Alex, she had thought that his project was deranged, irresponsibly foolhardy and that he should definitely be locked up. Her opinion hadn't eased much over time, but at least her sense of humour had eventually returned and she'd thrown herself into the new venture with gusto. But as he developed the concept and explained the economics, she'd slowly warmed to the idea. After all, they'd been through so much together, and her lover had lost virtually everything in the process.

They badly needed to shore up their bank accounts once again and move on. The finances were simple, Tarmin had assured her. He would separate out the land and divide it up into one hundred thousand one metre square plots, then lease them out, together with a hand-picked gnome host, for seventy-five pounds a throw. His back of a fag packet calculations had shown that the land currently valued at twenty five thousand pounds could, by dividing it in this way, generate over seven million pounds in income.

He would market Gnomeland as the ideal, totally unique gift and there was certainly a huge gap in the market, as far as he could see. Each gnome owner could visit their plots at any time, see them on the internet, order flowers, small fishing rods, or even send them on holidays and arrange their own special passports. Already someone had made a reservation to plant a mushroom plot. Everything, he told her, has its price. Their gnome shop would stock gorgeous gnomes from every corner of the world and in every shape and size.

Twelve o'clock raced to six, and still the press stragglers stuck around. Would they ever leave? Even in Tarmin's wildest dreams he'd not envisaged such a turn out. The afternoon had been opened up to locals and invited guests too, and they'd turned up in their droves. For some reason, the event had seemingly captured the imagination of even the most cynical and jaded of hacks. Although, perhaps it had been a mistake to include the lap-dancing fairies at the end; now the crowd would never leave. Tarmin had organised for a sprinkling of semi-clad lovelies to present the photographers with some salacious photo opportunities, and he and Alex looked on in amazement at just how creative these snappers could be when it came to a bit of pertly breasted goblin. On leaving, all VIP guests were presented with a keepsake passport together with their own gnome and the title deeds to its patch of land. By seven o'clock, the last of the dishevelled bunch were being ushered off the premises, filing out between the giant dwarf legs once again, and then saluted by Tarmin's security team, the gnome guard. Next week it would open for real, but now, and probably for the last time, Alex and Tarmin were left alone amongst the mass of debris.

Tackiness aside, the place looked amazing in the evening

light; fairy lights strewn amongst the branches and candlelit lanterns throwing dancing shadows across the lawns. From the garden view, no one would ever really have gnomed there'd been a party. Alex popped off her tunic and discarded her orange cap, letting her fair hair fall over her sweaty t-shirt.

'Wow. I've got to give you gold, my love. That was truly amazing. Any chance I can now have my own gnome de plume?' she quipped.

Tarmin put his head in his hands and groaned. They would have to be living with all these godforsaken gnome jokes as long as the business thrived. Alexandra stretched out her feet and wiggled her toes. Pointy boots were killers.

'I'll certainly be needing one, if Nathan Hunt picks up the scent that we're back. Let's pray that gnomes are off his collector's radar.'

Tarmin looked at her shambolic outfit and laughed. He loved this woman and could never get over the fact that she'd come into his life and managed to pave the way to get rid of Gayle, sticking through thick and thin. Here she was today, pandering to yet another of his crazy ideas. He gently kissed his queen, squeezed her hand and said: 'There's only one thing left to make this the most perfect day of my life.'

Alex smiled, her mind drifting to the playful waterbed in the master suite,

'Will you marry me, Alexandra?' he stuttered. It hadn't been this hard with Gayle. Mind you, they'd both been off their heads on Millers Gin at the time, so he'd have proposed to a warthog and not noticed.

'What sort of girl do you think I am?' she responded in nervous shock.

'Absolutely perfect' he whispered. God, he desperately hoped he wasn't coming across foolishly. All this dressing up lark had frazzled his brain, he was sure.

'Then I'd probably better make a perfectly honest man of

you'. Tarmin offered with more than a twinkle in his eye.

Alex rose from the sofa and picked out a chilled bottle of champagne from the bucket.

'Let's go up to your folly'.

'Can I take it that's a yes?' he asked her.

'What do you think, dumbo? I'm hardly going to the folly to get pissed on my own, am I?'

Jubilantly, Tarmin kicked the nearest gnome clean over the terrace balustrade, grabbed her hand and together, they headed out across the stone bridge to the fields

The sun was setting over Gnomeland and the life-sized figures cast their long shadows over the parkland. Tarmin and Alex reached the folly just as the sun faded behind the trees and the last vestiges of warmth slipped under the chilly covers of night. Tarmin sat her down on the stone seat in front of the folly's great open-air fireplace, gathered together some dead wood and, within a few minutes, had set a blaze going. The dancing flames flickered through the falling darkness and, after lighting some smaller candles in the stone niches, they sat together in comfortable silence and watched day fade into night. Alex knew words were not on Tarmin's agenda, just a loving closeness and the unspoken joy of a future unplotted but taciturnly understood.

Alex idly tossed a few sticks into the fire, whilst Tarmin poured the remnants of the champagne into their glasses. There was a sharp rustle in the bushes, the beating of wings from branches above, and faint bleating of far off sheep. The two of them sat entwined, slowly drifting into sleep, exhausted and pissed. Alex's hand dropped to one side and trailed in the grass, when a tongue started to gently lick her fingers.

'Don't Tarmin,' she murmured, at the same time as realising that superman lover he may be, but a three-foot tongue he certainly didn't possess. As the penny dropped, she jumped to her feet to the surprise of Tarmin and the affectionate black and white collie dog who was parked beside her.

'In God's name! Where the fuck has this come from?' she shouted, looking at the hugely fat sheep dog. The dog was frantically panting and stank of wet manure.

'Snuffer, Snuffer!' came a voice from the woods. "Ere boy!'

The shout was followed by a roughly dressed old man, thrashing a gnarled walking stick through the undergrowth. Tarmin and Alex took a step back and grabbed each other's arm.

'Hello there' Tarmin muttered, somewhat coldly.

'Evening to you both. You be Mr. Rimmell, I dare say? Snuffer, get your nose out of that poor lady's behind!'

Tarmin was so astonished that the vagrant appeared to know him, he totally ignored the fact that the sheepdog was causing poor Alex indecent hassle.

'Yes, that's me. How do you know that? Are you psychic or something?'

'Snuffer is my sidekick' the man answered. 'No, I knows who you are because it's my sheep that you let graze in them there fields, out yonder'.

'I've never been to yonder. Does it have a good pub?' Tarmin attempted to match the man's silly humour, appeased that he wasn't some nutter on the loose.

'Not officially, but sometimes I feels that my 'ome is like a fuckin' pub. Full of damn freeloaders around 'ere, take it from me.'

He smiled at Tarmin and extended a large, calloused hand in greeting.

'I'm Cyril Dunster and that there is Snuffer' he said pointing to the portly Collie, now cocking its leg against the empty champagne bottle. Tarmin immediately warmed to the strange man and shook his hand.

'Call me Tarmin, not Mr. Rimell. And this is my fiancé, Alex' he said, taking her by the hand. It was the first time that he'd used the betrothal word and it felt pleasing.

'Nice and cosy 'ere then?' Cyril shot a look around their little love nest. 'Very nice indeed. I bet your lady there is hoping for some fun by the flames, eh?! Big do you 'ad today, over at the big 'ouse? My sheep haven't stopped bleating all day, they were so disturbed by the comings and goings. I've been noticin' a few changes have been goin' on in these pastures 'ere. Anyways, I'm glad you never sold the place in the end. I went by last year to introduce myself to the new owner, but it didn't seem to be a match made in 'eaven. 'E was a weird 'un - horrible German type accent and up to no good, I reckoned. Snuffer can snuff a deceitful man from afar and he was right shook up.'

'You're right, 'said Tarmin, hiding his smile with his hand. 'He was an odd one and thank God the sale never went through. So you're stuck with me, I'm afraid'.

'And 'alf a million gnomes, by the looks of things. These 'ere sheep don't know what to think. OK if they still hang around then or are they disturbing the little people? We don't want to break with tradition now do we? My father, grandfather and great grandfather 'ave all had their sheep in the fields at Glencot. Whenevers you want a nice bit of nice lamb, you just asks me. That's my way of saying thank you.'

'Fine by me' Tarmin said, hoping the man would now move on. He could feel Alex shivering beside him and knew that the champagne had gone to her head, after he'd heard her quietly burping. Time to get her into bed. 'Yes, I'm quite partial to a nice shepherds pie or a lamb kebab'.

Cyril's face dropped at little at this insensitivity. This Mr. Rimell was nice enough but seemed a bit of a prat. That empty champagne bottle had a lot to do with it, he was sure. Still, he had to keep on the right side of him or his sheep might yet be ousted from their pastures by those ghastly gnomes that were popping up all over the place.

'You knows about this very place, then?'

'No not really, Tarmin said. 'I always thought it was just an old ruined cottage with a great fireplace, left deserted.'

'Well, no. It be much more fascinating than that. When I was a lad, there were still four walls standing, and then in the great storm of 1984, it took a direct 'it from that great oak over there,' he said pointing at a vast uprooted trunk. 'Smashed the place to bits, it did. But in truth, it weren't a cottage, you know. No, that there thing was a originally a small chapel datin' back to the time of Wookey Castle, which was rumoured to 'ave been built where your Glencot 'ouse now sits.'

He shuffled over to the fire and spread his wizened palms over the dying embers of the fire. Looking across at Tarmin and Alex, his half-lit toothless grin flashed across the silent night.

'See anything unusual 'ere?' he said, waving his hands in the direction of the fireplace.

Alex freed herself from Tarmin's clasp and moved over to where he was gesticulating. She peered at the fire's great lintel, brushing her fingers over the indecipherable and half broken inscription.

'Is this what you're referring to? It's all Greek to me' she observed.

'No, no my dear. Not Greek, Latin. My father, Ernie, was a bit of a know-it-all and 'e took a rubbing one day and had it translated by some nobby brainbox from Dorset. 'e told me that it said, in so many words, that the ruins was actually a 'oly resting place and rumour had it that deep down there...' The old man was pointing to a lone stone step half buried in the brambles, when all of a sudden the conversation came to an abrupt end. Snuffer had decided to pursue a rabbit that had stupidly popped his head out of a nearby burrow. The dog leapt across their path with amazing speed for an animal of such portly dimensions.

THE WOOKEY HOLE AFFAIR

'Snuffer!' Cyril squawked. 'Mind that 'eart of yours, boy. Those bunnies ain't worth the effort.'

Turning back to Tarmin and Alex, the shepherd picked up his staff and doffed his cap.

'I'll be off now, good night to you both' he said, and with that, Cyril melted into the dark undergrowth, disappearing as instantly as he'd first come.

Alex looked at Tarmin.

'Are you thinking what I'm thinking?' Tarmin said.

'Don't! Let's get out of here. We've got a hell of a lot of gnomes to put to bed.'

Tarmin stamped out the dying flames and kissed her on the lips.

'There's only one gnome I want to put to bed tonight.'

As they left the darkness of the woods, Gnomeland's distant lights looked hazy in the chilled night. Tarmin was beside himself with excitement. Was this it? Was the real McCoy - the hidden wealth he'd been so desperately hoping for - here on his doorstep all the time? Tomorrow morning at first light he would be down with his workman to take a closer look at the folly site. As they arrived back at the terrace, the muted tones of the gnomes choir drifted through the open doors and windows. It was only just after nine o'clock but they were both drained.

'I'm going for a long, long bath, Tarmin' Alex said. 'Will you lock up?'

'Go soak. I'll be up in a little while'

Tarmin walked out on the balcony overlooking the terrace, with a drink in one hand, and thought over the day. An occasional bat flapped its way through the house and, somewhere beyond the riverbank, he heard an owl making noise. He daydreamed on for another three cigarettes, reckoning that today had been the easy part, but soon the real graft would have to begin. There was no running away now. Now it would be marketing, PR, sales and so on. He'd staff up properly, have maintenance people on hand, retail suppliers and so forth. It was going to be a ghastly whirl of gnomes galore, but at least the short term plan was to cream the money for two years and then get the fuck out of there.

His thoughts slipped to Alex and the wedding; he could see it all. Hello! Magazine: 'AT HOME IN GNOMELAND WITH THE RIMELLS', and the tabloid press floating around Glencot taking pictures of the eccentric couple in various topical outfits.

Not so far away, he could hear a car choke into life and the powerful throbbing of the engine as it drove off. Must be a straggler, having finished a little nookey session with one of the lap-dancing gnomes in the woods, he thought. Piling his empty glass on top of the full ashtray, he set off to do the rounds of the house, locking and bolting the doors and turning off the sound system. As he walked through the hallway, he caught sight of himself in the large oval mirror and winced. He was still in that ridiculous outfit, only now he had wine stains on the hat, ash smeared across his face from the fire at the folly, and a large tear had appeared along one arm. He was shambolic. Slowly, he climbed the stairs, heading to their private world at the top of the house.

As he entered their bedroom, the enticing smell of scented bath oils wafted through the half open bathroom door. The soft operatic tones of Emma Shapplin were playing through Alex's Ipod, and beeswax candles of different heights dripped onto a huge oblong silver platter on top of the chest of drawers. It was dark and cosy, romantic and soporific. He dumped his exhausted body across the four-poster, prised off his shoes with great effort and lay dozing in and out of consciousness.

'Alex, bedtime!' he called weakly into the ether. 'You'll get all wrinkled in that hot water.'

When there was no response, he glanced over towards the

bathroom door and did a double take. That was odd - a tide of soapy water had begun to gush across the carpet and had just reached the mat by the bedside.

'Shit, Alex, the fucking bath's overflowing!' he shouted, jumping up and splashing through the oncoming tide. 'She's bloody well fallen asleep' he thought. His heart missed a beat as he skidded across the tiled floor towards the Victorian claw-footed roll top bath. No occupant; no Alex. For a moment, he'd had a rush of fear that she'd fallen asleep and drowned. Where was she? There were no scattered clothes on the floor. 'Silly cow,' he thought. She must have run the bath and left it absent-mindedly. She had been quite pissed from all that champagne.

Pulling out the plug, he killed the taps and piled towels against the door to stem the flow. He had a vision of a soapy waterfall cascading into the Fairy Room, immediately below.

'Oh fuck, fuck, fuck' he muttered angrily.

He ran downstairs to check, and to his relief, only a trickle of water was running down the gaudy fairy encrusted chandelier.

' Alex!' he yelled, 'Alex!' At any moment expecting to run into a sandwich munching semi-clad gnome. 'Sweetheart, where are you?' he called again at the top of his voice. Not a peep. It took him a good ten minutes to search the house and open all the doors again. He was greeted by nothing but eerie silence and hundreds of plastic eyes mocking his every move and thoughts. Now he'd run out of ideas. Where was the damned girl? If this was her idea of a joke he was definitely not finding it funny.

He pulled his mobile from his pocket and dialled her number. It went straight to ansaphone, so he left a curt message. 'Ring me back', he stuttered and hung up. This was the sort of thing that one saw on the movies; a couple stopping off at petrol station in the Australian outback, girl goes to the loo, man waits and waits; no girl, big mystery. But this was not the outback. This was a Wookey Hole in sleepy Somerset where the only crime was double parking outside the post office.

He spent the next half hour pacing the house, his aggravation levels rising and now turning to blind panic. Back upstairs for the fourth time, he half expected to find her lying naked on the bed, champagne glass in hand, awaiting his return. 'Joke!' she'd say and then seeing him so angry, would drop to her knees and make it alright again. But the room was silent, the towels still piled against the bathroom door, Shapplin drifting from the stereo on replay.

He felt his phone briefly vibrate in his pocket - a pre-cursor to the embarrassing gnome ring tone that he'd uploaded. He snapped it open, ready to play the stern fiancée.

'Yes' he said with some restraint, looking at her number on the display. 'Where the hell are you? You left the bloody bath running and the house has been washed down the hill and into the Mendips. It's not funny.'

'No Mr. Rimell, indeed it's not.'

A cold chill raked his body, ending in goose pimples and a tingling sensation he'd not experienced since the demise of Bambi in childhood.

'And neither is being deprived of half a million pounds.' Nathan Hunt's cool voice was rasping and hard. Tarmin could feel his blood draining away in pints.

'As you may have gathered, Alexandra is my guest at this time. Let me be brief. It's a very simple situation, Mr, Rimell. Five hundred thousand deposited into a Swiss account, the number of which will be texted to you, shortly and your girl-friend will come home. In fact, make that eight hundred thousand; there is interest to take care of too. Plus, I still have documentation of your oil scam in my hands, don't forget. I'm no fool Mr. Rimell, and I don't like being taken for one. Alexandra's future is in your hands. You have forty-eight hours to return the money and I can assure you that if I've not received satisfaction, you in turn, will be receiving no further gratification from the girl.'

The phone went dead.

Tarmin, who was standing rigid throughout the conversation, slumped back onto the bed, Hunt's words raced around his head. Deep down he knew that the Austrian had all the aces. The police were not an option for a multitude of reasons that Tarmin didn't even bother to contemplate. He'd have to pay up and he had only two days to do it in. This would spell the end of Gnomeland before it had even begun, and all his dreams of wealth. And Alex. What would that bastard be doing to her? Panic gripped his throat and sweat poured down his bloated face.

'Tarmin, Tarmin! Wake up! Do you want to get into this bath or not?'

Tarmin opened his eyes and looked at Alex, glistening with warm water and wrapped in a towel, standing at the end of the bed.

'You've been like a mad dog, dreaming of chasing rabbits' she said. 'Yelping and twitching like an epileptic. Bad dream was it?'